"You have never been afraid to talk to me before."

"That was different," Claire murmured. "It is not proper for a woman to discuss such things with a man."

Devon tipped up Claire's chin and brushed away a tear. His heart squeezed at the sight of Claire's pain. Clearly, she was in turmoil.

Had someone hurt her in the past, abused her or broken her heart? He struggled for a moment with the thought of simply leaving her alone. But Devon refused to accept that his feelings were one-sided. If Claire was truly repulsed by him, she would leave.

Instead, she stood before him, blushing, fidgeting and in general looking as if she was frightened to death.

Slowly, Devon drew her closer to his body. "You can stop me at any time, Claire. Tell me now, and I will never touch you again. Tell me to leave you alone, and I will disappear from your life, and you will never hear from me again. You can live in Fontjoy Square forever without any obligation to me. Or I will buy you a house elsewhere if you can't tolerate my presence in the neighborhood."

Her words came out in a tumble, a strangled cry as she fell against him. "No, no, Devon, I do not want you to disappear!"

Dear Readers,

In July of 1999, we launched the Ballad line with four new series, and each month we present both new and continuing stories set everywhere from medieval England to the American West—the kind of passionate, romantic stories you love best, written by the most gifted authors. At the back of each book, we tell you when you can find subsequent books in the series that have captured your heart.

First up this month is **With His Ring,** the second book in the fabulous new *Brides of Bath* series by Cheryl Bolen. What happens when a dedicated bachelor who marries for money discovers that his impetuous young wife has married for love—his? Next, Kelly McClymer returns with **The Next Best Bride.** A jilted groom marrying his errant fiancée's twin sister is hardly romantic, unless it happens in the charming *Once Upon a Wedding* series.

Reader favorite Kate Donovan is back with another installment of the *Happily Ever After Co.* This time in **Night After Night** a young woman looking for a teaching job instead of a husband finds the key to her past—and a man with the key to her heart. Finally, ever-talented Cindy Harris concludes the *Dublin Dreams* series with **Lover's Knot,** in which secrets are revealed, friendships are renewed . . . and passion turns to lasting love.

Why not start spring off right and read them all? Enjoy!

Kate Duffy
Editorial Director

Dublin Dreams

LOVER'S KNOT

Cindy Harris

ZEBRA BOOKS
Kensington Publishing Corp.
http://www.kensingtonbooks.com

ZEBRA BOOKS are published by

Kensington Publishing Corp.
850 Third Avenue
New York, NY 10022

All Kensington titles, imprints, and distributed lines are available at special quantity discounts for bulk purchases for sales promotion, premiums, fund-raising, educational or institutional use.

Special book excerpts or customized printings can also be created to fit specific needs. For details, write or phone the office of the Kensington Special Sales Manager: Kensington Publishing Corp., 850 Third Avenue, New York, NY 10022. Attn. Special Sales Department. Phone: 1-800-221-2647.

Zebra and the Z logo Reg. U.S. Pat. & TM Off.

First Printing: April 2002
10 9 8 7 6 5 4 3 2 1

Printed in the United States of America

This book is dedicated to Bruce V. Schewe

One

Fontjoy Square, Dublin
January 1871

The frigid night air scored Devon Avondale's lungs as he walked from one end of Fontjoy Square to the other. When he came to Number Three, he hesitated. Standing at the edge of the street, staring at Lady Claire Kilgarren's mushroom-colored stucco Georgian town house, his breath came in shallow puffs. As always, whenever he pictured Claire's sparkling blue eyes and upswept blond hair, his heart leapt. For nearly a year, he had enjoyed her friendship but concealed his physical attraction to her. Tonight, Devon meant to reveal the true nature of his feelings.

A light twinkled in Claire's parlor window, signaling that she was awake, no doubt working on a frame of embroidery or needlepoint, perhaps reading a romantic novel. Slowly, Devon walked the length of the brick path that led to her front door.

Assailed by doubt, he nearly turned and retreated to his own Palladian-style villa at the opposite end of the square. It would be so much easier to simply remain friends with Claire and ignore or suppress his romantic urges. He had lived for five years without a woman in his bed; he could live that way for the rest of his life if he had to.

Besides, Claire had made it abundantly clear that she was not interested in sex, romance or marriage. And nothing was worth the risk of ruining the friendship they shared.

But just as he turned to leave, his deceased wife's voice haunted his thoughts.

"Find someone to love, Devon," she'd told him, as she lay dying. "Someone else. Someone other than me, because I will soon be just a memory, a precious one, I hope. And when you do, Devon, love your new love very dearly, because life is also very short . . . and when we are getting close to its end, as I am now, I can assure you that the only thing that matters a whit is whom you have loved. . . . Oh, Devon, I have loved you so well."

Why Devon had chosen tonight, and not the night before, or the night before that, to reveal his feelings for Claire, he could not have explained. During the ten or so months he had known her, he had repeatedly concurred in Claire's denouncements of marriage, telling himself that he could never love again—*and nearly convincing himself of it, too*—despite Mary O'Roarke Avondale's deathbed admonition.

But this morning, after another restless, miserable night of reading Mary's diary, Devon had concluded that his wife, as usual, had been right. He did need someone to care for, someone to come home to, someone to make love with. That someone, he realized, lived at the opposite end of the square.

Lady Claire Kilgarren was his dearest, closest friend. Next to Mary, she was the most intelligent, witty woman he'd ever met. The enthusiasm she had shown toward refurbishing the garden in the center of the square endeared her to him. Her aristocratic bearing intrigued him. He couldn't be in her presence without experiencing a tingling in his groin. He woke up pondering what he could do to make her happy, and he fell asleep wondering if she was safe and sound. If that was not a sufficient basis for a loving relationship, what was?

Dry-mouthed, Devon gripped the brass knocker on the black lacquered front door of Number Three. His neck chafed beneath his heavy woolen coat and scarf, and his gut twisted. He did not have to do this tonight, he reminded himself. Claire was not moving anywhere. There was plenty of time to change his mind.

But Mary had cautioned him about living in the past.

Do not waste your time moping about what could have been. Do not wait for divine wisdom to visit you, or for some profound enlightenment to pop into your head, dear, because it isn't going to happen.

"The secret of life—if I may be so presumptuous as to suggest that dying has suffused me with some little

wisdom—is very simple; that is, there is no secret, and so you must create your own happiness, and the only way to do that is to find someone to love."

What was he waiting for?

Steadying his nerves, Devon took a deep breath and banged the knocker on the door.

His knock was hardly unexpected, even at this late hour. During the past few months, now that it was too cold to work in the garden and there was no other excuse for the two to visit, Devon Avondale had taken to stopping in at Lady Claire Kilgarren's house after he'd made his way round the neighborhood.

Claire likened him to a sentinel or watch; he didn't bellow out the hour of the night, thanks be to Erin, but his nocturnal meanderings surely gave the denizens of Fontjoy Square some peace of mind.

Pausing before the mirror in her foyer, Claire inspected her image. Devon was just a friend, she thought, patting her blond coiffure into place, but he was still a man, and she didn't want him to see her looking mussed or untidy. A flutter of nervousness spread through her middle as she opened the door.

"Is it too late?" he asked.

"Of course not. Come in." As always, Claire was momentarily stunned by Devon's overwhelming *maleness*. Her pulse skittered as she took in the sight of him. It wasn't just that he was a handsome man, though he certainly was, with his blue eyes and thick jet hair. It was his *attitude,* the fragile arrogance that he projected, that captured Claire's imagination.

How a man could exude fragility and arrogance at the same time, Claire did not know. She only knew that Devon was the sort of man whom women wanted to seduce or mollycoddle, or both. Men, on the other hand, recognized Devon for the dominant animal he was, and went to great pains to avoid angering him.

Tall, lean and broad-shouldered, with the grace and mystery of a panther, Devon Avondale did not *demand* respect—he didn't have to. Anyone who came in contact with him quickly understood that he was in total control of his surroundings.

"All's well in Fontjoy Square," Devon said, shrugging out of his heavy coat and hanging it on a rack beside the door. "But I could use the warmth of a good fire. Know where I can find one?"

Claire quickly closed the door, grateful as always to have Devon inside her home. She liked the comfort of his presence, the sound of his voice, even the manly smell of his skin and clothes.

"Oh, I think I can warm you up," Claire said with a chuckle. The flirtation that passed between them was playful and completely innocuous; theirs was a platonic relationship.

"Yes, and I believe you can, dear," Devon drawled.

While she enjoyed the banter, Claire knew that

Devon was no more interested in a romantic relationship than she. He might have once disagreed with her philosophy on marriage, but now that he was a widower, he had firmly declared that he would never marry again. The limitations of Devon's friendship, therefore, made him *safe*. Claire *felt* safe when he was around. Had she ever thought he viewed her as a sexual object, she would have tossed him out of her door in a flash.

As she led her visitor up the steps, she swished her hips a bit more than necessary. A man would have to be blind not to notice her provocative behavior. And in moments when she was completely honest with herself, Claire knew that she invited Devon's attention. She warmed beneath his admiring gaze. Yet she relied heavily upon his gentlemanly reserve and brotherly affection for her. Devon would never call her bluff, or make a physical overture toward her. He was far too kind and wise a man to do such a thing. She trusted him not to.

She could almost feel the heat of his stare on her behind as she ascended the steps.

Silently she chided herself for being so girlish and silly. *Devon was just a friend.* Had any of her female neighbors remained unmarried, she'd have been just as happy to spend her evenings with them. But Dolly, Millicent and Rose had all found husbands in the past year. By now, they had doused their lamps, extinguished their candles and snuggled up in bed with their husbands. As the only two unmarried adults in Fontjoy Square, it was perfectly natural that Devon and Claire would strike up a friendship. Just because they were single didn't mean they had to live like a nun and a monk.

"Have you ever wondered what our neighbors must think of our nightly visitations?" he asked her.

In her parlor, she settled on a sofa and picked up the square of needlepoint she'd been working on before Devon arrived. "I'm the least likely person in this neighborhood to inspire gossip," Claire replied.

"Ah, I had forgotten. You are the dedicated spinster of Fontjoy Square." Devon poured himself a snifter of brandy, then stood at the mantel. "But even spinsters get lonely sometimes, don't they?"

"Of course they do. That's what I've got you for, isn't it?" she teased.

"Just to keep you company?" Devon's eyes sparkled with mischief. "Is that all I'm good for?"

"Oh, no," Claire replied in mock seriousness. "You are good for much else. Like planting tulip bulbs and fertilizing rose beds. You're good at mending broken steps, too. And, let me see . . . oh, yes! I seem to recall that you sharpened my knives last week. Did a grand job, too! Did I ever tell you how much I appreciated that, Devon? No? Well, rest assured that you are not taken for granted 'round here."

"I am much relieved to hear you say that. I had

begun to think that my efforts had gone unnoticed."

"Never! What would we do without you?" She was joking, of course, when she suggested that she measured Devon's worth by his gardening and carpentry skills. He was much more to her than a handyman. During the past year, since she had lived at Fontjoy Square, Devon had become an important part of her life.

But her determination to remain a spinster was definitely not a joke. Devon was just a friend and nothing more, Claire insisted silently, reminding herself of that fact for the tenth time in as many minutes. Yet, glancing up from her sewing, she was chagrined by her own fascination with the tuft of dark hair that showed beneath the open collar of Devon's shirt.

"If by *we* you mean Rose, Dolly and Millicent, I am afraid that they are doing quite well without me." A wistful note sounded in Devon's voice. "I don't see nearly as much of the other ladies as I once did."

Claire signaled her amusement with a feminine little snort. "You've proven my theory. I'm afraid that is what happens when one enters the marital state. One becomes a dreadful bore."

"Really?"

"Millicent, Dolly and Rose have *changed* since they got married. It used to be so much fun to sit with Dolly and drink tea and gossip. Now all she wants to do is jump rope and hop about with dumbbells clutched in her hands—"

"Only woman I know who loves to exercise," Devon inserted. "Monstrous odd, if you ask me."

"Yes . . . and well, I shudder to think what she and that boxer husband of hers do to entertain themselves."

"What do you think they do?" Devon asked in a stage whisper.

"I'm sure I wouldn't know."

"Come on, Claire; what do you think Dolly and her pugilist husband do when they are all alone?"

A ripple of alarm ran through Claire's body. Despite Devon's tone, this was not appropriate parlor discourse. "I'm sure it's none of my concern. I am sorry that I brought it up."

"You're quite right, you know. Never mind Dolly and Dick Creevey. What do you think men and women who love each other do when they are alone? Kiss? Hold each other in their arms? Make love?"

Claire gasped. "Devon, how dare you?"

Impishly, he shrugged. "Don't you ever think you would like to be kissed, Claire?"

"What has gotten into you?" She put aside her needlepoint. "Have you been nipping at the whiskey, dear?"

He held up his glass. "Having made my fortune in the scotch whiskey business, I assure you, m'lady, that I can hold my liquor."

"I suggest you behave yourself. 'Tisn't proper to say such things to a lady." Claire's tone wasn't harsh, but she was firm. She felt as comfortable in Devon's society as she would have if he was her brother, but in the year since she'd met him, they'd never discussed anything more explicit than the vexing reproductive tendencies of stray cats.

Discussing sex with Devon was quite beyond the pale. Aside from being entirely improper and unbecoming between unmarried adults, it created an intimacy that both startled and disturbed Claire. As a wave of heat swept over her, she realized that she was on a slippery slope. Perhaps Devon was testing her. A niggling fear that he harbored some distinctly *unbrotherly* feelings for her took hold in Claire's mind.

But they were just friends. They had established those boundaries many months ago.

"Don't you miss it, Claire? Don't you ever wonder if you can live the rest of your life without it?"

"Miss what? And you'd better not say what I think you are going to say."

"Making love—"

"Stop right there!" Claire held up her hand. A man would never respect a woman who listened to such smutty talk. "You've gone entirely too far, Devon. If you persist in this foolishness, I will have to ask you to leave."

"You don't want me to leave and you know it."

"Are you challenging me, Devon?"

His laugh was low, velvety and a trifle menacing. "I'm calling you out, dear."

"Ah, a duel," she countered. Two could play this game. "What shall it be, then? Swords or pistols?"

Devon drained his glass and plunked it on the mantelpiece. Feigning seriousness, he bowed at Claire's feet. When he straightened, he rolled up his shirtsleeves, exposing his sinewy forearms, sun-bronzed and dusted with dark hair. "Neither. I intend to win this battle with my bare hands."

Then, so suddenly that Claire was surprised to feel his weight on the cushion beside her, he sat down, draped his arm over the back of the sofa and pressed his leg against her thigh. "And perhaps my lips."

A lump formed in her throat. "What are you doing, Devon?"

He reached for her hand. "I am going to kiss you, Claire."

Tiny pinpoints of heat prickled on Claire's skin where Devon touched her. "You think you can conquer me with a kiss?" she eked out.

"Yes. If you are willing to let down your shield." He leaned closer and planted a feather-light kiss at the corner of Claire's slightly parted lips.

She tried to turn her head, but he held her chin and kissed her again, this time full on her mouth. A surge of panic poured through Claire. She had never thought Devon was interested in her in that way. She had never anticipated being anything other than friends with him. She had never guessed that his lips were so warm, or that the smell of his skin—a mixture of wool, soap and maleness—would be so intoxicating.

Instinctively, perhaps even involuntarily, while her conscience, which sounded suspiciously like her father's voice, cautioned her to stop, Claire kissed Devon back.

Eventually, Claire would dissect her emotions, analyze them one by one and conclude that kissing Devon was highly improper, even foolhardy. But at the moment she could not think clearly. A part of her wanted to throw her arms around Devon's neck and never let him go. Who better than her best friend to help her explore these new and strange feelings? But another part of her, the part that knew the shame and embarrassment of being Lady Shannon Kilgarren's daughter, recoiled. Nice girls did not have the sorts of feelings that Claire was feeling now.

She feared she would faint.

"Tell me you don't like this." Devon's breath caressed her throat. His beard raised goose bumps on her skin. His whisper ignited her blood.

"You should stop," she said, clutching his shirtfront. But even she knew that her protests sounded weak. "Devon, please . . . stop."

"Do you really want me to, dear?"

Who could ever have thought Claire would have such difficulty answering a simple question? Claire, who was known among the ladies of Fontjoy Square for being the most opinionated and outspoken woman in the neighborhood, suddenly couldn't find her voice to speak.

Worse, the incredibly pleasant sensation of Devon's kisses warred with her determination to remain unaroused. Devon was quickly putting the lie to her long held belief that she was, in fact, *unarousable*.

Pressing her palms to Devon's chest, acutely aware of the thick, wiry hair beneath her fingertips, Claire managed to push him to arm's length.

"I thought we were friends, Devon."

"Friends can be lovers, too, Claire."

"This is not supposed to happen! I didn't want it to happen!"

"It was inevitable, dear. We've spent nearly every evening of the past ten months together. I've come to cherish you. I've come to look forward to the evenings just so I can hear your voice and watch your eyes light when you laugh."

"A bit of laughter here and there does not mean that we should—" Claire's voice trailed off. The last thing she wanted to do was rebuff Devon or drive him away. Indeed, she couldn't imagine living without him. But this leap from friends to lovers was too sudden and shocking to be taken seriously. Besides, she'd learned from experience that men held women who liked sex in low esteem. She couldn't risk losing Devon's respect; even if it meant hurting his feelings, she had to reject his overture.

"You've had too much to drink, Devon. In the morning, assuming you remember a word of what you've said, you'll laugh until your belly aches."

He drew back and studied her. "Claire, are you telling me that you feel nothing for me? I didn't imagine the sway of your hips as you led me upstairs, did I? I had hoped you wanted this. Good God, I had hoped you wanted *me!*"

"If I misled you, I'm terribly sorry." Claire scrambled to her feet, smoothing her skirts and patting her hair into place. "Perhaps you misunderstood, or misconstrued—"

"Or *imagined* that you cared for me?" He stood beside her, his expression darkening. "I did not imagine the way you looked at me. I did not imagine the way you reacted when I kissed you just now!"

"I felt nothing," she said.

His expression alternated from one of complete incredulity to one of intense anger.

A thread of apprehension wound its way up Claire's spine as she inched backward.

Devon halted her retreat by grasping her upper arms and drawing her into his embrace. Lowering his head, he covered her mouth with his and kissed her roughly.

She grabbed his shoulders, meaning to push him away. And she made a muffled sound of protest, intending to repel him. But when Devon's hold on her tightened, and his tongue slid deeper into her mouth, and his lower body hardened against her belly, Claire's protests turned to moans. Liquid heat spilled through her. Desire weakened her knees.

Fearful that she would collapse, she clung to Devon's shoulders. It was sinful to want a man the way she wanted Devon Avondale, and yet pushing him away was impossible. The longer Devon held her, the more she wanted him. The longer he kissed her, the more desperate she became.

At length, his kiss gentled and his arms relaxed. He stared at her questioningly, waiting for her reaction. Released from his embrace, Claire met his expectant gaze. If she told him to go and leave her be, he would. If she wanted more, he would give it to her.

"I—I don't know," she stammered.

"But you liked it when I kissed you."

Embarrassed, Claire looked down. But the bulge beneath Devon's trousers only raised her level of alarm. Beneath her high-necked woolen gown, she felt trapped in her own skin. She wanted to surrender to the feelings swimming through her body, but if she did, she would be repeating her mother's mistakes and fulfilling her father's prophecies, and she would never be able to live with herself.

"Devon, please." She covered her face with her hands. "I can't!"

"You can't, Claire?" he rasped. "Or you don't want to?"

Of course she wanted to. She wanted nothing else at the moment. But Lady Claire Kilgarren had spent most of her adult life pretending she was above such base, immoral impulses. Devon didn't understand that he was asking her to substitute his perception of the world for hers. And he didn't understand how frightened she was of the emotions that roiled through her. She wished she could explain it to him.

But she could never divulge the tawdry secret that inhabited her heart and soul, rendering her unfit to love or be loved by anyone as decent and kind as Devon Avondale.

Staring him straight in the eye, she took a deep breath and steeled her nerves. If she couldn't tell him the truth, she could at least spare him the pain and confusion of believing that there was any chance they would ever be lovers. "I love you as a friend, Devon, and I always will. Beyond that, I'm afraid I feel nothing. I hope you will understand."

A muscle flinched in the side of his face. His body stiffened and the light faded from his eyes. Slowly, Devon stepped around her and crossed the room. At the threshold, he paused but did not look at her. "I am sorry," he said. "I hope you will forgive me for imposing on you."

"We can forget this ever happened," Claire said, knowing even as she said it that what had transpired between them that night would never be forgotten.

"Yes, let's forget," he murmured.

His boots thudded down the staircase. A moment later, the door belowstairs opened and closed. Claire stood in the center of her parlor, her heart pounding, her head throbbing—her body aching with the need to feel Devon's body snug against hers again.

Two

Four days later

The fire on the hearth had long since faded to a pile of glowing embers, but Devon Avondale failed to notice the unhealthy chill that pervaded his study. A single lamp cast faint patterns of light on the thick Axminster carpet beneath his feet, but the vivid pictures flashing in Devon's mind required no illumination. A half-empty decanter of scotch whiskey sat on the table beside him, well within arm's reach, while a worn leather journal splayed open across his lap.

Devon's recent encounter with Lady Claire Kilgarren had sent him running back to the arms of his dead wife's memory. He'd made a terrible mistake. For half the night, sequestered in his study, he had sat in that chair, reading and re-reading Mary's journal, memorizing her words and imagining her emotions and experiences. Desperately, he had tried to understand her, and to divine who she had been and what she would have him do now. But the more he had read, the more confused he had become.

After nearly six years, tonight Devon missed Mary O'Roarke Avondale more than ever. Claire's rebuff had merely sharpened his anguish. His chest ached and his fingertips tingled with the frustration of not being able to summon his wife's presence, to touch her, to will her back to life.

He had so many questions for her now, now that he had read her journal, befriended her friends—*fallen in love with one of them and been summarily rejected!* He knew so much more about her than he had when she was alive. He wondered if, in life, Mary O'Roarke had been but a stranger to him. She was a mystery now, a beautiful enigma he would never figure out. Groaning, Devon thought he was going insane.

After all, only a crazed man would spend six years obsessing over his dead wife. Only a crazed man would devour his dead wife's diary, pour over every word she wrote, dissect every sentence, study the nuance of every phrase. Only a crazed man would do what Devon Avondale had done—track down the four women Mary O'Roarke Avondale wrote about in her diary and bring them together to live in Fontjoy Square.

Only a crazed man would thrust himself on a woman who had sworn for nearly a year that she was not interested in men!

Yet, despite the unconventionality of it, Devon's efforts in bringing together his wife's dearest friends had been his only consolation after she

died. Had Mary not suggested—no, ordered!—
that he search for the girls who had befriended
her as she grew up, Devon would still be wallowing
in self-pity.

Even on her deathbed, Mary had been watching
out for him. She had promised him that if he
would read her diary, he would find a reason to
live. She had told him that he would find someone
to love. And, as usual, Mary had been right.

Until now, the diary had given him comfort.
When Mary's words rang in his ears, when the
scent of her perfume wafted off the pages and the
slant of her letters spoke to him, Devon could pretend she was yet alive. He had read about her
childhood friends until he felt as if he knew them.
Mary told him what to do and he listened. Her
legacy gave him a purpose. Searching out Claire
Kilgarren, Dolly Baltmore, Rose Sinclair and Millicent Hyde had given him a distraction from his
grief.

Of course, Mary could not have predicted that
each of her girlhood friends would be on the edge
of poverty when Devon found them. That had
been a surprise. It had also presented a challenge
that Devon could not refuse. He had to pluck
these women from their necessitous circumstances; Mary would have insisted that he do so.

But he had to bestow his gifts on them without
revealing his identity because the last thing Devon
wanted was their *gratitude*. He only wanted to know
these women as Mary had known them. He
wanted to understand how they had shaped

Mary's life. He wanted to repay them for befriending her.

Which was why, some ten months earlier, Devon had delivered anonymous missives to the four ladies whom Mary O'Roarke Avondale wrote about in her diary. Without explanation, he had offered them homes in Fontjoy Square. The only condition he had placed on his donations was that the ladies refurbish their slightly shabby Georgian mansions and the neglected garden in the center of the square.

Not surprisingly, all of them had accepted this condition and promised never to divulge the source of their newfound largesse. Now, the four ladies were neighbors.

Only Lady Dolly Baltmore-Creevy had deduced that Devon had authored those notes. Perhaps because she had once been such an experienced imposter, Dolly had quickly sensed Devon's duplicity.

To Devon's knowledge, none of the other ladies knew that they were connected to one another by their friendship to Devon's deceased wife. After all, she had been Mary *O'Roarke* when they knew her. Devon was especially careful never to mention his wife's maiden name in the presence of his neighbors.

As he ran his fingers over the crinkled pages of his wife's diary, Devon questioned whether it was time to reveal his identity to the ladies of Fontjoy Square. The holiday season had been difficult. Claire's rejection of him had been devastating. Christmas without Mary was empty, and the charade Devon had created to amuse himself had lost its appeal.

For while Devon was pleased that three of the ladies he had invited to live at Fontjoy Square had found husbands in the past nine months, he could not suppress the sadness he felt at knowing they now had families and loving arms to turn to in the middle of the night. The rundown houses he had given them were now *homes*. He supposed it was petty of him, but he resented their happiness.

He sighed. The only remaining unmarried woman on the square was Lady Claire Kilgarren. Before she had rejected him, Devon had considered Claire his closest friend. He had spent more time with her than with any of the other ladies, ostensibly because she loved to garden more than her neighbors.

It was common knowledge in Fontjoy Square that Claire prized her unmarried status and intended to remain a spinster the rest of her life. Devon had been a fool not to take her at her word on that score.

For the first time, he was supremely irritated by the fact that Claire considered him a *friend*. Her reaction to his overture had bewildered and embarrassed him. Lifting the decanter to his lips, Devon concluded that Claire was beautiful and intelligent—and as cold as ice.

A splintering crack from belowstairs jolted Devon from his thoughts. Someone banged the heavy knocker on the front door. An unexpected caller in the middle of the night could only mean bad news.

Instantly, Devon conjured a handful of tragic scenarios. Mrs. Millicent Hyde-Wolferton had gone into premature labor while her husband was in London. One of Lady Rose Nollbrook's children had fallen ill. Dick Creevy, Lady Dolly's famous pugilist husband, had taken a brutal beating in the ring. *Maybe Claire had changed her mind.*

Wearily, he pushed himself up from his chair. Voices clashing in the foyer heightened his apprehension. Footsteps hurried up the stairs. As Devon crossed the room, the door to his study flung open.

The ashen-faced butler fidgeted in the threshold.

"What is it?" Devon growled.

"You've a visitor, sir. Says he's got to see you, face to face. Wouldn't take no for an answer."

"Hardly a social call at this hour," Devon said. "Who the devil is it?"

The butler opened his mouth but was silenced by the thud of boots ascending the steps behind him. Devon strode to the doorway and watched in growing agitation as a handsome young man with thick rust-colored hair materialized at the landing.

For a long moment, the two stared at one another. There was a hauntingly familiar cast to the younger man's features, and something mesmerizing about his intensely green eyes. Devon felt as if he had seen the lad before, but of course he had not.

"Who are you?" he asked at last.

"Name's Aidan, sir." The boy's houndstooth suit was clean if not a trifle worn at the knees.

The hair on the back of Devon's neck prickled. Yes, he knew this boy, he was certain. But from where . . . when?

"Aidan who?"

"Aidan Sullivan, sir. Though I suppose my name should rightly be O'Roarke."

"O'Roarke?" Devon's throat constricted. In the dimness of the corridor, he strained to see the boy more clearly. He waved his butler away, and the man went scurrying past the visitor and down the steps. Tension crackled in the air. "My wife's name was O'Roarke."

The boy seemed to breathe a sigh of relief. "Then I have found her at last."

"Found who?" But Devon already knew. "Who are you looking for?"

"My mother, sir. Mary O'Roarke." Aidan Sullivan closed the distance between himself and Devon, extending a chapped and raw-knuckled hand. "I'm sorry for pounding on your door in the middle of the night. I couldn't wait."

Shocked and numb, Devon listlessly shook the boy's hand. He did not know what else to do. He thought perhaps he was dreaming. This had to be some sort of supernatural experience, some hallucination inspired by too much brandy or fatigue. He even looked over his shoulder, into the darkened study, half-expecting to see himself slumped in the chair, snoring. But the chair was empty, and when he turned around again, Aidan O'Roarke was still there, watching him expectantly, his expression full of hope.

"You didn't know, then, did you?" the boy asked.

"Know what?"

"That Mary O'Roarke—your wife, my mother—had a child."

"On the contrary, I knew all about that episode in my wife's life. She was very young and frightened. It was not something we spoke of often." In fact, they never spoke about it. Mary had only revealed her secrets to Devon in her diary, and then, only when death was looming over her.

Aidan swallowed hard. "I didn't come here to cause trouble. I didn't think—"

Devon's emotions suddenly boiled over. "You didn't think that barging into my house in the middle of the night to announce that you are the bastard son of my wife would not cause trouble?" He wanted to grab the little punk by his lapels and shake him. He wanted to slap some sense into him. Strangely, he wanted to throw his arms around Mary's little redheaded boy and never let him go. But somehow he managed to check his impulse to do any of those things.

Besides, Aidan O'Roarke was hardly a little boy. He appeared to be at least twenty, and wise for his years, at that. His cheeks darkened beneath Devon's disapprobation, but his gaze remained level.

Squaring his shoulders, he said, "I assumed you knew because my mother wants to see me. Why else would she have written to me?"

"Written to you? Impossible!"

Aidan reached inside his jacket, withdrew a folded sheet of writing paper from his vest pocket and offered it to Devon. "I do not dissemble, sir."

The instant Devon glimpsed the handwriting, he knew it was Mary's. Slowly, he unfolded the paper. Noting the date, he realized that Mary had written the letter in the last days of her life. A chill passed through him. Why hadn't she confided in him? If she had wanted to see her son, why hadn't she told him? Had it been her child, the infant she'd thrust into Rose Sinclair's arms the moment it was born, whom Mary had wished for as she lay dying?

Had she missed the boy that much, never letting him out of her thoughts, always regretting that she hadn't kept him?

Had she been happy at all? Had she ever been satisfied with Devon and the life they shared?

Again, Devon wondered if he had known Mary O'Roarke Avondale at all. A sense of unrest welled up in his chest. He had some questions for Mary. Damme, he wanted some answers! But he wasn't going to get any.

Blinking back tears, Devon quickly returned the letter to its rightful owner. It felt like eavesdropping to be reading Mary's belated confession and apology to the son she'd rejected at birth. He knew the entire story anyway. He had read about it many times in Mary's diary.

"What are you doing here? What do you want?"

"I want to see my mother."

"Well, you are nearly six years too late, Mr. Sullivan." Devon's voice hardened. "She is dead, you see."

"Dead." Aidan's composure faltered. Inhaling deeply, he refolded Mary's letter. Then, he tucked it inside his jacket and stared at Devon. "Might I ask what my mother died of?"

"A sickness of the lungs. The doctors couldn't say for sure just how or where she acquired the disease, but she spent a great deal of time among Dublin's poorest folk, feeding them, clothing them, even nursing those who were ill. Most likely she got sick trying to help others."

"The doctors couldn't help her?" Aidan asked thickly.

"Perhaps they could have, had she gone to hospital sooner." Recalling how Mary coughed for months before she consulted a doctor, Devon cringed with guilt. He should have insisted that Mary seek medical attention earlier. He should have ignored her assurances that she would be fine as soon as summer arrived. Instead, Mary had continued her grueling routine of charity work. And by the time Devon realized how sick she was, she was beyond help.

"Did she suffer?" Aidan asked quietly.

"Not much," Devon lied. He couldn't tear his gaze from the young man's face; it resembled

Mary's to such a degree that Devon felt he was staring at a ghost. At the same time, Aidan's presence was indescribably painful. "Might I ask how Mary found you?"

"She didn't, really," the boy replied. "I found her."

"But she wrote you a letter—"

"She wrote the letter many years ago and posted it to me care of the Dorcas Society. Are you familiar with that organization?"

"Vaguely," Devon lied again. Having memorized Mary's diary, he knew that Rose Sinclair had taken Aidan to the Dorcas Society when he was a newborn. The teenagers had been frightened out of their minds by the arrival of Mary's child. In her half-crazed state, Mary might have cast the infant in the river. It was Rose who had possessed the presence of mind to wrap up the baby and deliver it to the Dorcas ladies.

Years later, after moving to Fontjoy Square, Rose had returned to the Dorcas headquarters and offered her services. It was there that she had encountered her recently adopted children, all of them the offspring of a beautiful drug addicted prostitute.

Rose had even married the father of one of those children, and now she was Lady Rose Sinclair Nollbrook. But she had not given up her charity work completely. Surely she had access to files and records that could connect Mary to Aidan Sullivan. Devon wondered what part, if any, she had played in Aidan's appearance in Fontjoy Square.

Puzzled, he asked, "But if Mary posted this letter to the Dorcas Society, how did you get it?"

"I went there looking for her. One of the ladies pulled my adoption file and the letter was found. It seems that Mary O'Roarke wrote to the Dorcas ladies many times over a period of years, begging them to release the names of my adoptive parents. She wanted to find me, you see. She was terribly persistent, writing as many as two dozen letters in the span of a year."

"Why on earth would you go looking for your mother at the Dorcas Society?"

"My adoptive father told me to."

"After all this time?"

A muscle in Aidan's jaw flinched. "Sure, and I wish he had told me before. I never knew until a few months ago that I was adopted. My parents did not want me to meet my real mother. I believe they feared somehow that I would love them less."

"And do you?" Devon blurted. "Now that you know? Do you feel any differently toward your parents?"

Aidan shrugged. For a moment, he fell silent, nibbling on his bottom lip, staring at his boots as if they fascinated him. "I don't know how to answer that question. All I can tell you is that when my adoptive mother died, I felt as if the wind had been permanently knocked out of me. Shortly thereafter, my father fell desperately ill, too. Just before he died, he told me about the circumstances of my birth—as much as he knew, anyway, which wasn't very much."

"But it was enough to lead you to the Dorcas Society."

"Yes. And now I'm here."

"Do you remember the Dorcas lady's name, the one who sent you here?"

"Rose something-or-other."

"Sinclair? Nollbrook?"

"Does it matter?"

"And when did you talk to Rose, lad?" Devon's heart thudded. The decision he'd been toying with—whether to tell his neighbors who he was and why he had brought them together in Fontjoy Square—apparently had been made for him. Rose had pieced together the mystery, and it was only a matter of time before she told her neighbors. He would be lucky if the ladies did not storm his door before sunrise. Queasily, he wondered what Claire's reaction to this revelation would be.

"This afternoon, sir. I came straightaway, you see."

"Yes, I suppose you did," Devon murmured, eager now to rid himself of the sight of Aidan Sullivan. He wanted to be alone, preferably in a darkened room, with his brandy and his thoughts. He needed time to absorb the shock of meeting Mary's baby boy face-to-face. A hundred emotions swirled inside him, but he could not identify any of them. He knew only that he needed to talk to Mary, but that was impossible.

Frustrated and confused, Devon's ordinarily impeccable manners deserted him. "I am afraid it is rather late, Mr. Sullivan. I'm sorry you have wasted your time. But, as I said, Mary O'Roarke is dead. You can see yourself out."

"Pardon me, Mr. Avondale, but if my mother is dead, I have some questions—"

"I am in no mood for questions, young man." Brusquely, Devon said good night and took a step back.

Aidan quickly advanced, placing his palm on the door to block its closing. "I came to meet my mother, sir."

"You're too late," Devon bit out.

"Perhaps. But if I cannot meet her, then I will at least learn something of her." Aidan looked around, as if he was searching the surroundings for signs of Mary's life, clues that might lead him to some understanding of who his mother had been. "I want to know more, you see, not just about my mother but about my father, too."

Instinctively, Devon shook his head. "If the ladies at the Dorcas Society couldn't tell you that, then I surely can't."

"Rose was less than helpful on that score," Aidan said petulantly.

Well, she was certainly the only one who *could* help, Devon thought. No one except Rose Sinclair-Nollbrook knew the name of Aidan's father, and if she wasn't talking, then Devon certainly wasn't going to divulge what little information he possessed regarding the callous young Romeo who had seduced Mary O'Roarke that fateful summer so many years ago.

"I hope you are not going to force me to physically evict you from my home," Devon growled, drawing himself up to his full height.

Suddenly sheepish, the young man retreated. "I'm sorry. I should have waited until morning, but I couldn't—"

"Understandable." Devon's tone softened. "I wish you the best of luck, Mr. Sullivan. Now, if you will excuse me . . ."

And with that, Devon shut his study door. Minutes passed as he waited for the sound of Aidan's boots on the stairs. When at last he heard the young man's departing footsteps and the crash of the door below, he breathed a sigh of relief.

Thank God the boy had gone when Devon asked him to. If Aidan had insisted on hearing more about Mary, Devon feared he might have been driven to violence.

The fact that his wife had nurtured secrets and harbored private desires during their marriage came crashing down on Devon like a ton of stones. For a split second he regretted ever having read her journals. The legacy she had left him—her memories, her diaries, her friends, *Claire*—led him to question his adequacy as both a husband and a lover.

Perhaps Devon Avondale finally knew more about Mary O'Roarke than he wanted.

Three

"No thank you, Dolly. I've drunk so much tea in the last few hours, I feel as if I might float away." Snuggling deeper into the corner of a camelback sofa, Lady Claire Kilgarren folded her arms across her chest and sighed.

With a shrug, Lady Dolly Baltmore-Creevy waved away her faithful servant. "That's all for now, Ferghus." As the man closed the parlor door, Dolly stared fixedly over the rim of her cup at her dearest friend.

The two women could not have appeared more dissimilar. Lady Dolly was petite, exuberant and, with her unkempt mop of blond curls, almost boyish in her appearance. Lady Claire Kilgarren was aristocratic in bearing, elegant and reserved by nature. Only on the subject of men and marriage was Claire animatedly outspoken. For nearly a year, ever since she had moved to Fontjoy Square, she had been extolling the virtues of spinsterhood and declaiming the treacherous institution of marriage.

At length, Dolly broke the silence. "How long has it been since anyone has seen him, dear?"

"Four days."

"Are you certain that he hasn't gone to London on business, or been called away by a sick relative, or some such thing as that?"

"He has no relatives," Claire answered, with a pout. "And it seems to me that he would have mentioned a trip to London. That is hardly the sort of thing one neglects to tell—"

As Claire's voice trailed away, Dolly suppressed a chuckle. For some time, she had noticed the long looks that passed between Mr. Devon Avondale and Claire. And more than once, she had amused herself with the thought that Claire had arrived in Fontjoy Square with the creamiest alabaster skin and the most delicate uncallused hands but had quickly developed into an avid gardener *under the close supervision and tutelage of Devon Avondale.*

During the warmer months, Devon and Claire had spent entire days trimming hedges, planting bulbs and nurturing roses in the center of the square. Dolly had grown accustomed to glancing out her window and seeing them bent over a flower-bed, their heads together, their fingers intertwined as they dug in the dirt. She could set her clock by Devon's nightly stroll, which invariably took him to Claire's house where, according to Claire, the two drank hot tea or chocolate and discussed how best to combat their aphid infestation.

Had Millicent Hyde-Wolferton and Rose Sinclair-Nollbrook not been so distracted with problems of their own, they might also have noticed Claire's growing alliance with Devon. Apparently, they had taken at face value Claire's vociferous opposition to marriage and men. After all, Claire had been so forthcoming and candid about her penurious circumstances, her past career as a paid companion and the events that led up to her moving to Fontjoy Square, it was difficult to believe she would lie about anything.

Dolly might have believed Claire, too, had she not been so well trained in the art of deception.

But, having once masqueraded as a boy in order to insinuate herself into the daily routine of the famous pugilist Dick Creevy, Dolly could spot an imposter a furlong away. Claire hated men about as much as Dolly did. And Claire had *not* acquired her house from her wealthy but emotionally distant father.

"Well, Claire, dear, have you sent 'round a message to Mr. Avondale's house? Perhaps he is under the weather, or preoccupied with work-related matters."

"Yes, and I've sent him a half-dozen messages," Claire replied, her blue eyes snapping. "He has not had the decency to respond to one of them. Can you believe how boorish and rude he is, Dolly? Refusing to do so much as pen me a single line, explaining his absence?"

"Is the man *obligated* to account to you for his whereabouts, dear?"

"Of course not! I did not meant to imply—" Claire's lashes fluttered. "Oh, Dolly, now you are over the top! You know that Devon and I are nothing more than friends. Nothing more, I tell you! Why do you insist on teasing me so viciously? Really, it is quite upsetting!"

"To paraphrase Shakespeare, I believe that you are protesting far too vigorously, Claire. If you and Devon are nothing more than friends, why don't you go knock on his door?"

"I have," Claire snapped. "His servant confirmed that Devon *did* receive my notes, but that he was *indisposed*. He does not want to see me, Dolly. It is as simple as that."

Dolly fell silent for an instant. It did seem odd that Devon would ignore Claire's overtures. If nothing else, the man was inordinately well mannered. Dolly had only ever heard of Devon losing his temper once, and that was when he believed that Rose Sinclair had fallen in love with a philandering cad. But when Sir Steven Nollbrook proved to be a decent man, Devon had fully supported his marriage to Rose.

"What do you think is the matter with him, Claire?"

Tears shone in the other woman's eyes. "I don't know. And if he will not speak with me, I don't know how I am going to find out. I suppose that I have offended him in some way."

"It is very likely that Mr. Avondale's disappearance has nothing to do with you, dear."

With a sniff, Claire brushed away her tears.

"Will you go over there, then, Dolly? Or send Dick, perhaps. Yes, that would make sense, wouldn't it? I just need to know that he is all right."

"Dick is at an exhibition match in Edinburgh and will not return home for three weeks. No, that won't work, Claire."

A discreet clearing of the throat sounded at the open door. Looking up, Dolly was surprised to see Rose Sinclair-Nollbrook brushing snow off her dark blue woolen gown.

"I hope I am not intruding." With an air of maternal efficiency, the dark-haired woman whisked into the room and gave both Dolly and Claire quick pecks on their cheeks. "Mind if I have some tea, Dolly?" After helping herself to a cup, she settled on the sofa beside Claire.

"Actually, you are the very woman Claire and I wanted to see." Dolly threw Claire a wink. "Mind if I ask what your husband is doing tonight?"

"Do you want to borrow him, Dolly?" Rose popped a lemon cookie into her mouth and smiled elfishly. "Well, you can't have him, dear; you'll just have to wait until your own lover comes home."

"I wasn't thinking of myself, Rose. It's Mr. Avondale we're worried about. He's been holed up in his house for four days and hasn't answered any of Claire's messages. She's worried about him, and to tell the truth, so am I."

"And you want Alec to go over there, knock the

door down and establish that Devon is still breathing?"

"Something like that."

"I will do it."

"You will?" Dolly asked, wondering why she hadn't volunteered to go herself. It wasn't as if Devon was a stranger.

Rose quaffed her tea, patted her lips with a serviette and stood abruptly. "Sorry that I can't stay longer, but the children will be awakening from their naps soon, and I promised their nanny I wouldn't be gone long."

"You just got here," Claire countered weakly.

Dolly didn't bother to argue, however. Lately, Rose's time was more precious than gold. With three newly adopted children and a busy barrister husband to care for, Rose barely had time to comb her hair. Indeed, her once perfect coiffure looked as if someone had recently thrust his very sticky fingers in it. Most likely, it was little Stevie, an adorable, rambunctious five-year-old. But even with her chestnut hair wisping around her face, Rose glowed with happiness.

"As soon as I know anything, I will pass my information on to you both." At the door, Rose paused and threw a smile over her shoulder. "Don't worry, Claire, I'm certain Mr. Avondale is all right. Probably in a bad mood, that's all. Sometimes life catches us all by surprise, and then we have to take a few days to sort things out."

Claire's cheeks flared with color. Clearly, she was embarrassed by her obvious concern for Devon.

Ducking her head and sipping her tea, Dolly hoped to disguise her own surprise. So Rose *had* noticed that there was more between Claire and Devon than a shared interest in tulips. The pretty brown-haired newlywed never ceased to amaze; just a few months ago, she had revealed that she'd been sneaking off to the Dorcas Society, where she counseled prostitute mothers. And then she'd brought home three motherless children, adopted them and married the father of one.

Rose could not be underestimated.

If she meant to find out why Devon Avondale had sequestered himself in his house for four days, she undoubtedly would.

Rose knew exactly what had precipitated Devon's disappearance. What she didn't know, of course, was how he felt after learning that his deceased wife had given birth to a child out of wedlock, and what he intended to do about Aidan Sullivan's sudden arrival in Dublin.

"Mr. Avondale is not receiving visitors," the grim-faced butler intoned.

"Tell him this is not a social call."

"He gave strict instructions, ma'am. He is not to be disturbed."

"Sick in bed, is he?"

"In his study, actually."

Shaking her head, Rose brushed past the butler, crossed the spacious marble-floored entry hall and headed for the staircase. Having never set foot in

Devon's house before, she had no idea where his study was. But she would find it if the butler refused to show her the way.

Behind her, the man sputtered, "Excuse me, ma'am, but Mr. Avondale made it quite clear—"

"He'll talk to me," Rose muttered, picking up her skirts. At the first landing, she paused as the butler skittered around her and stood protectively before a closed door. "Move aside, sir. I have no intention of being turned away."

Abruptly, and to the butler's apparent horror, the door opened inward. In the threshold stood Devon Avondale, cheeks unshaven, shirt open at the throat and with a scowl on his face that would have frightened off most grown men.

"I wondered when you would come," he growled.

Rose gave the butler a sympathetic pat on the arm as she entered the darkened study. What little warmth existed in the room emanated from a dwindling fire on the hearth. A single lamp battled the blackness but could not fend off the gloomy atmosphere. Noting that a book lay open beside Devon's armchair, Rose wondered how he could see to read it.

"Would you care for some tea, Rose?" Instead of looking at her, Devon stood before the fireplace. With an iron poker, he roughly stabbed the crackling logs.

Tossing off her cloak, Rose sank onto a sofa. "Claire says you have been holed up in here for four days."

"What concern is it of hers?"

"You don't mean that, Devon. She's worried, as we all are. We're your friends, you know."

"Are you?" He gave a harsh chuckle. "Then why did you send Aidan Sullivan here, Rose? Why not leave well enough alone?"

" 'Twas not my decision to make, Devon. Nor is it yours. The boy has a right to know the circumstances of his birth."

He threw a contemptuous look over his shoulder, one that sent a chill up Rose's spine. "Does he, now? Tell me something, Rose—do you intend on telling your three children everything about the circumstances of their births?"

A flood of heat suffused Rose's face. The impulse to leap off the sofa and stomp out of Devon Avondale's house nearly overwhelmed her. But the flash of emotion incited by Devon's reference to her adopted children was just as quickly suppressed by Rose's awareness of his pain and her sensitivity to his confusion. No doubt Devon had been shocked out of his mind when Aidan Sullivan materialized on his doorstep.

"You needn't turn your anger on me, Devon." Rose had vast experience dealing with the emotions of children. The emotions of men were amazingly similar. "Perhaps I should have told you that Aidan had visited the Dorcas Society. Indeed, perhaps I should have told him that his mother was dead."

"That would have been nice, Rose!"

" 'Twould have been nice if you had told me you were married to Mary O'Roarke, too, Devon."

"You knew her?" Devon asked, apparently startled.

"Quite well. We were classmates and friends. We spent a summer together with our families in Killiney when we were teenagers. Mary was very dear to me."

"I had no idea. But then, I had no reason to discuss my dead wife, now did I? And you had no reason to tell me that you knew her."

"I suppose not." A jarring suspicion entered Rose's mind. Was it pure coincidence that her mysterious benefactor had donated to her a home that was just down the street from the man who had married her dearest childhood friend? Had Devon Avondale been involved somehow in the strange events that led up to her moving to Fontjoy Square? Had he known from the beginning that Rose had once been close to Mary O'Roarke?

"At any rate," Rose continued slowly, "I was not entirely certain that Aidan would follow through with his plan to find Mary O'Roarke. I reckoned that if and when he did show up in Fontjoy Square, it was up to you to explain how his mother died. By the way, how did she?"

The question seemed to shoot through Devon like a blade of steel. His jaw hardened and his fists coiled at his sides. "A sickness of the lungs. Nearly six years ago."

"How sad," Rose murmured. Aidan's appearance at the Dorcas Society headquarters, the realization that he was Mary's boy and the subsequent discovery that Mary was Devon's deceased wife, had triggered a host of memories, not all of them pleasant. "She was a beautiful girl, Devon. I'm certain you loved her very much."

"More than you can ever know," he replied huskily. Turning his back to Rose, he thrust the poker into the brass fire set and fell silent

"I know what it is to be in love, Devon. I am sorry for you. But life goes on, you know."

"Does it?" He crossed his arms over his chest, refusing to look at Rose. "Tell me, how did you discover that Aidan was Mary's boy?"

"Aidan's adoptive father told him that he'd been born in Dublin to a young, unmarried woman, and that the adoption had been arranged through the Dorcas Society. Aidan figured we would have a record of his having been born and adopted, and he was correct."

"The file had Mary's name in it?"

"No, of course not. I did not—" Rose nearly bit her tongue. The fact that she attended Aidan's birth was none of Devon's business. "No, Mary's name was not in the record. But a letter she had written to her son was."

"Go on."

"Several years ago, Mary began sending letters to her son. She didn't know where he was, of course, so she sent them to the Dorcas Society. I suppose she hoped that one day he would come looking for her. And he did."

"But he came six years too late."

"I gave Aidan the letters. He found you from there."

"Without any help from you, Rose?"

"I did not need to tell him where you lived, Devon. Mary had affixed her address to her letters. You can imagine my surprise when I saw that address and realized . . ."

"Yes, I can imagine."

"Mary was very clever to send her letters to the Dorcas Society."

"Ah, yes. Clever Mary."

Unable to see Devon's expression, Rose was not entirely sure whether the sharpness in his voice was a result of bitterness, anger or just plain fatigue. "There's no point in turning your anger on Mary either, dear."

Suddenly, Devon wheeled around. Sneering his disdain, he pounded his fist into his open palm. "Isn't there, Rose?" His eyes snapped like leather whips and his face darkened with rage.

For a split second, she thought he might cross the room and strike her. But Rose's relentless maternal instincts muffled the fear she might otherwise have felt. "We—I mean, *she* was young, Devon."

"She should have told me before—"

"Before what, Devon? Before she fell ill and hadn't the energy or the courage to tell you? Before her son came looking for her? She must have been wracked with guilt and worried sick that you would someday learn of her indiscretion."

"She should have told me!" he roared.

Undaunted by Devon's fury, Rose stood and propped her hands on her hips. "What, that she had given birth to an illegitimate child when she was merely a child herself? That she'd been taken advantage of by some freckle-faced Romeo who promised her the moon? That she'd made a mistake? That she'd once been young and foolish?"

"I would have understood."

"Perhaps." A fierce urge to protect Mary's reputation galvanized Rose's nerves. She met Devon's gaze head on. "Not many men would have. We learned that from Millicent, didn't we? Her family tossed her out on her head just because she climbed out a window and ran off with some oaf who promised to marry her!"

"You don't understand, Rose." Devon's chest heaved with the exertion of his emotions, but his voice began to calm. "I don't care about the child. She deceived me by not sharing her feelings with me. She deceived me by—"

"By what?"

Devon covered his face with his hands. For a moment, he stood there, his body trembling. Then he thrust his fingers through his thick dark hair, pulling at the roots, looking as if he were on the verge of losing his sanity.

"I thought I knew her," he whispered, at length.

"Everyone has secrets, Devon."

His shoulders sagged. Stumbling backward, he fell into his armchair and stared dejectedly at the fire. "I want to be alone, Rose."

"You can't isolate yourself in this house, Devon. You can't build a wall around your heart simply because it is wounded."

"You don't understand, Rose. I have spent the past six years mourning my wife. Now I realize that she was a stranger to me. You knew more about her than I did, you and Dolly and Millicent and Claire, too."

"What are you talking about, Devon?"

His voice was strangely quiet, his expression that of a man perfectly resigned to his terrible fate. "Haven't you figured it out, Rose? Haven't you wondered who gave you your house in Fontjoy Square?"

Despite her suspicions, the final revelation of learning that Devon Avondale was her mysterious benefactor left Rose wobbly-kneed. Her heart thrummed and her stomach flipped as she struggled to make sense of what she was hearing. "It was you!"

"Of course, it was I," he answered sullenly. "Who else? Did you really think that some stranger, some guardian angel, some leprechaun perhaps, had taken pity on you and given you a house?"

"Why? Why did you do it?"

"I wanted to be near Mary's friends. Simple as that. And she wanted it, too, I believe. Just before she died, she wrote about the four of you in her diary, and she directed me to read it after she was gone. She said that if I would read her journal, I would find a reason for living. When I found the four of you, and realized you were all on the verge of poverty—"

"Poverty? Dolly, too?" Suppressing a chuckle, Rose recalled how Dolly had once bragged about the fortune her husband had left her.

"Well, the cat is out of the bag now, isn't it?" Devon's tone was sarcastic. "I suppose it doesn't matter, though, now that she is married to Dick, and living happily ever after—"

But Rose could not suppress her curiosity. "It was you in the black mask? You came to my door and gave me the letter that informed me that I had been given a home in Fontjoy Square."

"Yes."

"All because I once befriended Mary?"

"It was enough. I loved her. I wanted to show her friends a kindness."

"What exactly did Mary write in that diary of hers?" Rose's gaze fell on the open book.

But Devon shot her a warning look. "The journal is for me and no one else. Besides, she said very little about you, except that you were friends. That is all."

"I don't know what to say." A lump formed in Rose's throat. The depth of her gratitude toward Devon was indescribable, but why had he kept his identity a secret? She felt a trifle foolish for having lived beneath the auspices of his charity for nearly a year without knowing it.

"You needn't say anything."

"Thank you." Leaning over him, Rose touched Devon's arm, but when he flinched, she withdrew and straightened. Blinking back tears, she tried desperately to conceal her emotions. "Do I have your permission to tell the others?"

"Why not?"

"Thank you," she repeated in a whisper. The fire on the hearth warmed her cheeks, but the room had grown uncomfortably cold. Devon obviously had nothing further to say; his depression seemed to fill the room, forcing Rose out. Quietly, she gathered her cloak, crossed the study, and left.

Outside, the chill winter air stung her cheeks. The hour was growing late, and her children and their nanny were at home waiting for her. She longed for her husband. She wanted to crawl into bed with him, snuggle into his embrace and tell him everything.

But she owed it to Dolly, Claire and Millicent to tell them first that Devon Avondale was the man who had given them all homes in Fontjoy Square.

The stress of worrying about her encounter with Devon and his subsequent disappearance had driven Claire to the brink of insanity. Just that morning she had begun wondering whether it had been a mistake to rebuff Devon. She was miserable without him. She had lost her appetite, her sense of humor and her interest in anything other than Devon's condition.

Worst of all, his kiss had sparked feelings in her that she'd been pretending for years did not exist—in her *unarousable* body, anyway.

By nightfall, after suffering through a tepid bath followed by hours of pacing her bedroom floor, Claire had relived all the painful memories of her youth. In the proper perspective, she knew she had done the right thing in rejecting Devon's advances. Indeed, she had done the only thing she could do. She could not allow a man to seduce her; it went against her principles; it went against everything she believed in.

Exhausted from her fretting and intent on retiring early, Claire threw off her clothes and wrapped a woolen robe around herself. As she passed through the foyer en route to the kitchen for a cup of hot chocolate, a knock sounded on the front door.

"What on earth would take you away from your babies at this hour?" Claire asked, ushering Rose Sinclair in out of the blistering cold.

Without preamble—indeed, before she had even removed her bonnet—Rose informed Claire that Devon Avondale was Mary O'Roarke's husband. And that was when Claire knew with certainty that she had lost her mind.

"No, dear, you heard me correctly." Rose untied her cloak and tossed it over the banister in Claire's foyer. "Now come on, you're going to catch your death of cold in that flimsy nightgown. Get back in bed now, lassie! I'll go and fetch the chocolate and bring it up. Go, now! I know where the kitchen is."

A few moments later, Claire was sitting in her own bed, sipping hot chocolate and staring at her good friend and neighbor Rose Sinclair-Noll-brook. She should have felt safe and secure. *Why, then, did she feel as if she had entered a dream state in which everything was new and unfamiliar?*

Rose pulled up a chair and sat beside the bed. "Brace yourself, dearie."

By the time Rose had finished telling her story, Claire's initial disbelief had turned to shock. "Why didn't he tell me, Rose? Why did he deceive me in this manner?"

"Don't forget, Claire, he deceived all of us. But I do not believe his motivation was malicious."

Claire pressed her lips together. His motivation might not have been malicious, but his actions were inexplicable. For, while Rose, Dolly and Millicent had all found men and gotten married, she and Devon had devoted themselves to tending the garden and refurbishing the old Georgian neighborhood. They had spent whole days together; they shared a common interest. *They were friends.*

Now she realized she had not known Devon Avondale at all. Rather, he had been a stranger masquerading as a friend. He had not had her best interests at heart. His feelings toward her had not been chaste and brotherly; they had been lustful and deceitful. As shock turned to bitter realization, a sour taste surged up the back of Claire's throat.

Gently, Rose leaned over and took the china cup and saucer from Claire's trembling fingers. "Try to understand, Claire. Mary was a very special young woman."

"She was very beautiful," Claire said carefully.

"I loved her dearly myself."

"I've no doubt."

"And no doubt Devon was very much in love with her. Her untimely death devastated him. And isn't it just like Mary to leave him a journal with our names in it?"

"Just like her." Closing her eyes, Claire remembered her first and last encounter with Mary O'Roarke. *The* Mary O'Roarke. Twenty years earlier, she had been the most intriguing young woman in Dublin society. "Mary always did have the last word, didn't she?"

"What do you mean, dear?"

"Oh, I don't know. Never mind me; I am so tired I can't think straight." Eager to be alone, Claire feigned a yawn. Devon's overtures had confused and frightened her. His disappearance had perplexed and fatigued her. Rose's revelation angered her. She needed time and solitude to sort out her feelings.

On cue, Rose stood. "I'll run along, then. It's late, and Steven is waiting for me."

"When are you going to tell the others?"

"In the morning. Drop 'round about ten o'clock if you care to join the discussion. It's bound to be lively." With a wry smile, Rose leaned over and kissed Claire's forehead.

When she had gone, Claire extinguished the lamp and burrowed beneath the counterpane. The icy fingers that gripped her heart had little to do with the chill that seeped in through the windows. The tears she had been fighting since Rose told her who her mysterious benefactor was, and why he had given them homes in Fontjoy Square, now flowed freely. Claire's chest ached with bitterness and more than a tad of self-pity.

Why, she wondered, couldn't she leave her past behind her once and for all? Was it her fate to be ridiculed and cheated by everyone she loved? Was history repeating itself?

At last, the irony of her situation dawned on her. Many years ago, Mary O'Roarke had ruined Claire's chances of ever forming a respectable marriage connection; now the conniving little redheaded woman was ruining her life and stealing her best friend, too.

Claire's sobs gave way to hysterical laughter. Perhaps she was going crazy. Or perhaps she was cursed. For who else but Lady Claire Kilgarren would suffer this sort of evil luck?

Just when she trusted a man enough to be his friend, he betrayed her by wanting more. Just when she let down her guard, she was attacked and betrayed. Just when she had nearly regained her self-esteem, the very woman who had precipitated her fall from grace reached out from the grave and reminded Claire that she was entitled to *nothing*.

Perhaps her father had been right: Claire's flesh was weak, and the only way to avoid damnation was to stay away from Devon Avondale.

Four

The next morning was bleak and painfully cold. After a restless night, Claire debated whether to attend the meeting at Rose's house. An uncharacteristically nasty mood colored Claire's perceptions. She was not in the mood to hear the happy chatter of the other women. She would be physically ill if she saw Rose put her ear to Millicent's swollen belly one more time. And she feared she would become violent if Dolly made one more coquettish reference to Dick Creevy's sexual prowess.

The temptation to stay at home in bed was strong. But in the end, Claire could not stand to stay away while the other ladies discussed the perfidy that Devon had committed upon all of them. Surely she would find some support among Rose, Millicent and Dolly for her sudden animosity toward the arrogant man. Most likely they would band together in their denouncement of him, then move away en masse from this bloody rotten place called Fontjoy Square.

Entering Rose's parlor, Claire murmured a sullen greeting to the other ladies. Much to her chagrin, they all looked rather chipper, as if the world hadn't shifted on its axis just the night before, as if their very best friend—*and his deceased wife*—had not betrayed them. As if they didn't realize how utterly wicked all men were.

Dolly patted a space beside her on the sofa. Claire folded her arms and sat beside the pert, athletic-looking blonde. Rose stood before the fireplace while Millicent carefully lowered herself into an armchair.

"Are you all right, Millie?" asked Rose in that mother-hen manner that had never bothered Claire before but this morning made her want to scream.

"The baby's a mite restless this morning, that's all." Millicent giggled nervously. "I only hope he—or she—doesn't decide to make an appearance before Alec returns home."

"Off to London again, is he?" asked Dolly. "You must be terribly lonely, then. Dick's in Edinburgh and I can barely stand myself! Sleeping alone is for the birds, I tell you."

Rose and Millicent nodded their agreement. *Oh, yes, sleeping alone is a fate worse than death!* Clasping her hands in her lap, Claire silently mocked her neighbors' reliance on their new husbands. She simply could not understand how these seemingly independent minded and intelligent women could have allowed themselves to become so enmeshed in their husbands' lives. Why, they all acted as if marriage was the most wonderful thing in the world! Didn't they realize how vulnerable they were now? Didn't they see how tenuous their happiness was?

It's a foolish woman who loves a man to distraction, believes every word he says and has faith that he will never break her heart. Men tended to grow weary of the novelty of sleeping with the same woman each night. Women tired of their husband's unexplained absences and flirtations. Couples grew distrustful, or bored with their own duplicity. Husbands bought town houses for their mistresses and moved their wives to the country. In the most civilized of circumstances, some couples even achieved a sort of farcical politeness toward one another that bordered on absurdity.

But—and this Claire knew from experience—when the love between a man and woman was dead, it could not be revived. And no matter how polite the two were to one another, the emotions that bubbled beneath the surface of their fraudulent relationship were insidiously poisonous.

With a shiver, she glanced around the room again. Millicent, Dolly and Rose seemed oblivious to the danger of their situations. Or perhaps they believed they were different from other women, or that their husbands were different from other men. Well, Claire hoped to God they were right. She hoped her friends and neighbors would never experience the pain of being betrayed and rejected. She hoped they would never have cause to be as bitter as she.

"Well, as Claire already knows, I paid Mr. Avondale a visit last night." Rose related the details of her encounter with Devon, the discovery that he was Mary O'Roarke's husband and the mysterious benefactor who had given each of them her home in Fontjoy Square.

Millicent's cheeks turned bright pink. "Impossible! My father gave me my home! Through a private agent, of course. He did not want me to know—"

"I am sorry," Rose said sympathetically, "but your father did not give you that house, dear. You assumed that he did because it was what you wanted to believe. His pride prevented him from correcting you. But it isn't true. I hope you won't allow this knowledge to ruin your relationship with your father. He adores you, you know."

After a beat, Millicent turned her puzzled face on Dolly. "But I thought your dead husband left you your home! You said he did!"

Blushing furiously, Dolly said, "I lied. I did not want any of you to know that I was nearly broke when the house was offered to me. Why else would I have accepted such a strange offer from someone I had never met? I was desperate, I tell you! I'd have been on the street in another month if Mr. Avondale hadn't come along."

Claire rushed to Dolly's rescue. "Oh, good heavens, I lied too!" Throwing up her hands, she even forced a laugh. "And so did you, Rose."

Rose stiffened. "If you recall, I said nothing about how I acquired a house in Fontjoy Square."

For a moment, the women fell silent, their gazes skittering around the room. A round of nervous throat-clearing ensued, prompting Rose to pull the bell cord and order a tray of cookies and hot tea. At length, the tension in the room eased, and the ladies returned to the subject at hand, Devon Avondale. Rose recounted Aidan Sullivan's appearance at the Dorcas Society and his subsequent confrontation with Devon. She said the boy was Mary O'Roarke's illegitimate child, born as the result of a girlish infatuation with a freckle-faced Lothario.

"Mary O'Roarke got herself pregnant and didn't tell her parents about it?" Millicent asked, gaping.

"Is it so hard to believe?" Claire rejoined in as level a tone as she could muster.

"Mary was terrified of her parents," said Dolly. "As loyal a friend as one could ever hope for, and wild as a buck rabbit, but when it came to her parents—"

"She would have died before she'd have told them," Rose concluded.

"Poor, sweet girl," Millicent said.

"Yes, she was quite a special lass," Rose said in eulogy. "I'm certain we all miss her terribly."

Acutely aware that her feelings toward Mary O'Roarke were completely opposite to those of everyone else in the room, Claire folded her arms across her chest. Clearly, her neighbors thought Mary was a saint, or at least an angel. Could they have known the same Mary that Claire knew?

Millicent talked about how Mary had once befriended her during a summer in Vienna. The two girls shared a life-changing experience when a randy cad attempted to take advantage of Mary. In sounding the alarm, Millicent saved Mary from ruin. But Millicent damaged her relationship with her own father in the bargain. Oddly, Millicent said she would do it all over again if she had the chance.

And Dolly related a tale from boarding school in Switzerland, when Mary had cheated on an examination and Dolly took the blame. "My father couldn't afford the tuition any more, and I would have been sent home anyway."

Claire listened in awe as Rose described a summer spent with Mary at the seaside resort of Killiney. Headstrong and reckless, Mary fell in love with a young Romeo who got her with child, then vanished. Rose helped Mary keep the pregnancy secret, but after the baby was born and put up for adoption, the two girls fell out of touch.

At last, all eyes turned to Claire.

"When did you meet Mary O'Roarke?" Rose asked gently. "Can you tell us what you know of her?"

Baffled, Claire hugged her shoulders and shook her head. She had heard enough about Mary O'Roarke to justify her long-held beliefs. Mary had been cruel and arrogant when she entered Dublin society some twenty years earlier. Apparently, she hadn't been any different when Dolly, Rose and

Millicent knew her. "I'd rather not discuss Mary O'Roarke."

"Why not?" piped up Millicent.

"I just don't want to, that's all."

"That's not like you," Dolly said. "I have never known you to be reticent on any subject."

"She must have been a dear friend to you if your name was in her diary," Rose said.

Claire refused to answer. Indeed, she could not imagine why her name was in Mary O'Roarke's diary. Was it possible that Mary had documented that awful night twenty years ago, the night that changed Claire's life forever?

Slowly, Claire pushed to her feet. If she wasn't going to share her feelings about Mary O'Roarke, she might as well go home. She had nothing else to say to her neighbors, all of whom labored under the impression that Mary O'Roarke had been a sweet, kindhearted woman.

Before she left, however, she had one question for her friends. "After listening to what you have said about Mary O'Roarke, I admit I am more confused than ever. She let Rose do her dirty work and never spoke to her again. Dolly got tossed out of school on account of Mary O'Roarke. And Millicent was estranged from her father for years because she defended Mary's virtue. Why, then, do all of you speak of her as if she was some sort of saint?"

A stunned silence echoed throughout the parlor. Studying the faces of her friends, Claire realized that she had voiced an opinion shared by no one else. A tingly, red-hot bitterness nettled beneath her skin. Mary O'Roarke had trumped her yet again.

Pivoting, she stalked from the room without uttering so much as a good-bye. A fist of anger pounded her rib cage. Perhaps her friends, in their collective naïvité, had been blind to Mary's cruelty. Perhaps they had never felt Mary's sharp edge the way she had. Or perhaps, as Mary had once suggested, Claire didn't even know who her friends were.

Claire knew one thing, though. She was going to see what Mary O'Roarke had written about her in that damned diary if it was the last thing she did.

"Didn't I make myself clear?" Devon was tempted to bolt out of his chair and wring his butler's neck. "Tell that woman I am not accepting visitors!"

But once again the ineffective man sputtered his apologies as a pair of lady's boots pounded up the steps and into Devon's inner sanctum.

"Can't a man be left alone in his own home?" Bounding to his feet, Devon expected to see Rose Sinclair on his doorstep. Surprised to find himself scowling at Lady Claire Kilgarren, he added, "Can't a man enjoy a bit of privacy?"

"Not in a neighborhood populated mainly by women, dear."

"Haven't you women ever heard of an *invita-*

tion? Generally speaking, it *precedes* a visit to someone else's home."

"Given the degree of familiarity you and I have shared these last few months, I presumed I could dispense with protocol."

"We were hardly familiar, Claire. You made it clear you did not want to be my lover."

Claire slammed the door behind her, strode into the darkened room and tossed her cloak on the sofa opposite Devon's chair. "Does that mean we can no longer have a civil conversation? Is that it, then? I must consent to sleep with you if I want to exchange civilities? My, you're more of a brute than I had thought!"

With a bitter chuckle, Devon studied the pretty interloper who'd invaded his cave. Clad in the same dark blue winter gown she'd worn when he last saw her, she was a pleasant respite from the walls and pages he'd been staring at these past five days. But he was in no mood to entertain her company. His malaise, brought on by Claire's rejection of him and deepened by Aidan Sullivan's appearance, rendered him incapable of enjoying anything.

She stood before him, her arms crossed over her chest. "What's the trouble with you, laddie? You've been holed up in this house for nearly five days and you haven't even had the decency to send me a note of explanation."

"I'm not a laddie, I haven't got any troubles and I don't owe you any explanations. I just don't feel like talking to anyone, that's all."

"You might as well know, Rose has let the cat of the bag."

Of course. He had known that she would. Still, Devon's pulse quickened at the thought of being exposed. "Everyone knows?" he asked, startled by the emotion that roughened his voice.

"Yes, and we are all very grateful to you, as well we should be. It appears that you saved us all from poverty, Devon. How can we—how can I—ever thank you?"

"I detect a note of sarcasm in your voice, Claire. Something tells me you aren't grateful at all."

"What do you expect me to feel? Don't you understand what you've done to me?" She took a deep breath, apparently exasperated not only by Devon's generosity but also by his inability to comprehend the perfidy he had committed.

"Let me see," he began slowly. "I have given you a home to live in. I have kept you from starving to death. And I have been your friend this past year. What else have I done, Claire?"

"You lied to me." Her lashes fluttered uncontrollably. "And you tried to seduce me."

"Can we deal with one vile act of treachery at a time? I kept my identity a secret because I didn't want your feelings toward me to be based on gratitude. Or, God forbid, on sympathy."

"What *did* you want? What was your purpose in bringing all of us here?"

"I wanted to know you." Devon felt like a criminal being interrogated. He threw a furtive glance at the brandy snifter on the little table beside his chair; regretfully, it was empty. "I wanted to know the girls whom Mary had written about in her diary."

"You wanted to know Mary," Claire countered wistfully. "You thought by bringing her friends together, you would keep her alive, didn't you?"

He shrugged.

"You could have knocked on our doors, introduced yourself as Mary's husband and asked all the questions you liked. I'm certain that Millicent, Rose and Dolly would have been happy to regale you with stories about their childhood friend."

"They would never have been honest with me. They would have felt sorry for me, a bereaved husband who couldn't get on with his life. They'd have told me what they wanted me to hear, that Mary was a sweet, kind, loving person, that they cherished her, that sort of tripe. That's not what I wanted, Claire. And that's not what I got."

Swallowing hard, she twisted her fingers. "No, I suppose not."

"Don't be angry with me," he said quietly.

For a moment, she stood rigidly, her eyes tightly shut. Then she dropped her arms to her sides and stared intensely at Devon. "I thought we were friends! Now I realize that I was friends with someone else. How do you expect me to feel?"

"I have not changed, Claire."

"But our friendship has. The trust between us has been altered. I hadn't bargained for being seduced, you see."

Her accusing tone was like a sword through

Devon's heart. Slowly, he approached Claire. If she would let him, he wanted to hold her in his arms, to steep in the warmth of her body, to inhale the perfume of her hair. He needed to do that; he needed to know that she had not abandoned him.

"You are my dearest friend, sweetheart. I didn't mean to hurt you. I would never do anything you didn't want me to do."

She took a step back. "If you are my friend, Devon, you will never try to kiss me again. I-I don't like that sort of thing. I am not that sort of woman, you understand."

"What sort of woman?" He took a step forward.

"The sort who allows a man to—well, to kiss her and touch her."

"Is that a bad thing, Claire?"

She gave one of those nervous little snorts he found so endearing. "I won't judge anyone else. But I do not engage in such things. Truth be known, I don't believe in such things."

"You don't believe in them?" Devon tried to stifle his amusement. He didn't think for a minute that Claire lacked sexual urges. He had known her for the better part of a year, and she was as healthy and high-spirited as any female he'd ever met. "Are you telling me that you have an aversion to lovemaking?"

Her chin dropped to her chest. "I do not wish to discuss it, Devon."

He put his hand on her upper arm. God, how he wanted to pull her into his embrace and feel her lips on his. After what he'd been through the past few days, he needed the comfort of her friendship more than ever. "You have never been afraid to talk to me before."

"That was different. It is not proper for a woman to discuss such things with a man," she murmured. "Especially with a man she hardly knows."

He tipped up her chin and brushed away a tear. His heart squeezed at the sight of Claire's pain. Clearly, she was in turmoil.

Had someone hurt her in the past, abused her or broken her heart? He struggled for a moment with the thought of simply leaving her alone. But Devon refused to accept that his feelings were one-sided. If Claire was truly repulsed by him, she would leave.

Instead, she stood before him, blushing, fidgeting and, in general, looking as if she was frightened to death.

"You know me, Claire," he said, at length.

She dipped her head and studied the tips of her shoes.

Slowly, Devon drew her closer to his body. "Look at me."

When she lifted her head, her gaze was watery but direct, and heartbreakingly vulnerable.

"You can stop me at any time, Claire. Tell me now, and I will never touch you again. Tell me to leave you alone, and I will disappear from your life, and you will never hear from me again. You can live in Fontjoy Square forever without any obligation to me whatsoever. I will buy you a house elsewhere if you can't tolerate my presence in the neighborhood."

Her words came out in a tumble. "No, no, Devon, I do not want you to disappear!" A strangled cry escaped her throat as her body fell against Devon's. She clutched at his shirtfront and pressed her face to his chest. "Don't you understand? I thought I would go mad these past few days."

Caressing the top of her head, Devon sighed. "I have missed you, too, Claire."

Her sobs gradually subsided. For a long while, the two stood in the center of the parlor, Devon breathing in the perfume of Claire's hair and wishing he could convince her that his intentions toward her were honorable. But how *could* he when he did not understand the source of her fears? How could he make amends for what some other man had done?

How could he win her trust when he had been lying to her for nearly a year?

"Would you like me to walk you home?" he asked quietly.

When she looked up at him, her eyes were puffy and her lips moist. "Not yet," she whispered.

He wanted to kiss her so badly it pained him. "We are not in a hurry, then."

"We are friends, aren't we, Devon?"

"The very best of friends."

"I was wondering . . . I mean, you said that I could stop any time I wanted . . . that if you kissed me and I didn't like it—"

"Yes."

"If I wanted a kiss, *one* kiss, you would not think less of me, would you?"

"No."

"You wouldn't think I was a brazen harlot, would you?"

"Of course not." Claire *did* want him; his instincts had not been wrong. Yet she was apprehensive, embarrassed even, of her own desires.

Despite the heat coursing through Devon's veins, he hesitated. His deceased wife's voice sounded in the back of his mind.

"Women are taught to be chaste and innocent, dear," she had once reminded him. *"A woman is not supposed to want sex. Rather, she is supposed to grit her teeth and think of dear Queen Victoria as she does her duty to her husband and country."*

Of course, years earlier, when Mary had uttered that famous line, she had had her tongue planted firmly in her cheek and Devon's anatomy poised precariously at her lips. Mary O'Roarke might have been raised to believe that nice girls did not like sex, but she had certainly acquired a taste for it as an adult.

Nostalgia washed over him. Mary had not been immune to the hypocrisy society imposed on women. Indeed, she had developed a curious mixture of rebelliousness and submissiveness in response to her upbringing. Aidan Sullivan's appearance in Fontjoy Square had brought into focus the contradictions of Mary's personality.

Therefore, Devon was not shocked that Claire, a seemingly mature and candid woman, would be coquettish and awkward when it came to lovemaking. What he didn't know was whether the pretty blond aristocrat was *pretending* to be frigid, or whether she was really as innocent and inexperienced as she purported to be.

Seduction was a dangerous game. A man had to know when *no* was negotiable. More importantly, he had. to know when *yes* was an invitation to disaster.

Cupping Claire's face in his hands, he peered into her wide, unblinking gaze. "You are free to stop me at any time, dear."

"Do you promise, Devon?"

His pressed his lips to hers. "I promise."

Five

It was official. She was insane. She had stormed over to Devon's house with two goals in mind. First, she intended to tell him that he was a lying cad who did not deserve her friendship. Any man who would manipulate four women like puppets for his own pleasure and gratification was far too conniving a creature to be trusted.

Second, she meant to sneak a peek at Mary's diary, particularly the passage that related to that fateful weekend in the country some fifteen years ago. Morbid curiosity alone would have compelled Claire to do that, but, in addition, she needed to know what Devon knew about her. Had he discovered her secret? Did he know why Lord Kilgarren had disinherited her? Did he know what role Mary O'Roarke had played in Claire's downfall? And if he did, how could he have pretended this past year to be her friend?

But somehow, Claire's plan had gone terribly awry. Instead of casting off Devon's friendship, she had been swayed by his honeyed words and soulful eyes. Instead of excising him from her life, she had placed herself in his arms. With a sigh, she realized that her mother's legacy was truly inescapable. She ought to counter Devon's overture with a slap on his face, especially if he knew the reasons for her former penurious circumstances. Instead, she was living out her father's predictions and confirming Mary O'Roarke's hurtful epithets.

Everything her father had said about her and her mother, the countess, had been true, then. They were hot-blooded and oversexed, entirely incapable of controlling their passions. There was no point in even *trying* not to kiss Devon. That Claire would behave wickedly was inevitable.

All she could do now was negotiate the boundaries of her wantonness. She had to do *something* to protect her reputation. If Devon knew how badly she wanted to feel his hands exploring every inch of her body, he would be shocked—possibly even repulsed. If he knew how desperately she wanted to feel his lips on hers, he would be floored by her brazenness.

Better that he thought he was *persuading* her to kiss him. Better that he thought she was *giving in*, rather than getting what she wanted.

"If I say that I want to be kissed and nothing more, do you promise that you will refrain from attempting to pressure me into an, um, deeper involvement?"

"I will not take a mile where only an inch is offered."

Emboldened by his reassuring tone, Claire said,

"But if I want to be kissed, well, somewhere other than my lips . . . my throat, for example, do you promise that you will not attempt to parlay my request into a license to kiss me elsewhere?"

"Where, for example?"

Some very interesting places came to mind. "I do not precisely know. In this high-necked gown, there really isn't much available skin to kiss."

"Don't be so certain."

He had only yet touched her face, run his thumb beneath her lower lip and traced the arch of her brow. Yet Claire could feel the heat of his desire everywhere, even in places she would not dare discuss. "I intend to be certain about everything *before* it happens, Devon. A woman in my position cannot afford to be reckless with her reputation."

"You said you weren't worried about your reputation. Of all the women in this neighborhood, you are the least likely to be suspected of consorting with a man. Isn't that what you said?"

"It is widely known that I do not care for men."

"Ah." He chuckled. "I don't believe you. You would not be standing here with your body pressed against mine if you did not."

"Believe what you will, Devon, but I assure you that whatever happens in this room tonight will never happen again. Think of this as a farewell kiss, if you like. Now that I know who you are, and whom you were married to, I do not feel comfortable in Fontjoy Square. You did try to help me, though, and for that I am grateful. I suppose a little kiss of gratitude is in order. As long as you mind your manners, that is."

"Do you mean to say that you are going to allow me to kiss you because I gave you a house? Awfully expensive kiss, isn't it? What on earth would I have to give you in order to get you into my bed?"

A bubble of nervous laughter escaped Claire's throat. "Well, that is simply too ridiculous to think about, isn't it? You won't be getting me into your bed, Devon."

He pulled a long face. "I admit I am disappointed."

"Shall I turn around and walk out right now? Or are you going to honor my requests?"

"Dear, I intend to do whatever it takes to please you."

Tilting her head, she slanted him an appraising look. "And do you think you can do that? Please me, I mean? What makes you think you can do what no other man ever has done?"

"Because I will try harder than any man you have ever known, Claire."

"You should know at the outset that I am quite . . . unmovable. I mean, I would not want you to feel, er, inadequate if you are unable to excite me."

"Oh, my, you have thrown down the gauntlet now," he drawled, lowering his mouth to hers.

Gently, he pressed his lips to hers. For a long moment, he kissed her tentatively, fitting and shaping his mouth to hers. His breath was sweet and warm; he tasted vaguely of scotch whiskey and smelled of smoke and clover. He tasted good, and he felt better. But Claire could not easily abandon her long-held belief that it was unseemly to become excited about a man.

When his tongue stroked her lower lip, however, a tiny moan escaped her. Embarrassed, Claire turned her head. "I-I'm sorry—"

"For what, dear? Because you are enjoying yourself? Don't you understand that I want to give you pleasure?"

His stubbly jaw scraped the side of her face. He nuzzled her ear and nipped at her lobe, kissing her wherever her high-necked gown would permit. Claire's clothes felt hot and heavy against her body. She drew a deep breath and almost forgot to release it. Dizzied, she feared she would faint straightaway if Devon did not release her.

And she would have been sorely dismayed if he had.

His arms wound around her, one hand cradling her head, the other caressing her back. "Are you afraid of where your passions will take you, Claire?"

How does he know?

"Are you afraid of me?"

Can he hear my unspoken thoughts?

Her embarrassment tripled. Nodding, Claire squeezed shut her eyes and clung to Devon's shoulders. But that only drew her more snugly into his embrace, so that now his rigid penis pressed into her soft belly and his hard thighs framed her legs. Instinctively, Claire pushed her feet apart and drew one ankle halfway up his leg.

The urge to wrap herself around him was nearly irrepressible. Devon clearly sensed her need. Swiftly, he clamped his hands on Claire's buttocks, picked her up and swept her into his arms. Before she could blink, she was supine on the sofa, her head resting on a pillow, her lungs near to bursting with panic.

If kissing Devon had been unseemly, then lying on a sofa with him was surely unforgivable. "I do not think we should do this," Claire stammered.

Standing beside the sofa, he hovered over her. "I will stop if you ask me to."

Tension crackled between them. Claire had only to say the word *no* and Devon would retreat. He had promised her he would. She believed him.

"I think you should—" Her resolve faltered. "I think you should not—"

"Do you want me to stop?"

She moved her lips but no sound emerged. Staring up at Devon, Claire prayed violently—not for virtue, notably, but for courage to articulate her feelings. "Could I trouble you for a sip of whiskey?"

While Devon was at the sideboard, she marshaled her wits and analyzed her situation. Devon wanted to bed her, and she was practically panting to be bedded by him. Her upbringing and her deeply ingrained sense of propriety, however, would not allow her to enjoy a night of meaningless, casual sex. Or would it?

Apparently Devon was that rare man who did not judge a woman who wanted to be kissed. She thought he might be the only man in Ireland with such an enlightened view. He certainly wasn't like her father. An opportunity such as this might never arise again.

A novel realization struck her: Tonight was a *free* night, when morals and social mores could be ignored. Caution be damned! Whatever happened between Devon and Claire in this room would never be spoken of again. If she was going to pack her trunks and leave Fontjoy Square, she might as well find out what sex felt like before she went. She might as well find out what all the stir was really about, why her mother had been so enamored of men and why Dolly, Millicent and Rose—all apparently sensible women—had taken such tremendous risks for the men they loved.

Half-sitting, Claire accepted the drink that Devon offered her. As she sipped, her uneasiness abated. Warmth trickled into her limbs. After she drained her whiskey, she handed the glass to Devon, touched her sticky lips and smiled.

"Feel better?" he asked.

"Much." Languidly, she reclined, turning on her side so that Devon could lay beside her.

Nestled beside him on the sofa, Claire's anxieties continued to fade. She would have closed her eyes, but staring into Devon's gaze as he kissed her heightened their intimacy. His expression took on an intoxicating quality, and his kisses grew more urgent. When she was brave enough to run her tongue along his lips, he even groaned.

In her mind, she echoed his sentiments. The pleasure that came with Devon's kisses also created an exquisite sort of pain that pulsed through Claire's body. Between her legs, she experienced a disturbing heaviness. She wondered if other women had felt this way in Devon's arms. Though she knew it was not healthy to speculate, she could not help but wonder whether Mary O'Roarke had felt this helpless and needy in her husband's loving embrace.

Thoughts of Mary provoked an uncharacteristic jealousy in Claire. What would Mary say now if she could see her husband lying next to Claire Kilgarren? How would she feel if she knew her husband was practically breathless with desire for the girl whom Mary had referred to publicly as that "wretched little by-blow?"

Claire's bitterness toward Mary O'Roarke suddenly manifested itself in a lustiness that was equally uncharacteristic for her. Even as she parted her thighs and draped one leg over Devon's, Claire wondered whether her desire was motivated by revenge or petty jealousy. She should be ashamed for wanting Mary O'Roarke's husband. She should feel guilty for throwing herself at a dead woman's lover. She should be sorry for Devon's loneliness.

But she did not feel any of those things.

Instead, she had to suppress a chuckle. Fifteen years ago, Mary had predicted that Lady Claire

Kilgarren would never capture the attention of a decent man. Now, here she was, slipping undone the buttons of Devon Avondale's shirt and teasing goose bumps to the surface of his broad, muscular chest.

"You're smiling," he said.

"So are you," she replied throatily.

Mischievously, she yanked the tails of his white lawn shirt out of his pants.

Deftly, Devon shrugged out of his shirt and tossed it on the floor. Then he wrapped his arms around Claire's waist and hugged her against his naked flesh.

His belly and his chest were rock hard, covered with thick black hair. Caressing his sinewy forearms, bronzed from his gardening, Claire began the process of memorizing every angle and plane of the man's body. His biceps and shoulders were worthy of a Greek diorama; he looked as if he'd been carved from marble.

Yet he was warm to the touch and all too human. He didn't once flinch or pull away from Claire's exploring hands. He didn't grab, grasp or grope in response. Thankfully, he seemed content to indulge Claire's curiosity without demanding favors in return from her.

She caressed his back, scraped her fingernails along his spine and even cupped his derriere. And the more she touched him, the more she wanted.

Inevitably, her attention turned to his erection. Slowly, half frightened that Devon would pounce on her like a hungry tiger, Claire slid her hand over the bulge in his trousers. Without further coaxing, the hard muscle responded. Devon's hips jerked and he sucked in a mouthful of air through his teeth. Quickly, he controlled his reaction and, with a grimace, put his hand atop hers.

"Do you prefer that I not touch you there?" She hoped he wouldn't ask her to stop, but if he did, Claire knew she had to. It wouldn't be fair not to, not after Devon's promise to her.

"No dear, it is just that . . ." He swallowed hard. His forehead creased and his jaw clenched. "What you are doing . . . feels good. Very good."

Strangely, despite the pulsing need in her own lower regions, Claire discovered that pleasuring Devon offered its own rewards. "Do you like it when I do . . . this?"

Gritting his teeth, he managed to say, "Yes."

With her palm, she rubbed the length of his shaft until Devon's breathing was erratic. Muttering a mild imprecation, he rolled onto his back, released Claire's wrist and allowed her to stroke and massage him. Tiny beads of sweat appeared on his upper lip; his features were drawn and every fiber in his body seemed to tense. Claire wondered how much of this wonderful torture Devon could tolerate before he ripped off her clothes and took her.

As his hips lifted, her own desire soared. Her ability to excite Devon excited her. She felt powerful and feminine. She ached with the need to take Devon's body inside hers and love him. But losing her virginity to Mary O'Roarke's husband, the man who had deceived her about his identity for nearly a year, was quite out of the question, especially for a woman who did not even like men.

She wondered if she could put Devon out of his misery another way. It would be an act of kindness, she rationalized.

Her mind flashed on an image that she had never before conjured. She wondered if it was safe to unbutton Devon's trousers and put her hands on his naked penis.

Could she trust him not to molest her?

"Devon?"

"What, love?" His eyes fluttered open and he craned his neck to look at her.

"Do you suppose it is reasonable for a woman to expect a man not to attack her if she reaches inside his trousers and touches his naked body?"

His head fell to the sofa cushion. "No, it is most *unreasonable*. Most men would interpret the very question as a license to ravish you."

"You are not *most men*."

" 'Tis true." A slow smile spread across his face. "I can control myself. If you wish to touch me there, be my guest."

"And you promise—"

"I promise."

A little spurt of joy accompanied Devon's promise. Practically giddy, Claire sat up and reached for his waistband. The sofa was small, and Devon was hanging on the edge. To make more room, Claire straddled Devon's thighs and sat on top of him.

Vaguely, she wondered if it was possible to hate men in general and like one of them in particular.

As she worked the fabric of Devon's pants, Claire wrestled with the dichotomy of what she had long believed and what she was feeling for the first time.

Just because Devon Avondale's kisses were sweet didn't mean he was an honorable man worthy of her everlasting love and devotion. He had already proved what a scoundrel he was.

And just because she was voraciously curious to see and feel his naked body didn't mean she had to be in love with him.

Men often took their physical pleasure with women they didn't care a whit about.

Why couldn't a woman do the same?

Unbleached linen unmentionables peeked from beneath Devon's gaping trousers. A mild oath leapt to Claire's tongue. The man's bare flesh remained invisible.

As if he could read her mind, Devon lifted his hips and slid his pants and underpants down his thighs. Without warning, his male appendage popped into view. Engorged, it seemed to spring off Devon's belly. And though Claire had never seen an adult male penis, she knew enough to know that the one she was staring at was unusually thick and long.

"No wonder you wanted me to see that." She couldn't tear her gaze from it. "Good heavens."

His laugh was like velvet. "It is rather impressive, is it not?"

"I suppose," Claire replied grudgingly. "If you like that sort of thing."

"I am beginning to think you do, despite what you say."

She was beginning to think he might be right, and that was what alarmed her more than anything. After all, Claire's mother had suffered from an intolerable weakness of the flesh. Lady Shannon Kilgarren had been notoriously fond of men. Some unkind souls, such as Mary O'Roarke, had even referred to her as a *nymphomaniac.*

Well, at least Claire saw now what had intrigued her mother so.

Tentatively, she wrapped her fingers around Devon's anatomy. Uncertain how much pressure his shaft could withstand, she held him delicately at first.

"You won't hurt me if you hold it a wee bit more tightly," he drawled.

Carefully, she squeezed the hard muscle. "Do you like that?"

Devon's smile vanished, only to be replaced by an expression of intense concentration. "Do you want me to show you what I like?" he rasped.

Her sense of decorum abandoned her. Claire, the most proper and genteel of the ladies who lived at Fontjoy Square, was eager to learn everything that Devon had to teach her. Dimly, she wondered if she was slipping down the treacherous slope that had been her mother's downfall. Her father's voice was never completely silent. But she would worry about the condition of her impure soul later; for now, her attention was riveted to Devon's penis.

"Show me."

Watching, Claire experienced a thrill so wicked and wonderful she might not ever have believed it had she merely read about it, or been told about it by another woman. Devon's hand moved surely and expertly.

After a moment, he placed Claire's hand on his body, and she imitated his ministrations. The intimacy that had been growing between the two was now unbearably erotic. Claire had half a mind to toss off her knickers and impale herself on Devon's erection. But the other half of her mind clung to that old fear of letting go.

"Claire, if you are not careful, you will cause me to—"

"I have not been careful this entire evening, Devon."

Grasping Claire's wrist, he stilled her hand. "I do not want you to regret what happens. I'm afraid I know the limits of my control, dear. I cannot stand much more."

There was something poignant about the entreating tone in Devon's voice. Claire didn't want to stop now. She wanted to see Devon lose control. She wanted to experience that with him. "It's all right, then," she whispered. "Don't hold back."

His penetrating stare was full of questions. Sensing Devon's hesitation, Claire reached beneath his shaft and gingerly cupped the most delicate part of his anatomy.

Apparently unable to resist any longer, he groaned. Then he covered her hand with his and together they stroked him, slowly at first, then faster, until he said her name again, this time as if it was torn from his soul, and his body convulsed, and his eyes squeezed shut, and the evidence of his release poured warm and sticky onto Claire's fingers.

For a long while he lay on his back with his eyes closed. A look of total contentment spread over his handsome features. Uncertain what to say or do, for no one had ever tutored her in the etiquette of post-dalliance interactions, Claire fell silent.

With childlike wonder, she watched Devon's penis shrink to a less intimidating size. Had she not been so confused by her own emotions, she might have insisted that Devon do something to appease the pulsing need between her legs. But she had no idea what he could do in that regard other than make love to her. And, now that her wits were returning and she was thinking more clearly, she reckoned she was lucky he hadn't molested her.

He snored.

Good God, what have I done?

"Devon?" Carefully, quietly and moving as stealthily as an intruder, Claire lifted herself from Devon's body. Standing beside the sofa, she leaned over him. He was, as she had suspected, asleep. She thought of awakening him, or tossing a cover over his half-exposed body. It seemed rude to leave the man in this condition and sneak out of his house in the dead of night without bidding farewell.

It seemed equally rude that he would fall asleep and ignore her after they had shared such an intimate experience, after Claire had reversed all her long-held beliefs about men and acquiesced in Devon's attempt to educate her sexually.

"Devon?" she repeated softly, half wishing he would wake up, half wishing he would remain asleep.

He looked so sweet and innocent and boyish.

Now she knew why her mother had such a weakness for men. They were terribly alluring when they were asleep, their features smoothed into boyish repose.

"Devon?" She touched his shoulder.

"Mary?" he asked groggily, rolling to his side, clutching at a sofa pillow as if it were a woman's soft, rounded body.

Mary?

The shock of hearing that name nearly knocked Claire over.

And now she knew why her father preached abstinence, sobriety and celibacy.

Wounded, Claire drew a deep breath and straightened. She turned and scanned the room, noting the brass fire poker that would have been a perfect instrument to skewer Devon right where he lay. The big Chinese vase on the mantel would have crashed beautifully over his head. The iron walnut cracker on the sideboard would have neatly crushed his—

Her gaze lit on a well-worn leather-bound book,

splayed open and resting on the floor beside Devon's armchair. Was it possible that he had left his dead wife's journal laying about? Could it be? Claire's violent fantasies evaporated. Glancing at Devon, satisfied that he was still dead to the world, she padded across the carpet and picked up the book. As she ruffled the gold-edged pages, she caught a glimpse of her own name, and those of her neighbors', written in a distinctively feminine slant.

Claire's need to know what Mary O'Roarke had written, and what Devon Avondale knew, was suddenly stronger than ever. Clasping the journal to her breast, she picked up her cloak and stole out of Devon's study.

Plunging into the cold outside, she mentally scolded herself for allowing her physical urges and her curiosity to get the better of her. What had she been thinking? She should never have let down her guard, or allowed herself to think she might have been wrong about men in general or, at least, one in particular. She should never have doubted her own instinct for self-preservation.

The Duke of Kilgarren had been right to condemn women who liked sex.

The duchess had been foolish to let men use her.

Claire was not going to let Devon Avondale make a fool out of her.

Six

Devon had awakened and found himself alone,
sprawled on the sofa before a dwindling fire. Hurt
that Claire would have left without saying good-
bye, and feeling vaguely guilty for having committed some dreadful faux pas that he couldn't
remember, he had stumbled to the sideboard in
the middle of the night. Now his head ached from
the whiskey he'd consumed and he didn't feel any
better about Claire's wordless departure.

As the first rays of daylight streamed through the
windows, he slumped in his armchair. His mind
flashed on an image of Claire, hunkered over him,
her gaze riveted to his body. As weary as he was, the
memory created an uncomfortable weightiness in
his lower regions. Claire undoubtedly had the potential to be one of the most sexually responsive
women he'd ever known. She just needed to let go
of her inhibitions, a goal Devon would be happy to
assist her in achieving. He wondered if, after last
night, she would still attempt to assert that she did

not like men. The thought made him smile. Knowing Claire, the answer was *yes*.

Naturally, the idea of lovemaking brought to Devon's mind a picture of his beloved Mary. For years after her death, he hadn't thought he would ever even *have* sex with anyone else.

Melancholy swept over him as he recalled their first encounter. Though Mary had not been a virgin, she had been nearly as self-conscious and shy as Claire. Her previous sexual experiences had clearly been traumatic. Devon and Mary had been married for several years before she fully trusted him—physically, that is. When she finally did, their sex life was incredibly rewarding.

Why did she have to die?

All he had now were her written words. Engulfed by loneliness—in part because Mary had abandoned him in the middle of his life, and in part because Claire had left him in the middle of the night—Devon reached for the journal he'd left on the floor. His fingertips searched for the familiar leather binding. With a frown, he leaned down and ran his palms over the thick oriental carpet.

"She has stolen Mary's diary!" Standing, Devon slammed a fist into the palm of his other hand. He couldn't believe that Lady Claire Kilgarren would be so deceitful as to steal Mary's journal. Yet there was no one else who could have. It was in this room when she arrived, and now it had disappeared.

Stalking from the study, Devon shouted for his butler. "Bring me a pot of coffee, will you? I'll

have it in my room. And draw me a bath, someone! Lay out my clothes!"

His household staff erupted with busy efficiency. Within minutes, servants bustled about
with armloads of fluffy towels. They laid out Devon's freshly laundered unmentionables and ran
hot water in the tub. Fontjoy Square was surprisingly modern; just before he had invited the four
ladies to live there, Devon had installed new
plumbing and water heaters in all the houses.

Now he wondered if he'd made a mistake in
inviting Dolly, Millicent, Rose and Claire to live in
Fontjoy Square. He had thought they would en-
rich his memories of Mary—not *steal* them.

Handsome in a sharp-edged sort of way, Aidan
Sullivan stood in Claire's foyer, snatching off his
glove and extending his hand. "I hope I am not
intruding."

He was, actually. When her butler had an-
nounced the arrival of a young Mr. Sullivan, Claire
had been in her bedchamber reading Mary
O'Roarke's journal. Having slept later than usual,
she'd eaten a quick breakfast, then returned to
her room where she'd been for the past hour, unable to put the journal down. Mary's recollections
of her boarding school days in Switzerland made
for interesting reading, and Claire hadn't even
found the part about that infamous season in Dublin fifteen years ago. She would have liked to read
the entire journal in one sitting.

But she was too polite to turn Aidan away. From what Rose had said, he'd been sorely disappointed to learn of his mother's death. And Devon's boorish reaction to the boy's appearance had surely devastated him.

Claire harbored a great deal of sympathy for Aidan. And since Devon had wounded her feelings, too, she felt a sort of camaraderie with him.

"It's no imposition at all, Mr. Sullivan." As she slipped her fingers in his, Claire was surprised at the rough texture of Aidan Sullivan's hands. Surmising that he made his living with his hands, a degree of trust was instantly established.

"I was hoping that I could speak with you for a few moments."

"Of course. There's a fire going in the parlor. Just up the steps and to the left." Ushering her guest abovestairs, Claire marveled at the oddity of being visited by Mary O'Roarke's long-lost son. What in Erin's name could he want from her?

But, she concluded wryly, this episode was no more bizarre than the other recent events that had toppled her tidy little world.

First had come Devon's unexpected romantic overture. Then came the astounding news that he'd been married to Mary O'Roarke, upon whose inspiration he'd given Claire a house in Fontjoy Square. Next was the erotic encounter with Devon that had badly shaken Claire's long-held beliefs about men. And, finally, came the confirmation of her deepest suspicions about the ignominy and untrustworthiness of men, and the dangers of falling in love with one. When Devon had fallen asleep and murmured his wife's name, Claire had thought she would go mad with anger and shame.

"Please sit down, Mr. Sullivan."

He sat on the sofa, and while she poured the tea, he looked around the room with unabashed interest. "You have a beautiful home, Lady Claire."

"I'm glad you like it." Claire sat opposite Aidan, appraising him over the rim of her teacup. "What can I do for you, Mr. Sullivan?"

"I came to talk about my mother. I understand that all of the ladies in this neighborhood befriended her at one time or another."

"Who told you that?"

"I've spoken with Rose Nollbrook, and she's told me quite a bit about my mother. I'll allow, she's silent on the subject of my father. Can't understand why. She is the only person alive who could tell me his name."

"And what has Rose chosen to tell you about Mary O'Roarke?" Claire tried to modulate her tone of voice, but it was difficult to speak about the woman without sounding overly acidic.

Leaning forward, Aidan clasped his hands together and spoke earnestly. "Rose—Lady Nollbrook, that is—said she was very beautiful."

"Yes, she was. You favor her, I suppose." Claire studied her guest more closely. She thought he probably bore a greater resemblance to his father. Mary's features hadn't been as sharp as Aidan's.

And she had had a broad, smooth forehead, whereas his was like an overhanging ledge.

"That is what Mr. Avondale said the moment he saw me."

The mention of Mr. Avondale made Claire uneasy. "What else did Mr. Avondale say? About Mary O'Roarke, I mean."

Aidan lifted one shoulder. "Very little, really. I won't say he ordered me out of his house, but he was not at all eager to discuss my mother. I thought at first my existence might have shocked him. But that wasn't it at all. Apparently, he knew his wife had given birth to a child out of wedlock long before he met her."

"Knowing about a child is one thing; seeing him in the flesh is quite another."

"Yes." After a pause, Aidan said, "Tell me, did my mother ever mention my father?"

"For heaven's sake, no."

"Did she talk about her family? About her own parents, that is?"

"Not that I remember."

"Do you know anything about any of her other relatives?"

"Honestly, Mr. Sullivan—"

"Please call me Aidan."

"I did not know Mary as well as Rose did. Or Millicent or Dolly, for that matter. I believe Dolly went to school with her in Switzerland when they were quite young, and Millicent met her one summer in Vienna. My association with Mary O'Roarke was extremely short-lived—I'm sorry I can't help you."

" 'Tis urgent that I know more about my mum."

"What's the urgency, Aidan?"

The boy's cheeks darkened and his gaze flickered about the room, as if he was suddenly flustered. "I-I did not want to have to tell anyone—"

"What is it?" Once again, Claire's sympathy for the boy was aroused. He looked positively miserable, uncomfortable in his own skin.

His voice fell to a hoarse whisper. " 'Tis my lungs, you see. The doctor says—"

A floorboard in the hallway creaked. Twisting in her chair, Claire was stunned to see Devon standing in the parlor doorway, his arms folded over his chest, his expression dark and forbidding.

"Yes, what does your doctor say, young Master Sullivan?" he drawled malevolently.

With widening eyes and a nervous gulp, the boy slowly stood. "I was having a private conversation with Lady Claire, if you don't mind."

Devon strode into the room and stood beside the sofa. "Well, I do mind. I'm not at all interested in your physical ailments, and I'll thank you not to bother any of the residents of this neighborhood with them. Now get the hell out of here, and don't let me see you in Fontjoy Square again!"

Claire leapt to her feet. "You can't tell him to leave, Devon! This is my house—"

"It's all right, m'lady. I was just about to go." Careful to avoid brushing Devon's shoulder, Aidan practically ran from the room, pulling the door shut behind him.

Seconds later, the front door opened and closed.

Furious, Claire stood toe to toe with Devon. Had she not been certain that he would never hurt her—physically, that is—she would have recoiled from the anger rolling off him. Most men, perhaps even Dick Creevy the famous pugilist, would have backed away from the hateful look on Devon's face. A muscle in his jaw flinched, and his eyes were as black as coal. But Claire instinctively knew that Devon Avondale would never lift his hand to a woman.

"How did you get in here?"

"You don't think your servants are going to stop me, do you, *my lady?* After all, they are paid by me, indirectly if not directly."

"They do not know the source of my income."

"You should have known that once you and your neighbors identified the source of your collective largesse and started talking about it, it wouldn't be long before all the servants in this neighborhood knew about it, too."

He was right, of course. Domestic servants were notoriously loose-lipped. But that was no excuse for Devon's entering Claire's home uninvited. "Do you think you have the right to barge into my home any time you please?"

"Are you telling me that I am unwelcome here?"

"You weren't. Last week."

"Ah, much has changed since last week, though, hasn't it? You have learned who your mysterious benefactor is."

"Yes. It is Mary O'Roarke."

His brow arched. "Well, that is one way of looking at it. Although I was the one who actually gave the house to you, I can easily understand why you would feel that Mary O'Roarke is responsible for your current condition."

"Indeed." Unable to meet Devon's gaze, Claire whirled and faced the mantel. Mary *was* responsible for her present circumstances. And Devon's sarcastic tone suggested that he knew precisely what role his precious wife had played in Claire's downfall.

Tamping down harsh words, she wished desperately that she'd stayed up the entire night and finished reading Mary's journal. She needed to know what Devon knew. "What do you want from me, Devon?"

"I want that journal back."

Fear prickled at the back of her neck. She thought of blurting out a confession, then quickly changed her mind. She would just have to brazen out Devon's challenge; she was determined to read that diary. And after she did, she just might burn it. "I do not have your wife's journal."

"It was in my study last night when you arrived, and this morning it has gone missing. I do not believe that the diary got up and walked out of my house on its own."

"You never know. Perhaps a leprechaun stole it."

"Give me the diary, Claire."

Grateful he could not see her face, Claire stood

before the hearth and chafed her hands in front of the fire. "I do not have it."

"Do not lie to me," he said menacingly.

Hot tears welled behind her eyes, but Claire proudly suppressed them. It wasn't in her nature to lie, and she detested herself for deceiving Devon. Yet it seemed that she'd been lying since the moment he kissed her, and she couldn't help herself.

"I would like for you to leave," she whispered.

"Look at me."

She didn't want to. She couldn't.

"Look at me, Claire!" He took one giant step, grasped her upper arm and turned her to face him. "Where is that diary? Is it in your bedchamber? Well then, I shall go up there myself and find it!"

Desperate, frantic to keep the journal in her possession until she had read it and certain that she was about to be caught in a damning lie, Claire grabbed the front of Devon's jacket. "No! You cannot go up there!"

His voice dropped to a low growl "Why? Because it is improper for a gentleman to visit a lady's boudoir?"

That was reason enough. But Claire had a much more practical motive for banning Devon from her private quarters. He would find Mary's diary on her bedside table, and he would know that she had pilfered it from his study. Worse, he would confiscate it. And she wasn't about to let that happen.

Extreme measures had to be taken. Her mind flashed once again on the poker in the brass fire-set behind her, but even in her most distraught moments, Claire was not a violent person. Still, she had to do something, and quickly, to prevent Devon from pounding up the steps and searching her bedroom. She had to do something to pull his attention away from that journal.

Seized by panic, she wondered if she could use Devon's sexual longings to her advantage. As risky as it was to trifle with a man so much more sophisticated than she, Claire concluded that she had to do whatever it took to keep Devon away from the journal. Mary O'Roarke would not get the last word this time.

If she had to let Devon make love to her . . . well, then, that was just what she had to do.

Pulling herself a bit closer to Devon, she saw that he had nicked his chin with his shaving razor. Inhaling, she was momentarily distracted by the clean male scent of his skin. His hair, obviously freshly washed, was thick and gleaming. His neck-tie was neatly starched and elegantly tied. As much as Claire despised what he had done to her—deceived her by failing to tell her who he was and to whom he had been married—she couldn't deny that Devon Avondale was an attractive man.

As much as she resented Mary O'Roarke's posthumous meddling in her life, she had to admit that she was grateful for her home in Fontjoy Square and the small stipend she'd been receiving each month for nearly a year.

And, finally, as much as Claire would like to believe she did not need a man, she couldn't help thinking that it would not be entirely unpleasant to kiss Devon Avondale again.

For a long moment, Claire hung on to Devon's lapels while he cuffed her arms and held her captive against his chest. The logs in the fire crackled and popped, emphasizing the scorching heat that surrounded the two. Claire's pulse quickened and her face burned. She found it strange that she could be so angry with a man one moment and so mesmerized by him the next. She reminded herself that her feelings toward Devon were based on friendship, but the longer he stared at her, the more difficult it was to think of him as a friend.

In her heart, she knew that no matter what happened to them in the future—whether she moved away from Fontjoy Square or not—their relationship would never again be platonic.

Devon was not oblivious to the change in the atmosphere. On the contrary, the hardness prodding Claire's belly told her that his arousal had already diminished his anger—and, she hoped, his memory. If her words would not convince Devon of her innocence, perhaps her kisses would make him forget about Mary's diary.

Swallowing hard, she watched his expression change from one of pent-up fury to one of seething desire. His eyes were half-lidded, his lips moist. Her breasts crushed against his jacket front as he tightened his grip on her arms. He bent his head, his gaze riveted on Claire's lips. It wasn't Devon's strength that held her captive now; it was the magnetism of his need for her.

Oh, what a tangled web! As Claire raised up on her tiptoes, she silently regarded her newly discovered aptitude for duplicity with a mixture of awe and dismay. Was she merely giving in to her mother's legacy of wantonness? Or was she responding in kind to the underhanded tactics of a seductive sharpster who had tricked her into moving into his neighborhood just so he could indulge in a nostalgic fantasy of life as it had been with Mary O'Roarke?

A wave of jealousy rolled over Claire as it occurred to her that he still loved Mary O'Roarke, and that he would never love any other woman as dearly as he had his dead wife.

If she was going to trifle with this man, she'd better safeguard her heart. The last thing she wanted to do was fall in love with a man who would never give his heart and soul to her fully.

Falling in love with a man gave him unlimited power over a woman. That was the mistake her mother had made—repeatedly.

"I hope you know, Devon," she said, her voice surprisingly husky, "that this means nothing to me."

He did not answer right away. Instead, he kissed her—deeply, passionately, greedily. Then he pressed his lips against her neck and whispered, "You are a terrible liar, Claire."

She was, and she knew it. She was a terrible liar because she was such an unpracticed one. Dissembling did not come naturally to Lady Claire Kilgarren.

Nevertheless, she continued her deception. "You should not think that just because I am allowing you this liberty—"

"—allowing me this liberty?" His breath was hot on her neck. "Are you trying to tell me, Claire, that you are showing me some sort of kindness, *doing me a favor*, as it were?"

"As I said before, I am grateful for what you have done for me."

"Grateful, eh?" His jaw was smoother than it had been the night before, his beard less abrasive. Yet the texture of his skin as he nuzzled Claire's throat drew goose bumps to her flesh. "Ah, Claire, when are you going to give up that coquettish act?"

" 'Tis not an act," she tried to say stiffly, but her voice sounded more like a kittenish mewl. "I told you that I have no interest in a romantic entanglement, and I have not changed my mind."

"Not even a little bit, Claire?"

"No." She gasped, though, when his tongue lapped at the corner of her mouth.

"You didn't know how much you enjoyed being kissed, did you?" He nipped at her lower lip, sending a jolt of erotic lightning through her body.

Claire clung to Devon now, not because she was trying to keep him from running up the steps to her bedchamber but because she feared her knees would collapse if she released him. Tilting her head, she exposed her sensitive neck and nape.

With a heavy sigh, Devon pulled her even more tightly into his embrace. And as he rained kisses along her delicate flesh, Claire began to imagine how sinfully delicious it might feel if he were to kiss other parts of her body.

Reluctantly, Claire admitted to herself that she enjoyed being kissed by Devon Avondale. *Damn him!* Had he only left her alone, had he been content to be her friend, she would not be so confused and miserable now. But, as she wrapped her arms around his neck, the irony of her situation dawned on her: If Devon had not been her friend for nearly a year, she would never have trusted him enough to let him touch her.

The truth was, she didn't know what she felt. She only knew that it was wickedly exciting.

He wondered if Claire knew how difficult it was to resist sweeping her into his arms and carrying her up the stairs to her bedchamber. Not to look for Mary's diary—he would worry about that later—but to toss Claire onto the bed and make love to her for the rest of the day.

"Do you think that we can sneak up the steps, darling?"

"The servants will know."

"To hell with the servants. We are adults, and what we do is none of their concern."

Her gaze darted nervously toward the open door. "You said yourself, servants talk. I wouldn't want it going 'round the neighborhood that I am—"

"I suggest you not worry so blasted much about your reputation, Claire."

Hurt and wariness flashed in her eyes. "That is easy for you to say, sir. When a woman loses her reputation, she also loses her self-respect. And then she has nothing."

Devon had hit a nerve, but he wasn't entirely certain why. Startled and instantly remorseful for having hurt Claire's feelings, he cupped her face in his hands and kissed the tip of her nose. "I did not mean to overset you, Claire. 'Twas a careless remark."

Her eyes closed, and after a tense moment, a tear sparkled on her lashes. Tenderly, Devon removed the tear with a kiss. There was pain hidden in Claire's past, but he didn't know where. Mary's history of her had been rather sketchy. In fact, she had written less about Claire than she had any of the other women who lived at Fontjoy Square.

Devon knew only that Claire and Mary had arrived on Dublin's social scene together fifteen years earlier, and that they had come out, during the same spring season. They met one another at a fancy dress ball, traded a few laughs and danced with the same fellows. Mary had described Claire as "charming, funny and amazingly elegant." There had been a touch of envy in her tone. But beyond the florid descriptions of Claire's fashionable gowns and coterie of suitors, Mary had written little.

Had there been more time, perhaps she would have written more. But Mary's memories of Claire were recorded shortly before she had died. She had been weak, her mind muddled. She had only written that she and the popular Lady Claire Kilgarren became fast friends, and that at the end of the season, they had shared a room one weekend at a grand country house party given in Mary's honor. Afterwards, and for some reason that Mary had not recorded, the girls never spoke after that weekend. Devon did not know why.

"Are you all right?" he asked, fearful that he had ruined the moment. "Should I leave?"

Her eyes fluttered open. "Do you think that I am bad, Devon? Too brazen? Fast? A Jezebel?"

For a heartbeat he wondered if she was serious. It was such a ludicrous question. Why, the woman was as virtuous as a nun! In the year he had known her, she had not entertained one gentleman caller. But he could see in Claire's expression that she had serious doubts about the quality of her virtue. "Why would I think that?"

"Perhaps because of what you have read in Mary's diary."

"Mary's diary?" Puzzled, Devon gave Claire a long, searching look. Perhaps she had not stolen Mary's journal after all. Touching her cheek, he experienced an overwhelming spasm of tenderness for the woman he had so rashly judged. "I am sorry if I wrongly accused you of taking the diary. If you had, you would have read it by now. And had you read it, you would have discovered that Mary said little about you."

She took a deep breath, as if she were about to

dive underwater. "Then do you think I am bad because of what happened last night? And because I enjoyed it?"

"My dear, I would be very disappointed if you had not enjoyed it. Indeed, I would feel like a cad for having enjoyed it so much myself."

Her eyes narrowed suspiciously. "Do you mean that? Or are you just saying it so that I will allow you further liberties?"

"Dear God, but you are a difficult woman to seduce!" When Devon saw the slightly wounded look on Claire's face, he took pains to quickly correct his statement. "No, no, that is not what I meant. But must we search our souls and gnash our teeth every time we have the desire to kiss one another, Claire? 'Tis a perfectly natural impulse between two people who care for one another. And you are very beautiful, you know."

Her cheeks were scarlet, as if this entire discussion was deeply humiliating. Averting her gaze, Claire said in a very tiny voice, "I think you are very beautiful, too, Devon."

"There, now, that is what I like to hear."

"My reputation is very important to me, though."

"You needn't worry about your reputation. I won't tell a soul."

"Do you promise?"

"I promise."

She lifted her face and met his gaze directly. "Then do you want to come abovestairs to my bedchamber?"

The very question excited him. As he tasted her lips, he murmured, "What about the servants?"

"Wait here. I will go downstairs and announce that you have left. I'll send the maid to the market and the butler to the docks to fetch a sack of oysters for tonight's dinner. Then I will meet you in my bedchamber in a quarter of an hour. Don't be late, Devon," she added flirtatiously.

His lower regions tingled. "Late? Darling, I shall be watching the clock."

Seven

Claire closed the parlor doors behind her, hitched up her skirts and dashed down the steps. Within minutes after she'd given instructions to her servants, Number Three Fontjoy Square was as quiet as a tomb.

As she hurried back up the stairs, passing the doors behind which Devon waited, a dizzying sense of unreality stole over her. She could hardly believe that she had actually invited a man to her bedchamber. Again? After all these years? Was she so foolish as to make the same mistake twice? *And this time with Mary O'Roarke's husband?*

For years, Claire had been telling everyone that she did not want a man, that marriage was repugnant to her. But she had not always felt that way. When she was young, she had wanted very much to be in love. She had changed her mind and sworn off men only after that hideously painful and humiliating weekend in the country with Mary O'Roarke.

Now she could not seem to resist her attraction

to Devon. She wished he had never kissed her, but he had, and that kiss had forever changed the nature of their relationship. Long-suppressed urges had boiled to the surface, and Claire could not seem to put a lid on her emotions. Pausing at the top landing, she struggled to steady her breathing. What she was doing was insane, completely uncharacteristic of her.

Or had she finally just given in to her true nature?

Whatever the cause of her sudden and confounding need to explore her sexuality, Claire was unable to control her passions. She might resent Devon in the future for having unleashed these wild feelings. She might hate herself for being so reckless and wanton. She might grow to be so disgusted with herself that she never wanted to see Devon again. She might—as she had already suggested—be forced to move away from Fontjoy Square.

On the other hand, if she allowed Devon to make love to her once, she might become addicted to him. A shudder wracked Claire's body. Depending on a man for financial security and social status was bad enough; depending on him for sexual satisfaction would be thoroughly humiliating. Yet Claire feared that if she indulged herself too freely in the pleasures that Devon offered her, she might well grow so attached to him that she would never be able to live without him.

Her insides churned as she hurried to her room. Her door was ajar, signaling that her maid had tidied the room. Indeed, her bed was freshly made, the top quilt smooth, the pillows and bolsters plump against the headboard. But Mary's journal, which she had left on her bedside table, was nowhere in sight.

Frantically, Claire searched her chambers. Perhaps her maid had slipped the diary into a drawer. But before she could find it, Devon's footsteps sounded on the steps behind her.

She stood beside the bed, her heart thumping.

In the doorway, Devon hesitated, his expression questioning.

"Come in," Claire said in a tiny voice.

"Are you certain?"

Her nod was a lie. She wasn't certain at all. She had no idea if what she was doing was wrong or right. She might be making the biggest mistake of her life. She only knew that she had gone too far to turn back.

Devon shut the door behind him. Slowly, he closed the distance between them, his gaze riveted to Claire's. When he stood in front of her, his penetrating stare ignited a fire in her belly. Embarrassed, she wanted to run and hide. Aroused, she wanted to strip off her clothes and lay naked beside him. The contradiction of her emotions made sensible conversation impossible.

Luckily, Devon was not as confused and nervous as she. His half-smile was warm and reassuring. Gently grasping her shoulders, he pressed his lips to hers and kissed her.

Vaguely, Claire hoped that her servants stayed

in town the rest of the afternoon. She could have gone on kissing Devon for hours, perhaps days. By listening to her moans and sharp inhalations, he learned quickly how she liked to be kissed— slowly and tenderly at first, then harder and more urgently. She had never known a man could be so sweet and attentive. Devon's tongue was deliciously skillful. His taste and smell excited her; when he gazed into her eyes and kissed her, she felt as vulnerable and helpless as a kitten.

Clinging to him, Claire tilted her head. Obligingly, Devon nuzzled the crook of her neck, scraping his beard along her sensitive skin. The tingling that exploded between Claire's legs nearly knocked her off her feet.

His voice was like whiskey, warm and intoxicating. "Wait here, darling."

Blinking, she watched him step into the spacious bathroom that adjoined her room. If nature had summoned him at this most inopportune time, she was grateful for her modern plumbing. Few homes outside London had such modern fixtures. In fact, the tubs and toilets in Fontjoy Square were rather anachronistic, given the general state of disrepair the grand old Georgian houses were in. More than once the ladies who lived there had remarked on their luck at having such luxurious bathing areas.

The splash of running water bewildered Claire. What in the world did Devon have in mind? When he reappeared, he had thrown off his jacket and rolled up the sleeves of his white linen shirt. Hugging her again, he whispered something scandalous against her ear.

"You want to do what?" she asked, drawing back to stare at him incredulously.

"I want to give you a bath." The gleam in his eyes was slightly wicked.

"Dear man, I have already bathed today!" Was he trying to tell her that she needed another?

"This has nothing to do with cleanliness, Claire. Come on now, I tossed some lavender into the water. Turn around. There, that's a good girl." His fingers moved at the nape of her neck.

Before she knew it, Claire's dress was unbuttoned and a wisp of cool air licked at her spine. Trembling, she stood as still as a statue while Devon smoothed her woolen gown off her shoulders and over her hips. Wearing nothing but a thin linen chemise, garters and thick cotton stockings, Claire shivered against the chill in the room. A warm bath *did* sound inviting. And the idea of being bathed by Devon *did* sound wickedly appealing.

Kissing her bare shoulder and neck, Devin murmured, "Come with me."

Taking his hand, Claire stepped out of her puddled gown and followed him to the bathroom. The tile beneath her feet was cold, and the sun that slanted through the oval stained glass washed everything in a clear, golden glow. This was Claire's most private room, and Devon's presence in it seemed exceptionally wicked. Her breath caught and her skin prickled with anticipation. Frozen, she stood at the side of the tub and waited for Devon to direct her next movement.

He untied the lace drawstring at her waist, reached for the hem of her chemise and drew it over her head.

Now she was naked except for shoes, stockings, garters and knickers.

Bending over, he unbuttoned her shoes and slid them off her feet. Squatting, he ran his hands up her legs and unsnapped her garters. Then he rolled her stockings down her bare legs to her ankles and, as she lifted each foot, over her instep.

"You are beautiful," he whispered, kissing the inside of her thigh.

Claire's skin rippled and her knees wobbled. When Devon grasped the waistband of her unmentionables, she steadied herself by grasping his shoulders. When he drew them down the length of her legs, exposing her patch of silky blond hair, she clung to him. As she stepped out of her knickers, Claire feared she would faint. When Devon pressed his nose to the juncture between her legs, she gasped.

"Dear God in heaven, what are you doing, Devon?"

He breathed in greedily, then sighed, as if her scent were a drug that had induced in him an altered state of being. Only when the water rose to the edge of the tub did he reluctantly pull away from her.

"Get in the bath," he told her. Reaching, he

turned the brass spigots and cut off the flow of water.

Obediently, Claire stepped into the tub, sat down and slid beneath the water. The warmth of the bath enveloped her, soothing her nerves. The lavender bath salts eased her anxieties. Her inhibitions faded as she met Devon's dark erotic gaze.

On his knees, he leaned over the edge of the tub with a bar of soap in one hand and a small towel in the other. Lovingly, as if he was bathing a child, he picked up one arm, then the next, lathering her skin and rinsing it. He held her feet and washed her legs, caressing her limbs, rubbing the tension from her muscles. He sluiced water on her shoulders and breasts. He ran his hand towel over her flesh until the heat of the water, combined with the heat generated by her desire, was unbearable. When she thought she couldn't tolerate any more, he reached beneath the surface of the water and rubbed the soap against her throbbing womanhood.

The sensation of the hard slab of soap against her body catapulted Claire into a state of sexual panic. Leaning her head back against the porcelain, she grabbed onto the sides of the tub and slid farther down so that her pelvis was tilted and her legs were parted.

"That's it, darling, just relax." Devon's honeyed voice merely accelerated her ecstasy. Releasing the soap, he used his fingers to pleasure her.

Claire hadn't known that such exquisite sensations could be produced so easily, simply by touching and caressing that tiny nub of flesh. Unable to stifle her moans, she arched her back and spread her legs, opening herself even wider to Devon's manipulations.

"How is it that you know how to do such a thing?" she asked between ragged breaths.

"Intuition," he replied with a devilish chuckle.

"Poppycock," she drawled. Devon's skill was the result of experience, and Claire knew it. Dimly, she thought he must have bedded many women. Or perhaps Mary O'Roarke had been a more amorous wife than she was a loyal friend. The thought might have dampened Claire's ardor had she not been in the throes of passion herself. "You seem to know more about my body than I do."

His eyebrows arched at that. "No one has ever touched you here?"

The lump in her throat prevented her from speaking. Claire shook her head; she had never even *imagined* being touched that way.

With one hand, he separated the folds of her body. With the other, he caressed the most sensitive part of her body. Apparently, Devon had all the patience in the world. Most of the water in the tub drained out while he indulgently teased, stroked and pleasured Claire in ways she'd never dreamed of.

"Devon," she managed, at length, "can we adjourn to the bedroom?"

"Of course, darling. Put your arms around my neck." With casual ease, he lifted her from the tub, carried her to her bed and laid her atop the quilt. His eyes hungrily scanned the length of her body while he unbuttoned his shirt and yanked the tail of it from his trousers.

Claire thought of asking him to disrobe completely. She wanted to see his nakedness and feel his hard, bare muscles against her belly and breasts. But her self-control teetered on the verge of nonexistence, and she feared her lust could spiral out of control if some flimsy shield of fabric didn't separate them.

He kicked off his boots and climbed onto the bed, where he kneeled between her bent legs. With his hands on her knees, he pushed her thighs apart again, and this time he was in a position to see every inch of Claire's anatomy.

Only twice before in her entire life had Claire allowed a man to examine her private parts, and that was in the setting of a doctor's office. She had been nervous and self-conscious then, and she was now, albeit for entirely different reasons. Devon was not staring at her with the clinical detachment of a doctor. Instead, he gazed at her ferally, almost predatorily, as if he wanted to consume her. The glint in his eyes aroused Claire even more.

Gazing at Devon, Claire experienced an unprecedented combination of trust and trepidation. Clearly, he knew what he was doing; she did not. But before Devon had ever kissed her, he had been her friend, and she knew he would never hurt her or press her to liberties she did not agree to. While her pulse galloped, her fears eased. Devon's bronze forearms, sinewy and dusted with dark hair, looked strong and capable. His broad shoulders comforted her. Closing her eyes, she gave in to him wholly, confident that he would take care of her needs.

At length, he slipped one finger inside her and angled it toward her navel. Fascinated by her body's reaction, Claire murmured her approval.

"You must tell me what you like, Claire. Don't turn into a shy miss, now."

"Have I ever held my tongue, Dev?"

"Not when we were *just friends,* no. Lately, you have taken to harboring secrets."

"You seem to be exposing them all," she replied lazily.

"Ah, well, I am trying, dear." He wriggled his finger inside her. "Do you like that?"

Whether by accident or design Claire would never know, but Devon seemed to have found a mysterious spot hidden deep inside her, rife with nerve endings and exquisitely sensitive. Her inner muscles clutched at his finger and her hips lifted instinctively. Opening her eyes, she tried desperately to articulate her feelings.

But words could not adequately describe what she felt, and her speech was halted by the acute sensations pulsing through her body. Clasping Devon's wrist, she could only eke out a mild oath and a high-pitched cry.

His expression was taut, his features drawn. "Do you want me to stop, darling?" he whispered.

"No." On the contrary, she held his hand for fear he would withdraw it. Tilting her pelvis, she positioned herself so that Devon could easily reach her most sensitive place, that secret spot she'd never known existed until just minutes earlier.

"Are you ready now? Do you want to *come?*"

Having never heard that phrase before, Claire hesitated. "Come where?"

His lips curved and his gaze softened. "To me, sweetness. Let it go; that's right, be a good girl. Yes, close your eyes and let it all out and come to me, I'm right here."

Quickening his movements, he thrust his finger in and out of her slick passage, stretching her inner muscles, drawing her to the edge of her control. His knuckles bumped against her thighs and his thumb massaged her little nub of flesh. The sensation that Devon's touch gave her was powerful, all-consuming, and so intense that Claire ached for a release from it.

Unable to contain her emotions a second longer, Claire ground her lower body against the heel of Devon's hand. Clawing at the quilt beneath her, she bucked and thrashed as a convulsion of pleasure-pain swept over her. Any thoughts she might have had of being demure or ladylike flew out the window. A sudden blinding and primeval need to get what she wanted directed her actions. Propping her feet on Devon's shoulders, she pushed rhythmically against his hand. Contractions seized her lower body. Hot juices poured from her, drenching her thighs and Devon's fingers. Crying out, she released the tension that had been building up inside her and came in Devon's hand.

For a while, while Devon whispered soothing words and Claire attempted to regain her senses, they rocked together gently. When he slowly withdrew his fingers, Claire shivered. In the aftermath of their passion, she did not know what to say.

She had no idea whether other women experienced the intensity of emotions she just had. She did not know whether her responses had been normal or excessive. Perhaps she had been cursed with her mother's mania for men and sex. Embarrassed, she rolled to her side, her back to Devon, and clamped her knees together.

"Are you all right, Claire?" He sat on the side of the bed, stroking her hair.

The storm that had twisted through her body still ravaged her emotions. Nodding, she struggled to beat back a flood of tears.

He leaned over and kissed the top of her head. "God help me, I fear I have hurt you. Claire, I did not intend—"

"You have nothing to apologize for, Devon. I am an adult woman. I could have put a stop to this tomfoolery had I wished to."

"Tomfoolery? I had hoped you would enjoy it." His voice was tinged with regret.

"I did, I suppose." She squeezed her eyes shut. She *had* enjoyed their lovemaking, if that was what it was. But now that it was over, she was stunned by the strength of her response.

Surely the copious amount of fluid that had

flowed from her body was abnormal. She found it difficult to imagine that most women thrashed about and keened like exotic primitives, as she had. Devon probably thought she was depraved. The more she thought about her behavior, the more mortified she became.

"Then why are you sad, darling?"

She couldn't say because she didn't know. Her heart continued to thump wildly and her inner muscles ached. Strangely, she had the urge to throw her arms around Devon's neck and sob, but he would think her fit for Bedlam, so she ground her teeth together and remained silent. She wished she had not enjoyed her sexual release so much. There had to be something wrong with a grown woman who could not control her *animal urges*. If she was not careful, she would wind up like her mother, vilified, ostracized and humiliated.

"I—I feel *dirty*," she whispered at length. "I feel so naked and exposed! I feel as if I have done something terribly wicked and should be punished for it."

Silence spun out between them. After a long while, he asked her to look at him, but she refused. He had already witnessed her weakness.

"Well then, I can only deduce that this was an unpleasant experience for you. Indeed, I am sorry. Once again, it seems that I have imposed myself upon you. I confess I am hopelessly confused. Whenever I think that I am doing precisely what you want, it turns out that I have offended you. I hope you will forgive me, Claire."

"You must think me terribly loose and unprincipled," Claire said.

"What in God's name would make you say that?"

"I know what is in Mary's diary," she replied.

Behind her, he stiffened. His hand, which had been stroking her hip, withdrew. "Then you do possess the diary."

"I do not have it, Devon. I only know what it is in it. Remember, *darling*, I was there, all those years ago."

"I want it back, Claire."

"I told you, I do not have it."

The rustle of his clothes told Claire that he was dressing. She felt his presence at her bedside. His stare, even when she was not looking at him, was full of heat. His voice was deep and vaguely menacing. "I want you to give me that journal. Now."

"I do not have it."

"Where is it?"

"How would I know?"

"Because you took it from me, that is why. Claire, don't do this to me! I thought we were friends."

"Friends don't lie to one another about who they are!" Claire's words slipped out before she thought about what she was saying. Suddenly she seemed as powerless to control her words as she had been her physical responses.

"Why is that damned diary so important, anyway? Why don't you just let her go, Devon? She's been gone nearly six years now, and yet you still allow her opinions to color your own, her wishes to control your actions! Will you ever be free of her, Devon?"

"How dare you speak ill of my Mary! How dare you steal her journal and deprive me of my precious memories!"

The urgency in his voice reminded Claire of how much Devon had loved Mary O'Roarke. Rolling over on her back, she met his angry gaze. She watched his fists clench at his sides. A muscle leaped in his jaw. He looked as if he wanted to smash his fist into something—or someone.

"How dare you trifle with me as if I were a puppet, Devon! What am I to you? A memento? A reminder of how sweet and wonderful and beautiful your late wife was? Does the contrast between the two of us affirm your knowledge of how perfect she truly was? You have spent this past year pretending to be my friend. But, in truth, you were waiting to see if what Mary said about me was true. Isn't that right, Devon?"

"I do not know what you are talking about."

"Do not pretend you do not know what Mary did to me."

His brow furrowed and his eyes narrowed. "Mary said you were friends. If you read the diary, you know what she said."

"I have not read it, Devon. And I do not have it. So I cannot return it to you."

The look on his face was murderous, but Claire

was not afraid of Devon. Not in the physical sense, anyway.

What did frighten Claire was the power that Devon clearly exercised over her. He had demonstrated not only the ability but also the willingness to pull her strings, to control her and manipulate her.

For his own purposes, simply to indulge his romantic obsession with his dead wife, he had uprooted Claire, plucked her from poverty and given her a home. For nearly a year he had pretended to be her friend when in reality she was nothing more than a curio in his macabre fantasy. She ought to hate him for having deceived her. She ought to move away from Fontjoy Square and never speak to him again.

She ought to leave him behind while she still possessed the fortitude to do so, before she became completely enraptured by him, enthralled by his sexual mastery, enslaved by her own needs.

Her mother had not been strong enough to resist temptation, but Lady Claire Kilgarren vowed that she would be.

"I think you should leave now," she said coolly.

He took a step back. "When you decide what it is you want, Claire, let me know."

"I know what I want. I want to be left alone."

"You are a confused little girl in a full-grown woman's body. Why don't you admit that? You crave intimacy, yet something in your past has left you scared to death of men."

" 'Tis you who are living in the past."

"That's a bloody lie!"

"You have accused me of stealing your memories, Devon. Obviously, your memories are more important to you than the present."

"One of these days you will learn that we cannot fully appreciate the present unless we understand the past."

"I left my past behind me a long time ago. I have no wish to live it again with you."

He gave her a curt nod, turned on his heel and stalked toward the door. On the threshold, he said over his shoulder, "Neither of us can change the past, Claire."

"Between the two of us," she countered, "it is not I who am sleeping with ghosts."

Eight

Three days of rain had intensified the pungent aroma of the stables behind Devon's house. Too irritable to accept visitors or pay calls upon his neighbors, and unable to shake his depression, Devon sought the society of his cattle and a spotted dog named Cicero, who had the annoying habit of getting underfoot and yelping each time his tail was trod upon by man or beast.

Grooming his horses was a chore ordinarily left to Devon's footmen, tigers and drivers. But, after the series of shocks and disappointments he'd suffered, Devon needed to exercise his muscles and sweat out some of the whiskey he'd poured into his body. His exertions eased his tension, and the quiet, unconditional acceptance of his animals soothed his jangled nerves. As he ran a brush over his favorite mare's coarse brown coat, Devon's mind replayed the events of the past week.

Claire's ambivalence bewildered him. One minute, she wanted him; the next minute, she wanted nothing to do with him. No doubt he had made a terrible mistake in revealing his intimate feelings to her. She had responded to his overtures by mocking him, stealing from him and rejecting him. He had tried to give her pleasure, and in return, she had besmirched his memories.

Surely Mary O'Roarke could not have predicted that Claire's true nature would turn out to be so cruel. Had Mary known what Claire was about, she would have warned Devon. But Claire had fooled Mary, too. God, how he wished he could talk to his wife now. He needed her more than ever. He needed her journal, the only remaining physical manifestation of her thoughts and wishes. Desperately, Devon needed someone to talk to, someone other than Cicero. Loneliness twisted his gut like a screw.

Behind him, footsteps shuffled through the straw. "Mind if I join you?"

Turning, Devon was mildly surprised to see Aidan Sullivan, bundled in a woolen jacket and muffler.

The younger man extended his bare hand.

"You had best get some gloves on, Sullivan. In this sort of weather, your hands will be raw if you're not careful."

Shrugging, Sullivan looked around the stables, inspecting the tack on the wall, the fine leather saddles and bridles that hung from pegs and, in the corner, Devon's gleaming black rig. Something about the boy's inquisitive nature piqued Devon's interest. *Why the hell did the boy always scan his surroundings as if he were attempting to commit ev-*

erything he saw to memory? Was he that desperate for clues to what his dead mother's life was really like?

"Was there something you wanted to see me about?" Devon asked at length.

" 'Tis a mite cold out here," Aidan replied. "Mind if we go inside? I wouldn't mind a cup of hot tea, or some mulled wine, if you have it."

"I came out here because I did not want to be inside." For a half-second, Devon considered sending Mary's son away again. He hadn't the patience necessary to tolerate the boy's manners, which, if not exactly rude, were hardly sophisticated. But, after three days of hammering shoes on hooves, combing tangles out of manes and shoveling manure out of stalls, the potential for human conversation held a small degree of appeal. Besides, he could do with some mulled wine himself.

"Follow me, then." Assuming that Aidan had come down the alley that bordered the house, Devon led him through the back door and up the rear staircase to his study. The men shed their heavy coats and warmed their hands before a fire that blazed on the hearth. When a maid had delivered mugs of hot, spicy wine, smoked salmon sandwiches and a whiskey infused fruitcake, Devon and Aidan sat in chairs opposite one another and enjoyed an afternoon repast.

"I apologize for popping in the way I did the other day, without announcing myself first." Aidan spoke around a mouth full of black soda bread. "It must have been a shock for you."

"As I told you, I knew what my wife had gone through that summer. Your existence was hardly a shock."

"Still, seeing me in person—"

"Yes." Devon put aside his plate and cup. "It brought to mind certain memories. But that is all in the past. I am sorry that you never knew your mother."

"The news of her death came as a shock to me." Aidan gave a wistful half-smile. "So near, yet so far, isn't that what they say? To have come all this way—"

"And where precisely did you come from?"

The boy cleared his throat, set his plate and cup on a side table and wiped his fingers on a linen tea towel. "Spent the last few years in the north, in the country, scratching out a living as best I could, working in the factories, that sort of thing."

"And your parents?" Devon inquired. "Your adoptive parents, I mean. What did they do?"

With a shrug, Aidan shook his head. "Me old dad? Went from job to job, I'm afraid. Mum did her best to keep him out of the bottle, but it was a losing battle. So you can understand, can't you, when I learned me folks weren't really me folks, how I must have felt."

"No. How did you feel?"

"I wanted nothing more than to meet them, me mother especially. It became somewhat of an obsession, finding me real mum and hearing her tell me what a horrid mistake she'd made. I know, it wasn't a very realistic hope, but it kept me going."

After a moment, Devon said quietly, "I'm sorry, then, that you came too late."

"Yes, but I have learned quite a bit about Mary O'Roarke in the past few days."

A thread of tension wound its way up Devon's spine. "And what exactly have you learned, Mr. Sullivan?"

Leaning forward, elbows on knees, Aidan tapped his fingertips together. His voice was just above a whisper, his gaze suddenly intense. "Quite a hellion in her youth, wasn't she?"

"Just because she was seduced and had a child out of wedlock? It happens, Sullivan. Oftentimes to the nicest of girls."

"From what little I have read, she got herself into some terribly messy scrapes."

"That is your mother you are talking about!"

"Just so. Perhaps that proves the old saying, *the apple doesn't fall far from the tree.*"

Indignant, Devon fought the urge to box Aidan's ears and kick him so hard in the pants that he would never be able to sit down again. Instinct told him to hear the little rapscallion out. Besides, no matter how ill-mannered and disrespectful the boy was, he remained Mary O'Roarke's son. If Aidan didn't respect his mother, Devon still respected his wife.

"What the devil are you talking about?" he seethed between clenched jaws.

"I have read her diary, Mr. Avondale."

"I do not believe I heard you correctly."

"I have read her diary."

Tension thickened the air. Anger heated Devon's blood to near boiling. "Oh, you have, have you?"

The boy nodded.

"Mind telling me where you got it?"

"I think you know."

"Tell me anyway."

"One of your neighbors."

"Which one of my neighbors?" It was not a question, but a demand, and if this little upstart interloper did not answer Devon's question—and quickly—he was going to regret it.

"Lady Claire Kilgarren." Aidan's eyes widened, and he reared back, as if he truly expected to receive a blow.

But a tiny voice in Devon's head reminded him that Aidan Sullivan was Mary O'Roarke's child. Besides, the boy's upbringing had been less than privileged and his adoptive parents less than nurturing. How else could Mary's own son have turned out to be such a weasel? Perhaps he wasn't entirely to blame for his stupidity.

Slowly, Devon rose to his full height. "Give me the diary."

Scrambling to his feet, Aidan replied, "I'm sorry, Mr. Avondale. I cannot do that."

"You'll give me that diary or else I'll pound it out of you." Coiling his fists, Devon took a step toward the boy, then halted. Never before had he experienced such profound difficulty in controlling his anger. But if Aidan did not produce that journal, there might, indeed, be bloodshed.

Swallowing hard, Aidan snatched his coat from the back of his chair and took a side step toward the door. "With all due respect, I believe that journal belongs to me."

White spots exploded before Devon's eyes. "Are you daft?"

"Perhaps so. But that diary is the only thing left of my mother, Mr. Avondale. Mary O'Roarke was my mother—"

"And my wife."

"You had her for nearly fifteen years, by my estimation. I never even met her."

"Too bad. Give me the diary."

"I did not journey this far just to go away empty-handed." Aidan backed across the room, his cheeks pink, his gaze locked on Devon's. "I spent every penny I had to get here."

"I will reimburse you for your expenses. Just give me the diary."

"That diary, it seems, is as precious as gold." Aidan gulped. "To both of us."

"Give me that damned diary!"

With his hand on the door handle, Aidan said, "A thousand quid, Mr. Avondale. That is what it will take for you to get your precious journal back. Until then, the journal has been hidden in a very safe place. Only I know where it is, and only I can produce it for you."

Stunned, Devon stared wordlessly as Aidan Sullivan exited the study. Then he stood at the top of the landing and watched the redheaded young man scamper down the stairs and out the front door.

He hated Mary O'Roarke's son. The boy had no respect for his mother and no comprehension of what her life had been like. He had called her a hellion. He had suggested that she had loose principles and low morals. He had insulted his own mother, for God's sake!

Offended beyond measure, Devon gripped the banister and closed his eyes. Now that Aidan was out of his sight, his thoughts turned to Claire. How could she have stolen Mary's diary? How could she have given it Aidan? Worst of all, how could she have looked Devon straight in the eye and lied to him?

He swayed with disgust. An acrid taste burned the back of his throat. Claire's betrayal sickened him. Once, he had thought she was a friend. He had even hoped their friendship might grow into something more, something more intimate and special. Now Claire had proved herself utterly untrustworthy. Not only had she stolen his memories, she had cheapened them, too. She had given Mary's journal to Aidan Sullivan, a crass, unfeeling lad who hadn't the vaguest notion what Mary O'Roarke was about.

Now Lady Claire Kilgarren was Devon Avondale's enemy.

Rose Sinclair was breathless when she entered the parlor of Number Five Fontjoy Square. Having been abruptly summoned to a late morning tea at the home of Millicent Hyde-Wolferton, she'd just managed to get the children fed and bathed and settled in the classroom before rushing across the street. Tucking a stray hair into the bun on her head, she greeted the other three ladies, poured herself a cup of tea, and sighed as she sank onto a sofa.

"Rose, I believe those children are running you ragged," Lady Dolly Baltmore-Creevy remarked.

Millicent stood at the mantel, warming her posterior before the fire and self-consciously holding her lower belly. "Oh, Rose, I can only pray that I will be as good a mother as you are."

"You'll do fine, dear." Rose missed talking to her younger friend. But her new family occupied all of her time and energy. "By the way, how are you feeling?"

"Sick every morning," Millicent replied. "And I miss Alec something fierce! If he does not return home from London soon, I swear I shall go out of my mind."

All of the women chuckled except Claire. The pretty blonde wore a look of complete discontent.

"Is something the matter, Claire?" Dolly asked.

"I did not call this meeting to order," Claire said sullenly. "Millicent did."

Dolly interjected. "Actually, dear, it was my idea. We decided to meet at Millie's house because of her morning sickness. The last thing she needs is to be out traipsing around the neighborhood, getting chilled and overset."

" 'Tis you we really wanted to talk to," Rose added.

"If you have something to say to me, why not just say it?" Claire asked. "Why call a meeting of everyone in the neighborhood?"

Dolly smiled apologetically. "It seems to me that this matter does affect the entire neighborhood. We've all just recently learned the identity of our mysterious benefactor, but instead of bringing us together, it appears that the news has caused a rift between us all and Devon. Mr. Avondale has hidden himself in his house again. Perhaps you can shed some light on what is going on, Claire. Why isn't he responding to our notes and invitations? Is he angry? Does he regret what he has done?"

Rose watched with interest as Claire crossed her arms over her chest. For as long as Rose had known her, Claire had never exhibited such an ill temper. Now, the duke's daughter, who had foresworn marriage and men many years before, looked as if she was miserable.

"I suppose he is upset because of Aidan Sullivan's recent appearance."

"He knew the boy existed," countered Rose. "He had Mary O'Roarke's diary."

"I'd like to get my hands on that diary," said Millicent. "I'd like to read what she wrote about me. Just out of curiosity. Wouldn't the rest of you?"

"I would," Dolly agreed.

"So would I," Rose murmured. Mary's account of that summer in Killiney would be interesting ndeed. "But the diary was not written for our eyes. 'Tis Devon's diary now."

"Not any longer," said Claire. All eyes turned to her. "I stole it from him."

"You what?" Rose felt like shaking the younger woman by her shoulders. "Whatever for, Claire? What were you thinking?"

"I was thinking the same thing Millicent was thinking! That I would like to read what Mary O'Roarke wrote about me!"

"Well, whatever it was, it was sufficient to inspire Devon to give you a house and set you up in it."

Scowling, Claire replied, "Well, that's a bit odd in itself, if you ask me. Mary and I weren't exactly good friends."

A hush fell over the room. At length, Millicent said, "I loved Mary very much."

" 'Twas *you* who stood up for *her*, Millie." A tear glistened in Claire's pale blue gaze, but she quickly dashed it away. "And it was Dolly who took the blame for her when she should have gotten tossed out of school in Switzerland. And it was Rose who helped her hide her secret and find a home for her baby when she hadn't the courage to deal with the problem herself. I don't understand why the three of you regard Mary O'Roarke as a saint."

"No one said she was a saint, Claire," answered Rose softly. "She was flesh and blood, entirely human, capable of making mistakes just like the rest of us."

"When I first met her, I envied her. But then I

discovered that she was just a scared little girl. Like me," said Dolly.

"She had a bit of a wild streak," said Millicent. "But she was basically a good person."

"The three of you were better friends to her than she was to you, don't you see?" Claire cried.

"See what, Claire?" Dolly asked.

"Oh, I don't know!" Dropping her head, Claire covered her face with her hands. A long silence spun out while Rose, Millicent and Dolly stared at one another quizzically. Then, at last, just when Rose was about to adjourn the meeting, Claire took a deep breath, clasped her fingers in her lap and looked up. "Why does he love her so much?"

"Good heavens, you're in love with Mr. Avondale," blurted Dolly.

"Well, that's a relief," inserted Millicent. "I was beginning to think you actually believed all that nonsense about marriage being such an onerous institution."

"I am not in love with Devon Avondale," Claire ground out.

But the other women in the room could see that Claire was lying. What Rose did not understand was why Claire resented Devon's affection toward his deceased wife. "Mary O'Roarke Avondale is dead, darling," she gently reminded her. "You needn't worry about competing with her for Devon's affections."

" 'Tis clear that he is smitten with you," said Millicent.

"I've known it for months," concurred Dolly.

"Don't be ridiculous, all of you," scoffed Claire. "I have told you many times that I am not interested in having a romantic relationship with a man. I assure you that I have not changed my opinion."

Again, the other three women exchanged knowing looks.

"Well then, dear, why does Devon's affection for his dead wife disturb you?" asked Rose.

"He gave me a house, presumably at her direction. I would just like to know why, that's all."

"Why don't you ask him?" suggested Dolly.

"I don't think he would speak to me right now," Claire replied, her cheeks darkening.

After a moment, Rose smoothed her skirts and cleared her throat. "Well then, I think it is time I pay another visit on our friend Mr. Avondale. If the mountain won't go to Muhammad, then Muhammad shall go to the mountain, or some such nonsense. And I, for one, am tired of seeing Claire and Devon estranged from one another for no good reason at all. Claire, are you certain there is nothing else you are not telling us?"

"Please don't speak to him on my account, Rose. I have no wish to be reconciled with the man. If it does not offend the rest of you that he has used us as props in some twisted fantasy he has about his dead wife, then that is your business. But I am highly insulted that I have spent nearly a year regarding this man as a close friend and confidante only to learn that his interest in me is solely a product of his obsession with Mary O'Roarke."

"You say Mary O'Roarke's name as if it leaves a bad taste in your mouth," Rose observed.

Standing, Claire met Rose's gaze and said, "I wish I had never met Mary O'Roarke."

"Have you stopped to think that had you never met her," Rose countered, "you would never have met Devon Avondale?"

Head held high, Claire left the room without another word.

Three days later, Rose pinched her nose and stomped into the stables where Devon's servants had assured her she would find him. "What the devil's the matter with you?"

Rather than turn and look at her, he continued brushing his horse's coat. "I assume you are referring to my recent secession from the feminine society of Fontjoy Square?"

"I am referring to your spat with Claire."

His hand stilled and his body tensed. "Claire told you we had a *spat?*"

"Not in those words, but 'tis obvious that the two of you have had a falling out. I would have come sooner, but Katie has the croup."

"Sorry to hear it. As for Claire, I cannot tolerate her disrespect toward Mary."

"Oh, that is bull—"

Pivoting, Devon's brows shot up and his expression very nearly cracked into a grin. "Why, Rose

Sinclair Nollbrook, that sort of language is hardly becoming to a new bride and mother of three. What would your esteemed barrister husband think if he heard you using such expressions?"

"He is the one who taught them to me, Devon. I had no idea how salty lawyers' tongues were until I met Steven."

Sighing, Devon laid his brush on a rickety table. "I don't suppose you are going to forget about this topic and simply go away if I refuse to discuss it?"

"Not a chance."

"We might as well go inside, then." Devon summoned a groomsman who took over his chores. Then he ushered Rose into his house and led her to his study. When the two were seated before a warm fire, he crossed his long, lean legs and stared expectantly at his guest. "And what have the neighborhood ladies sent you over here to say to me now, Rose?"

"I allow that we are all rather bewildered by the recent turn of events. It seems that the moment we discovered you were our mysterious benefactor, you disappeared."

"Aidan Sullivan caused me to show my cards a bit sooner than I had hoped."

"Perhaps, but we would have found out eventually. You can't have hoped to keep it a secret forever."

"No, but I did not intend to make public all the intimate details of Mary's life. Sullivan's determination to insinuate himself into Mary's life, even after she is dead, disturbs me. He had no business making the rounds in the neighborhood to speak with Mary's old friends."

"He might be pushy, but he is Mary's son. He came a terribly long way from Edinburgh just to discover that his mother was dead."

"Edinburgh?" Devon scratched his chin. "He told me he came from up north."

Rose shook her head. "You must have misunderstood him. His adoptive parents moved to Edinburgh when he was an infant. The Dorcas Society tries its best to keep track of the children it places. The records reflect that Mr. Sullivan was an apothecary by trade, but when his own father died and left him a small milliner shop in Edinburgh, he moved his family there."

"I could have sworn—" Devon's voice trailed off, and he rubbed his face as if he were in a groggy trance that he could not snap out of.

"Is there something else bothering you?"

"Ah, well, there is Claire's reaction to learning that I was married to Mary. She seems to view it as some sort of betrayal on my part."

"Perhaps it is none of my business, Devon, but what does Mary say about Claire in her diary?"

"That they made their debut into Dublin society the same year. That they met at some silly hothouse rout and flirted with the same boys. That they attended a country house party and shared a room and that afterwards they fell out of touch and never spoke again."

"That seems rather strange, doesn't it?"

Devon made a long face. "I never gave it much thought. Apparently, Mary did not stay in touch with any of you. She wrote that after you helped deliver her child, Rose, she gave her servants instructions not to admit you into the house. I think she wanted to pretend that she had never given birth to little Aidan, don't you?"

"Exactly. But there must be a reason she no longer wanted to see Claire."

"Are you suggesting that Mary omitted something when she wrote about Claire?"

Glancing at the clock on the mantel, Rose suddenly sprang to her feet. The time had passed quickly, and she'd promised Mrs. Bleek she would return before the children's lessons were finished. "I am suggesting, Devon, that you talk to Claire and find out what is bothering her. If you love her, that is."

As she hurried down the steps and out of Devon's house, Rose's discomfort grew. She needed to go to town and visit the Dorcas Society's headquarters and take another look at Aidan Sullivan's file. She remembered reading that his adoptive parents had moved to Scotland shortly after he was born. But it was possible that she was wrong.

Clutching her coat around her middle, Rose practically ran the short distance between Devon's Palladian mansion and her more modest brick house at Number Four. With three children and a new husband, she had a hundred things on her mind and not nearly enough time in the day to accomplish all the things she meant to do. Pushing open her front door, however, she paused long enough to inhale the comforting aroma of freshly baked bread and to enjoy the faint sounds of the children's voices filtering from upstairs. Rose Sinclair loved her new life. She was nothing but grateful to Mary O'Roarke. She couldn't comprehend Claire's diffidence toward the poor woman, God rest her soul.

Leaning back against the door, Rose closed her eyes for a moment and smiled. Her weight rocked back on her heels, but the door wouldn't shut.

Rose slowly turned and pressed her palms against the black lacquer.

Opening her eyes, she found herself staring into Aidan Sullivan's ruddy face.

Nine

"Sorry if I startled you." The boy's boot was wedged between the door and the frame.

With a gasp, Rose took a giant step backward, allowing the door to swing open. She hadn't even heard Aidan Sullivan follow her up the steps and onto her porch. She had no idea how long he had been behind her, or where he had come from. An unsettling sense of trepidation overtook her as she gaped at him.

Quickly, Aidan stepped inside, shut the door behind him and blew on his bare fingers while he rubbed them together. "Didn't mean to frighten you, mum, but it's colder than a faerie's arse out there—"

"Excuse me?"

His eyes widened. "I am sorry. Sometimes I forget when I am in the presence of a lady. I hope you will forgive me."

Flustered, Rose nodded. "Yes, yes," she stammered. "Come in and take off your coat. I've some questions for you anyway."

In her parlor, Rose poured the shivering man a cup of hot tea. As anxious as she was to check on her children, she could not pass up the opportunity to question Aidan about the conflict in the information he had given Devon Avondale concerning his adoptive parents.

But before she could raise the subject, he surprised her by strolling about the room, examining pictures on the walls, the sterling silver samovar she had inherited from a distant aunt, a framed certificate showing her husband's admittance to the Dublin bar. He even paused before a bookshelf where he tilted his head to read the titles and ran his fingers over the leather bindings.

"Are you looking for something?" Rose asked, her voice sounding more tart than she had intended.

When he faced her, a tear sparkled in his eye. "I can't help myself, I'm afraid. When I am in this house, *with you*, I feel closer to her."

He was referring to his mother, of course. Uneasily, Rose sank into a chair while Aidan continued to pace the room. "It must have been difficult for you, finding out that your adoptive parents weren't your real parents."

"Unimaginable." He paused at the secretary's desk where Rose often sat and wrote out her ubiquitous lists. With his back to her, he murmured, "And then finding that Mary is dead. I've come too late."

"Would you care for some more tea, Mr. Sullivan?"

"I did not come here for tea and idle chatter, Rose." He turned and crossed the room. Standing at the mantel, he stared at her through narrowed, glistening eyes. "I came here for information. I want to know my father's name."

The tightening in Rose's chest wasn't relieved by the gulp of tea she managed to get down before answering. Her cup and saucer rattled as she placed it on the table beside her. Averting her gaze, she said, "I do not know your real father's name."

"I do not believe you," he replied quietly.

"I do not care whether you believe me. Your father's name is not on file at the Dorcas Society. Mary did not tell anyone who your father was. I have given you all the information I can, Mr. Sullivan. There's no use trying to find out more; you'll only drive yourself to distraction."

"I have already been driven to distraction. What I want now are answers. Who was my father, Rose? What was he like?"

"I don't know," she lied. "And I wouldn't tell you even if I did."

His face contorted in an angry snarl. "That's not fair!"

"There are many things in life that aren't fair, Mr. Sullivan." Rose stood, her hands clasped at her waist. "Now I've a few questions for *you*—"

In a flash, Aidan was nose-to-nose with her, grasping her upper arms, shaking her as if she were a rag doll. "To hell with your questions! Tell me my father's name or else I will—"

"Or else you will what?" Sir Steven Nollbrook's deep courtroom voice boomed through the room. More quickly than Aidan had moved, he crossed the floor and, with one swat of his arm, sent the boy crashing backward into a chair. "If you ever touch my wife again, I will see to it that you spend the rest of your days in prison."

Fearful that her husband was going to lunge after Aidan and pound him into mincemeat, Rose clung to Steven's lapels and quickly explained, "That's Aidan Sullivan. Mary O'Roarke's child. You remember, I told you—"

"What's he doing here and why did he have his hands on you?"

"He wants me to tell him his father's name."

For a stunned moment, Aidan slumped in the chair. Then, slowly, he scrambled to his feet and lurched toward the parlor door. "I didn't mean yer wife no harm," he said sullenly. "I only wanted to know who me real pa was. Guess I got carried away. Sorry."

Aidan's expression was so childlike and his voice so pitiful that Rose almost felt sorry for him. But she feared him, too, and she was immensely grateful that her husband had materialized before Aidan had had the chance to coerce any more information out of her. Now she was more eager than ever to get down to the Dorcas Society headquarters and retrieve Sullivan's adoption papers.

"Get out!" Steven threw up his arm and pointed toward the stairs. "And do not ever darken my doorstep again."

As the boy shuffled out the door and down the steps, Rose fell into her husband's arms. With her face pressed to his chest, she inhaled the familiar aroma of his clothes and skin. "Thank you, Steven," she whispered.

He kissed the top of her head. "There is something about that boy that is not right, Rose. I will instruct the servants not to admit him to this house again."

"He's just a very confused and desperate boy, dear. I don't think he actually would have hurt me."

Steven held her at arm's length. "You are too trusting, Rose. Do not let that young man back into this house, do you understand?"

Nodding, she rose on her tiptoes and received her husband's kiss. "By the way," she murmured, "What brought you home in the middle of the day?"

"My afternoon appointments were canceled. I have a few hours before I have to return to town. I am afraid I will be home later this evening, but in the meantime—" He wrapped his arms around her waist and held her snugly against his body. "I thought that perhaps Mrs. Bleek could keep the children in the classroom for a couple of hours."

"Oh, you are a very bad boy," Rose replied,

smiling as her husband led her to their bedchamber.

As the afternoon wore on, the weather worsened. By nightfall, snow blanketed Fontjoy Square. Unable to sleep, Claire pushed herself up in her bed, lit the small lamp on her table and opened a novel. Her eyes scanned the pages, but she could not concentrate. Her heart ached and her stomach flip-flopped as outside the wind howled. Just a few weeks earlier, she could have counted on Devon to knock on her door after his evening stroll, share a pot of chocolate with her and put her fears to rest. Now she was alone.

Turning a page, she shivered. The fire on her hearth had dwindled and required some attention. But Claire couldn't even find the energy to pull the bell cord and summon a servant. Instead, she tossed aside her book and sank deeper beneath the covers. Staring at the flickering shadows on the ceiling, she tried to make sense of the recent events that had forever altered her life.

If Devon was there, she would ask him why he suddenly decided to kiss her. What made that night different from all the others, when he had simply stood at the mantel, watched her sew and engaged her in conversation? Had he been thinking of kissing her for many days, perhaps weeks? Had he really expected her to kiss him back?

She wondered, too, whether he had ever believed her when she said she didn't want a man. Had Devon secretly mocked her each time she denounced the idea of romantic love? Had he known all along that she was lying to herself? Had Mary O'Roarke's diary already convinced him that Claire Kilgarren was a loose, wanton woman whose passions could not be controlled?

Biting her bottom lip, Claire stifled her tears. She had not been lying when she said she didn't want a man. She really hadn't—not until Devon kissed her, that is. After that horrid house party so many years ago, when Claire's reputation was damaged and her mother's completely destroyed, she'd resolved never to let another man touch her. Claire was not the sort of woman to make the same mistake twice, or so she had thought until Devon had wrecked her resolve.

One monumentally sordid experience had imbued her with cynicism and suspicion toward men. One kiss had given her hope.

Yet she couldn't allow herself to fall in love with Devon Avondale. The notion was preposterous. He was once married to Mary O'Roarke, the very vixen who had ruined Claire's prospects for a respectable marriage. Claire detested Mary O'Roarke and detested even more the knowledge that Mary had given her a house.

Given her a house?

As some sort of peace offering? As a token of Mary's contrition? As a symbol of Mary's superiority?

Oh, she could almost see the smug look on Mary's face, her condescending tone of voice, her sly little smile when she had instructed her husband to find poor little Claire Kilgarren and lift her up from poverty! And she could hear Mary's chuckle as she wrote in her diary.

The diary that Devon had read. The diary that exposed Claire Kilgarren and her mother as Jezebels.

Pulling the covers over her head, Claire wished she had never opened her door the day that mysteriously black-clad man arrived on her doorstep and handed her the thick vellum envelope, the one that contained the offer of a fine Georgian mansion in exchange for nothing other than refurbishing the garden in the center of Fontjoy Square.

She cursed the day she had crossed the Liffey Bridge in a hackney cab with her entire wardrobe packed in one trunk. She would have been better off had she remained where she was, patting babies' bottoms and fending off the advances of the men who employed her to raise and educate their children. She had become an expert in detecting and deflecting the unwanted desires of men.

In her former life, the worst she had to fear was an empty pocketbook and a growling belly. Now she feared the power of her own desires and where they might lead her.

Her own desires? Just weeks earlier, Claire would have laughed if anyone had suggested that she—

the dedicated spinster—would burn with sexual desire. She had not thought it possible. She had not wanted this complication in her life. She had not bargained for the pain her desire had caused her.

And she could not stop thinking about Devon. She couldn't stop thinking about how warm his breath had been against her neck, and how safe she'd felt in his arms. She couldn't erase from her mind the image of his half-naked body, the velvety sensation of his penis in her hand, the excitement she'd experienced when he'd reached his climax. She couldn't forget the erotic pleasures he'd given her. In truth, Claire couldn't think of anything else *but* Devon and the friendship they'd shared before that first kiss had ever occurred.

A knock at the door jolted Claire from her obsessive thoughts. Belowstairs, excited voices mingled in the foyer. Claire had thrown off her counterpane and quilt and was searching for her slippers when her bedroom door opened.

"Mum, it's Millicent Wolferton's maid! And she's all in a tizzy, let me tell you!"

"What's the matter?"

"Somethin' wrong with the babe, it appears. The lady's in a bad way, and Sir Alec is still in London!"

"Has Rose been summoned?"

"Yes, ma'am, and Lady Dolly, too. They're already at the Wolferton house, waiting for you!"

"Good God, I can't do anything! What we need

is a surgeon or a midwife!" Frantic, Claire pulled on a pair of her gardening trousers and stuffed the hem of her gown inside them. Clad in a heavy woolen coat, her throat and head covered by a scarf, her hands protected by leather gloves, she raced down the street to Millicent's house.

Ten minutes later, she stood beside Millicent's bed. Flanking her were Dolly and Rose, both of whom wore grim, worried expressions as they watched Millicent writhe in pain.

"We need a surgeon," Claire repeated, frightened by the pallor of Millicent's skin.

"But the snow has made it impossible to get a carriage through the streets," replied Dolly softly. "Dick is undoubtedly stuck in the city, unable to get home."

"Steven was summoned back to his office late this afternoon when a porter delivered a message that one of his clients had been tossed into jail. He can't get home, either. I'm afraid we're just four women without a man to help us." Rose pressed a damp cloth to Millicent's forehead. "Her fever is dangerously high. She doesn't even know where she is, poor dear. If we don't get help soon, I fear that she will—"

"Don't even say it, Rose." Claire pulled her coat more tightly about her. "If she needs a doctor, we'll get her one. We don't need men to help us."

"What do you intend to do?" Dolly asked.

"Don't do anything foolish," Rose cautioned her.

But Claire was already halfway down the steps. She wasn't going to let Millicent die in that bed. That simply wasn't going to happen, not while there were surgeons in Dublin who could save her, and not while Claire possessed the strength to find one.

Devon had been sitting in his chair and staring at the fire so long that his eyes itched and his cheeks felt sunburned. Had he been able to, he would have spent the night reading Mary's diary, but that memento had been taken from him, so that all he could do now was revisit his memories and drown his sorrows with whiskey.

He had no idea how long he'd been asleep. He awoke with a start, quickly sensing that something was wrong. Instantly, his body tensed. As his eyes flew open, the dour face of his butler sharpened into view.

"I'm sorry to disturb you, sir, but I thought you would want to know."

"Know what?"

"Kevin, the groomsman, and Hannah, the scullery maid, say there is someone in the stable."

Groggily, Devon rubbed his eyes. "What the devil are you talking about?"

"Seems Kevin and Hannah were planning to retire to the hay loft for a bit of sport, if you know what I mean."

"In this weather? Why not do it in the kitchen, before the fire, if they can't find any other place?"

"Can't understand it meself, sir, except to say that Cook has threatened to disembowel anyone she catches swyving on her butcher board, and apparently, Kevin promised Hannah that he could warm her up. Had a flask of scotch whiskey, the lad did, and a bundle of blankets. At any rate, the two crept out the back of the house and toward the stables but were put off by the sound of someone inside."

Devon sprang to his feet. "A horse thief! I'll put an end to that."

It appeared that the butler had more to say, but Devon pushed past him. In the foul mood he was in, he was only too eager to get his hands around the throat of the cheeky bastard who thought he could saunter into Devon's stables and steal his cattle. Without hesitation, he grabbed the small pistol his servant handed him, tucked it in the waistband of his trousers and pounded down the steps.

Devon's blood roared in his ears. A good fight might even clear his head. He almost hoped the arrogant horse thief in his stables was stupid enough to engage him in hand-to-hand combat.

Stepping outside, Devon took a quick breath. Icy air cut through him like a knife, reminding him that he hadn't even bothered to throw on a coat before he rushed from his house. But Devon didn't care. The faint light that flickered inside the stables affirmed Kevin's and Hannah's suspicions. Someone was attempting to steal

Devon's livestock. That someone would pay dearly.

Stealthily, Devon picked his way over the cobbled stone apron that connected the rear of his house and the stable area. At the stable entrance, he paused, peering around the open door, allowing his eyes to adjust to the semidarkness. Inside, footsteps rustled through the straw that covered the floor, while horses gently whuffled and fidgeted in their stalls.

Aidan Sullivan's unwelcome face popped into Devon's mind, piquing his anger. Already the boy had tried to extort money from him by selling him Mary's diary. Devon deduced that his refusal to pay the boy was the inspiration for this insanely risky criminal endeavor. Was Sullivan truly foolish enough to think he could get away with horse thievery?

Stepping around the corner, Devon crouched low and moved silently toward the center of the stable. He hid behind a wooden partition, then slowly raised himself up and peeked over the edge.

The horse thief, his back to Devon, stood just a couple of yards away. He hung his lantern on a peg on the wall. A circle of golden light illuminated his activities as he slipped a bit between the teeth of Devon's favorite gray mare, led it from the stall and began saddling it.

For a while, Devon watched, amazed that Mary O'Roarke's natural son could have grown up to become such a disreputable fellow. Devon's fingers closed around the butt of his pistol, but out of respect for his dead wife, he left the weapon tucked inside his pants. He would not shoot the little villain unless he had to.

Straightening to his full height, Devon stepped from behind the wooden partition. "Lift your hands above your head, or else I will shoot you."

The boy's body went still. Then, slowly, his leather gloved hands reached upward.

It stood to reason that the interloper would possess a gun or weapon of some sort. No thief in his right mind would attempt to steal a horse without one. Swiftly, Devon closed in on the boy and patted his sides, searching for any suspicious bulges beneath that thick woolen jacket. He ran his hands down the lad's legs and back up his inner thighs. For a boy, Aidan Sullivan was surprisingly soft.

When Devon reached around and slipped his hand inside the boy's jacket, groping for the pistol that he suspected was tucked inside a breast pocket, he got the shock of his life.

"Good Lord, you're a woman!" Devon's hand cupped a female breast—a very firm and shapely one, at that.

"Release me, you callous oaf," a familiar voice seethed. Over her shoulder, Lady Claire Kilgarren scowled hatefully.

Only then did Devon notice the wisps of blond hair tucked beneath the horse thief's knitted cap. Despite his chagrin at finding Claire in his stables, his lower regions tingled. Mentally, he scolded himself for his inability to even be in her presence without wanting to ravish her. "Care to explain why you are stealing my mare?"

"If you'll take your hand off my breast."

"And what if I refuse?" It was cold as the North Pole in that stable, but like Kevin the groomsman, he would have made do if Claire had been willing. "You're at my mercy, you know."

"You're not that kind of man, Devon."

Unfortunately, she was right. Slowly, Devon's hand slid from beneath her jacket. With a sigh, he took a step back.

Claire faced him, her back to the horse. "Millicent needs a surgeon. She's got a terrible fever and she's in tremendous pain. Something's gone wrong with the baby."

Instantly, Devon sobered. "And how was stealing one of my horses going to help Millicent?"

"We can't get a carriage through the streets. Dick Creevy and Sir Steven can't even get home from the city. But a horse could get through. And there is bound to be a good doctor at Meath Hospital. I thought if I could get to him—"

Before she finished her thought, Devon had reached for the lantern on the peg and grabbed the horse's reins. "I'll need to put on some warmer clothes," he said, leading the horse toward the stable door.

"Where are you going?"

"To Meath Hospital, where do you think?"

"You don't have to do this, Devon."

"Of course I do."

"We're not your responsibility, Devon."

Pivoting, he stood so close to her that he could hear the rattle of her teeth. The urge to pull her into his arms, warm her bones and dispel her fear was strong. But there would be time for that later—*perhaps*.

Or perhaps not. Clearly, Claire did not trust or even like Devon. If there was any doubt in her mind as to the way he felt about her, Millicent, Dolly and Rose, she had completely misunderstood him. It pained and disappointed him to know that she would rather have stolen his horse and ridden into town than ask him to help her. Somewhere along the line, he had failed her as a friend. But he didn't know how he had done that. Other than being married to Mary O'Roarke, he didn't know how he had offended Claire. He certainly couldn't undo his marriage. And even if he could, he wouldn't have wanted to.

"Surely you don't expect me to allow you to go riding around in the middle of the night, especially under such treacherous conditions! Frankly, I am offended that you did not come to me first, Claire. Haven't I done everything I could for the four of you ladies? Good God, don't you realize that you're the only family I've got?"

Her lashes, dotted with specks of snow, flickered guiltily. "Why, yes, but I thought that . . . well, under the circumstances . . ."

"Claire, no matter what happens between us,

you will always be my friend. And so will Millicent and Dolly and Rose. I hope you will remember that."

"Yes." She followed him as far as the alley, then hung back when the kitchen door opened and light spilled out from the house. "I'll be at Millicent's house, Devon. I'm not certain what I can do for her, but there's no use in my going home. I wouldn't be able to sleep."

"I will bring the doctor back as soon as I can," he promised her, handing the horse's ribbons to an unhappy looking groomsman. "Bring the horse around front, will you, Kevin?"

Minutes later, Devon swung his leg over the mare's back and carefully set off toward Meath Hospital.

A half block away, Claire stood at the edge of the street and watched Devon disappear into the darkness. His trek to Meath Hospital would be dangerous. When he got there, he would have to find a doctor and bribe him handsomely to come out into this nasty weather. Yet he had not hesitated to make the journey. Nor had he given Claire any serious chastisement for her attempt to steal one of his horses.

She wished she did not admire Devon Avondale as much as she did.

She wished he was not so selfless, brave and generous.

Most of all, she wished she had not felt so good

when he reached around her and squeezed her breast.

Devon Avondale was everything she could have wanted in a man. Were he not so obsessed with Mary O'Roarke, Claire might have been willing to amend her view of marriage and allow herself to fall in love with him.

But Mary O'Roarke's vicious behavior had been the precipitating factor in Claire's social disgrace and public humiliation. Undoubtedly, Devon Avondale had read Mary's version of those events. If he believed Mary, then how could he have any regard for Claire? There was simply no way that Devon could love Mary and respect Claire at the same time. And there was no way that Claire could forgive Mary for what she'd done.

Pulling her cap over her ears, Claire trudged back to Millicent's house, where a light burned in the upstairs window and shadows passed behind the curtain. A sense of foreboding shrouded the neighborhood. Millicent's ordeal had just begun, and Claire couldn't be distracted by her own problems.

Besides, Devon had been right about one thing: The denizens of Fontjoy Square formed a family. And no matter what happened between Claire and Devon, the rest of them had to stick together.

As Claire pushed open Millicent's front door, a blood-curdling scream split the air. Furiously, she pounded up the steps. At the threshold of Millicent's room, Claire drew up short and gasped. Millicent's bedclothes were soaked with blood and her entire body trembled convulsively. Rose quietly gave orders while Dolly scurried between the bed and the bathroom. A maidservant busied herself with tearing sheets into long strips of linen.

"Is she going to be all right?" Claire blurted.

Dolly's blue eyes were wide with terror.

Rose glanced up and said confidently, "Of course, dear. Now where the hell is that doctor you promised us?"

Ten

The next few hours ticked by slowly. The women filled a bath with cool water and got Millicent into it. Her fever subsided, but she continued to moan and clutch her abdomen. With her arms thrown around Rose and Dolly's necks, she stumbled back to her freshly made bed. Feebly, she sipped at a glass of fortified wine that Dolly held to her lips. Then her head fell back on the pillow and she closed her eyes.

"She is asleep." Straightening, Dolly wiped the perspiration from her brow with her sleeve. "Where is that doctor, Claire?"

"Are you certain Devon said he would go to Meath?" Rose asked. "Only a fool or a hero would venture out in this weather."

"I have no doubt that he will do what he promised," replied Claire. "He will return as soon as humanly possible."

Shortly before daybreak, a knock sounded belowstairs. Claire, her eyes tired and scratchy, pushed off the settee she shared with Dolly. Rose, who was keeping a vigil at Millicent's bedside, stood, too, just as Devon and an older bespectacled man appeared in the bedroom door.

"This is Dr. Flannagan," Devon explained.

Both men were covered in snow. Their faces were blistered by the violent weather, and they moved stiffly, as if every muscle in their bodies ached. The return on horseback from Meath Hospital, pushing constantly against a raging snowstorm, had evidently been brutal.

Dr. Flannagan, clutching a black leather valise, leaned over Millicent, lifted her eyelids and frowned. "Could I ask to have some privacy with my patient?" he asked over his shoulder.

Everyone, with the exception of Rose, departed Millicent's bedchamber.

In the parlor, a servant produced a pot of hot tea, but Devon preferred whatever the sideboard had to offer. After knocking back several gulps of whiskey, he stood on the hearth and rubbed his hands before a blazing fire. Slowly, the tension in his posture faded, and his skin took on a more natural color. But his expression remained grim and inscrutable.

The room was mournfully quiet until a porter, a raggedly dressed boy of about ten years of age, burst into the room and handed Dolly a folded vellum note. She dug in her pocket and pressed a few coins into his grimy palm. Then she quickly scanned the note. "My husband has made it home from the city," she said excitedly, leaping to her feet.

"I will walk you home," Devon offered.

"Good heavens, I can dash across the street without a protector."

Devon smiled wistfully. "Of course."

"Come and fetch me if anything changes, Claire."

"I will."

With Dolly gone, the parlor fell silent again. For a long while, Claire sat on the sofa sipping tea while Devon stood before the mantel, his lips turned downward, his jaw stony. She seriously considered asking him to leave. Being in Devon's presence was uncomfortable and unnerving.

What do you say to a man with whom you have been intimate, but with whom you have nothing in common?

His voice, when he spoke, was so low and gravelly that Claire had to lean forward to hear him.

"You dislike me that intensely, do you? That you would rather steal a horse of mine than ask me to do Millicent a favor?"

"As I said, Devon, it was not your concern."

"Everything that goes on in this neighborhood is my concern."

"Is that so?" A needle of irritation pricked at Claire's gut. "Just because you gave us these houses, Devon? Do you think you own us just because you *rescued* us from poverty? Well, perhaps that is why I did not ask you for another favor. I no longer want to be beholden to you, Devon. I no longer want to be thought of as your *favorite charity.*"

His gaze was black and gleaming. "You don't give yourself much credit, do you, Claire?"

"I know why I am here. 'Tis not because you like me. 'Tis because of Mary O'Roarke and your obsession with her."

"She was my wife," Devon bit out. "You act as if you resent my affection for her. You seem to think my love for her is somehow an affront to you."

"I know only that with one slip of her pointed little tongue, Mary O'Roarke destroyed my youth. And, fifteen years later, with one stroke of her pen, she destroyed the rest of my life."

"Your coming to live in Fontjoy Square represents the *destruction* of the rest of your life?" Devon crossed his arms over his chest.

"Your betrayal of me has quite crushed my spirit, Devon."

His voice dropped to a hoarse whisper. "How have I betrayed you, Claire?"

"You lied to me."

"You stole from me."

Indignation and anger poured through her. Though her body ached from lack of sleep, Claire shot to her feet. Her heart pounded and her knees wobbled as she stood in front of Devon. "I have stolen nothing from you."

"Return the diary and all will be forgiven."

"Damn Mary O'Roarke's wretched diary! You ought to burn the damn thing, and if you cared a whit for me, you would!"

His thick, wiry brows shot up. "How dare you—"

Claire drew back her arm to slap him.

Her gaze locked with his. Her emotions were dry kindling to the spark of his accusation. She hated Devon because he had hurt her. But he had the power to hurt her only because she loved him so much.

Stunned by this insight, Claire hesitated. Slowly, her hand fell to her side. God, but Devon Avondale was a handsome man, and never had he been more handsome than he was now, with his dark eyes flashing and his dampened hair curling thickly at his neck. His skin was scrubbed raw by the arctic winds, his beard was coarse and stubbly, his smell thoroughly masculine. He had put himself in great jeopardy to save Millicent's life. Anguish and fatigue was etched on his face. Had she not been so proud, Claire would have melted into his arms and kissed him.

Instead, she faltered backward, her chin trembling. "I am sorry, Devon. I would never have hit you. I am tired, and worried about Millicent. My mind is cloudy."

His expression softened. "What happened between you and Mary? Tell me, Claire."

"Are you telling me you don't know?"

"I don't know."

"Mary didn't tell you?"

"It is not in her diary, Claire. I thought you knew—"

"I don't believe you."

"Tell me anyway. Tell me *your* version, why don't you."

"She ruined my reputation, Devon. She ruined my mother's, too."

After a moment, he pinched the bridge of his nose and said, "All right. So she said some unkind things about you. Does that mean you cannot care about *me*, Claire? It was not I who said those things!"

"Unkind things?" Claire scoffed. "That would be a gross understatement, Devon."

"Care to tell me what she said, Claire?"

Unable to face him, Claire whirled and marched to the sideboard where she poured herself a neat shot of scotch. The heat from the liquor spread through her blood, warming her, imbuing her with courage. Yes, she wanted to tell Devon what his precious little Mary had done to her! She wanted to see the shock and revulsion on his face when he realized that the wife he'd practically canonized since her death had once been a malicious tabby and conniving social climber. She wanted to disabuse him of the notion that Mary O'Roarke was perfect!

But when she returned to him, her bravado momentarily faltered. Was it fair to impugn the character of a woman who had been dead six years?

"Tell me, Claire," Devon practically growled.

"All right, then. Mary O'Roarke and I shared a room that weekend; that much you know already. My mother attended the party also. She was ensconced in a room at the other end of the hall.

And Mary's father came along. As fate would have it, his temporary lodgings were opposite my mother's."

"Go on."

"It seems that my mother and Mary's father hit it off quite nicely. They were having a jolly time that evening in a grand casino that our hosts had arranged in the dance hall. It was like a holiday. Mother was happy to be away from Father, who was as strict a Methodist as ever came from Manchester, I can assure you. Mr. O'Roarke was a handsome fellow with charming manners and an eye for the ladies, if you know what I mean. I knew that Mother was drawing attention to herself. People were watching, ladies were whispering behind their fans. Our host and hostess were getting nervous."

Devon pursed his lips knowingly. "I think I see—"

"No, you don't see," Claire said, more harshly than she intended. "At the same time Mary's father was flirting with my mother, Mary was flirting her own head off with some young Scotsman she'd once met in Killiney."

Devon's brows shot up. "What was his name, can you remember?"

"I've long since forgotten. But I remember vividly that the young man wasn't at all interested in her. Mary made a cake of herself, batting her eyelashes, hanging on his arm. At last, he extricated himself from her and asked me to dance. Twice in a row, if you want to know, an almost unheard of overture in those sorts of settings. Tongues set about wagging that the boy was paying me too much attention, that it appeared we were too friendly, that I ought to be more circumspect and dance with the other boys."

"And did you?"

"No, I thought it all an amusing game. I had no idea that my reckless disregard of the so-called rules of etiquette would have such unpleasant and long-lasting consequences."

"What happened then?"

"When the party ended, I said good night to my new suitor and left the casino. I was halfway up the stairs when I heard Mary screaming. She had barged into her father's room and found him in a compromising position—with my mother. I am glad that you are at least decent enough to look embarrassed."

"I am sorry for you," he replied gruffly.

"Oh, dear, it didn't end there. Mary wouldn't stop screaming until half the guests in the house ran to see what was the matter. My mother's reputation was ruined, of course."

"And what about Mr. O'Roarke's?"

"I'm sure the incident had no effect on him whatsoever, except for the inconvenience it caused him that night. I doubt anyone ever had the nerve to even tell his wife."

"Ah. But someone obviously told your father."

"That, and more. Mary was determined to get her vengeance, you see. She told anyone who would listen to her that she'd seen me in the gardens with that redheaded Scotsman, sitting on his lap with my knickers around my ankles and my breasts spilling out of my dress. It was nonsense, of course. I never even talked to the boy after that night."

"Didn't your father believe you?"

"I suppose you would have to know my father to understand. He was a man who did not tolerate scandal, a man who believed that if thine eye offended thee, then pluck it out. He'd have had me in a chastity belt if he could have done so legally."

"Are you saying your father ostracized you because of the idle gossip of some young debutante?"

"I am saying that he *disinherited* me, Devon." Claire's voice was a hiss of pent-up pain. "And tossed my mother into the streets."

"Where is your mother now?"

Shrugging, Claire tossed her head. She wasn't sure she knew herself, but she had a pretty good notion. Somewhere in Monto, most likely, making a living the only way she knew how, *on her back*. "I'm sure I haven't spoken to her in years."

"Don't you know where she is, Claire? Aren't you worried about her?"

Of course she was worried about her mother. But she was embarrassed by her, too, which was why she had gone to such pains to be different from her. After the duchess had been cut off by Lord Kilgarren, she descended shamefully into a life of complete decadence. Claire, on the other hand, had reacted to her own disgrace by vowing never to let another man touch her.

Only Devon had been able to touch her. And ever since he had, Claire had been racked with guilt and frustration. She was terrified by her own desires and by the possibility that she was just like her mother. Her confusion was rampant. One minute she ached for Devon's kiss; the next she despised him for having awakened these dangerous new impulses.

"Claire?" he prodded. "Where is your mother now?"

A chill slid up her spine. "My mother and I do not communicate."

"Why not?"

"She disgraced herself. I always thought my father was overly harsh, puritanical and cruel. I swear I do not understand how he wound up married to my frivolous mother. But, in the end, Father's suspicions were well-founded. Imagine how I felt, Devon! My mother cavorting with my friend's father . . . in front of everyone! She had no shame, I tell you! None at all! She got what she deserved!"

"And did you?" he asked quietly. "Did you get what you deserved?"

"What do you mean by that?"

"Experience and your father have taught you that only bad women enjoy sex. You believe your own mother to be a harlot."

"How dare you—"

"Perhaps you should talk with your mother, Claire. Find out why she did what she did."

"I know why she did it. She couldn't control her animal impulses."

"Maybe she didn't want to. She had a choice, Claire, and she understood the consequences of her actions. Presumably, she was not forced to have sex with Mr. O'Roarke. But, for whatever reason, she chose to."

"She thought she wouldn't be caught."

"You told me she was flirting outrageously, publicly, openly—"

"She had always been a notoriously reckless woman."

"I think you don't understand her, Claire. I think you will not understand yourself until you talk to her."

A sudden, inexplicable fear enveloped Claire. It was bad enough that Devon had touched her where no other man had. Did he have to probe her soul and her psyche as well? The invasiveness of his questions made her slightly queasy. "Well, that is not going to happen," she said with finality. "And I am finished talking about it. You asked me how Mary ruined my reputation and I told you. I owe you no further explanations."

Neither of them spoke for a long while. Devon stared absently at the fire, and Claire, physically exhausted and emotionally drained, collapsed onto the sofa. Telling Devon what had happened at the house party had humiliated her. She fully expected him never to speak to her again. After all, not only had she confessed that her mother was a woman of loose morals, but she had also maligned Mary O'Roarke's virtue as well. She would be lucky if Devon didn't stalk from Millicent's parlor right now.

Instead, he leaned against the mantel and said wearily, " 'Tis a startling revelation. But enough of that for tonight. We are all of us under a great stress. We can discuss it later. For now, allow me to walk you home."

"No, I would rather stay. I can sleep on the sofa. If there is any change in Millicent's condition, I will be right here."

"Go ahead, then, lie down. There's a coverlet over here."

He strode across the room and picked up a blanket strewn across the back of a chair.

Claire collapsed onto the sofa, her bones weary, her chest aching. She murmured, "Thank you," as Devon tucked the blanket around her.

He unlaced her boots and gently pulled them off her feet. "Get some sleep. I'll awaken you if anything happens."

Her head barely hit the bolster before her eyelids closed. As she fell asleep, Claire was dimly aware of Devon's hand on the top of her head and his voice, as soothing and sweet as aged whiskey, floating all around her.

"I won't leave you, Claire. Try as you like, you see, you cannot rid yourself of those who love you."

Devon sank into the chair opposite the sofa. Claire's lashes fluttered for a moment, then stilled completely. Her bosom rose and fell, her lips parted slightly and her features smoothed in repose. As tired as he was, Devon could not take his eyes off her.

As angry as he was at her because she resented Mary O'Roarke, he could not deny that he loved Claire.

Staring at her, he wondered when he had first fallen in love with his flaxen-haired neighbor. Not at the very first sight of her, that was for certain. Oh, he had realized the moment he saw her that she was beautiful, far more beautiful than the other ladies of Fontjoy Square, with the exception perhaps of Rose Sinclair-Nollbrook, who was older than Claire, a good bit *rounder* and more . . . maternal.

No, Claire was different. Different from Mary O'Roarke, whose wild copper curls and flashing green eyes had incited Devon's sexual desire the instant he met her. Different from Dolly Baltmore-Creevy, whose petite, muscular figure and close-cut cap of blond ringlets created an androgynous look that piqued Devon's interest but also made him uncomfortable. Different from the wide-eyed, naive Millicent of whom he had once been so protective.

Aristocratic, serene, surprisingly earthy, unruffled and outspoken, Claire was like no woman Devon had ever known before. He hadn't meant to fall in love with her, and she had not meant to fall in love with him. Indeed, their friendship had blossomed in part because they had both agreed on one thing: they had no interest in romance.

But Devon *was* interested in romance now. It had been nearly six years since Mary died and he was lonely. Rose, Millicent and Dolly had found husbands. The women he had brought to Fontjoy Square had married and made families. He was happy for them—and envious. He had loved being married to Mary O'Roarke, and he wanted to feel that same contentment again. *With Claire.*

There was only one small problem: Claire disliked Mary O'Roarke so intensely that she could not allow herself to fall in love with Devon. The irony wasn't lost on him. Mary had known that Devon would be slow to let go of her memory, and so she had penned a diary in which she introduced him to four unmarried women.

Mary had known her last wishes would be honored, and that Devon would find those four women and offer them homes. She had instructed him to find someone to love; she must have known that he would find someone among the four women who had befriended Mary during her lifetime, the women she respected, the *women who had shaped her own character.*

Well, he had found her . . . and she was near but very far away. The incident that had changed Claire's life forever had been omitted from Mary's memoirs. And until he rectified the wrong Mary had committed, or at least convinced Claire that he did not share Mary's views, he had little hope of changing Claire's mind.

* * *

"Where is your mother now?"

Devon's question rang in Claire's ears, jolting her from her sleep. She half sat, peering into the darkness. The fire had dwindled and the room was cold. Opposite her, Devon slept in a chair, his head lolling to the side, the sound of his breathing filling the room.

Was that really her problem, her unresolved relationship with her mother? And was it any of Devon Avondale's business whether she ever spoke to the duchess again?

Pulling the blanket up to her chin, Claire stared hard at the man who threatened to topple the defensive rampart she had so carefully constructed around her heart. Was he a rapacious invader intent on conquering her, or was he her rescuer? She did not know.

A part of her wanted to fight him, reject him and send him away. Another part of her wanted desperately to be protected and cherished by him.

His eyes suddenly opened. "I make you uncomfortable, don't I?" he asked, his voice rasping.

The cold she felt in her bones instantly turned to fire. "Yes, you do, sir."

"Change is not always a bad thing, Claire."

"I did not ask for it."

"You cannot prevent the world from changing. If you do not change, you will be left behind."

"I control my own little corner of the world, Devon, as do you. I have no intention of relinquishing sovereignty of it to you, or to any other man."

"You are so afraid of losing control that you would push me away?"

She hesitated. She did not want to expel Devon from her life, but she did not want to lose herself completely in him, either. "Women who devote themselves exclusively to their men always wind up with broken hearts."

"Not always. What about Rose—"

"Her first husband was a notorious whoremonger who treated her like dirt."

"But her second one adores her." Devon sighed. "Do you think she was afraid to fall in love again?"

Claire made a derisive little snort. "She has the luck o'the Irish, I suppose."

"You're Irish, too, Claire."

"A woman who depends on luck instead of her wits is a fool. Forget it, Devon; I am not going to fall in love with you."

"Then our lovemaking . . ." He shifted in his chair, crossing his long legs, gazing hungrily at her. "Our lovemaking was nothing more than sex? Pure animal lust? Meaningless rutting?"

Claire's cheeks burned. Beneath the blanket, she crossed her arms over her chest. "You were my friend before all this happened. Perhaps we should pretend it never occurred. We could go back to being the way we were, Devon."

"I told you, I cannot do that." He pushed off the chair and crossed the distance between them.

Sitting on the sofa, he leaned over her and touched her face. "I don't think you can, either."

"Yes, I can," she said weakly, not believing herself for a second. But she could try. She had to. If she let her sexual impulses dictate her decisions, she would wind up like her mother, ostracized, unwanted and without a shred of self-respect.

"Kiss me, Claire," he whispered.

Despite her continued protestations, Claire wanted to kiss Devon. As she lifted her chin and fixed her attention on his lips, her father's voice warned her that she was in grave danger of losing her soul to the devil. She knew her actions were wildly contradictory to her assertions that she did not want a man. Yet she could not resist one last kiss.

One last kiss, she told herself. And tomorrow she would make plans to leave Fontjoy Square. Because as long as she was around Devon Avondale, as long as she could see him and feel him and *smell* him, she simply could not control her physical urges. In order to escape temptation, she would have to run away.

His mouth covered hers, obliterating all conscious thought of her father's warnings and her mother's misdeeds. The tension in her muscles eased, only to be replaced by a different kind of tension. Her pulse quickened and her skin tingled. She slid her arms out from beneath the blanket and wrapped them around Devon's neck. She parted her lips, encouraging and inviting him.

With a moan, Devon deepened their kiss. As his

tongue explored her lips and mouth, his breathing grew more ragged and irregular. His lashes flickered and, in the nearly non-existent firelight, Claire saw that his gaze had taken on a drugged, lethargic quality. His arousal aroused her. Scraping her fingernails along his nape, she arched her back and pressed herself more tightly into his embrace.

Suddenly, he straightened, crossed the room and shut the door.

The click of the latch startled Claire. "This is insane," she murmured, half aware that she was in another woman's home.

Devon returned and bent over her, his expression strained. "Claire, I want to make love to you. Completely. Tell me to stop if you don't want me to."

She answered by running her fingers up his chest, dipping them inside the throat of his shirt and deftly unbuttoning the top button. He responded by ripping the rest of the buttons open and shrugging out of his shirt. Then he stood, pulled off his boots and unbuttoned his pants.

Claire watched with unabashed fascination as he removed his clothes. Her throat went dry as he pushed his unmentionables down his thighs, exposing his erection. The promise of feeling Devon's body inside hers filled her with anticipation.

In the back of her mind, she wondered if she should tell him that she had never been with a man before. Quickly, she concluded that a man like Devon, a gentleman at heart despite his seemingly unquenchable sexual thirst, would attach a great deal of significance to her virginity. No doubt he would feel tremendously responsible for ensuring that Claire's first real sexual experience was painless and pleasurable. He might even not want that responsibility; he might choose not to make love to her at all.

The sofa was uncomfortable and too small for two bodies. As Devon scooped her up in his arms and laid her gently on the carpet, Claire decided not to tell him she was a virgin. She wanted him to focus on making love to her, not protecting her. She wanted to be treated like a woman, not a child.

Eleven

The house was quiet. Abovestairs, Millicent lay desperately ill, battling for her life and the life of her child. Rose and the doctor were with her, fighting fatigue and the odds in a brave attempt to make her well. Claire should have been there, too, holding Millicent's hand, pressing cool compresses to her feverish brow. Claire should have been able to suppress her desires just long enough to see her friend through this dreadfully dangerous night.

Instead she was lying on her back, kicking off her boots and practically panting with eagerness to feel Devon's naked body against hers. Guilt tugged at her but could not draw her out of Devon's thrall. As she rolled down her stockings and wriggled out of her gown, Claire realized how frighteningly powerful her sexual attraction to Devon really was. So powerful that she would not tell him she was a virgin. So powerful that she would rather suffer the pain of losing her virginity than endure the disappointment of his withholding his love from her. So powerful that she could think of nothing else but the heat that pooled between her legs as he hovered over her.

She parted her thighs, and he lowered himself onto her. His erect penis pressed against her belly, his strong muscular legs wedged between hers. For a long time, they kissed, their tongues and teeth clashing, their breath mingling, their bodies moving rhythmically against each other.

At length, Claire reached down and wrapped her fingers around his pulsing shaft.

Supporting his weight on his elbows, Devon shifted his position. The tip of his penis nudged Claire's drenched flesh. His fingers toyed with that tiny, incredibly sensitive nub of flesh between her folds. As his hips rocked against hers, the pressure building inside and out of her body increased. Her need emboldened her. She grasped Devon's hips and buttocks, pulling him closer to her.

The next few moments passed in a blur of exquisite pleasure and pain. Devon's penis slid easily into her feminine opening, but then her muscles tensed and her inner body resisted his penetration. Claire gasped as the sensation between her legs sharpened. Closing her eyes, she grit her teeth and tried to relax.

"Are you all right?" he asked softly.

Swallowing hard, she managed to reassure him that she was. "It feels good, Devon. Please don't stop."

"I don't think I could," he nearly growled.

Then, with a strangled cry, he slid deep inside her, up to the hilt.

Her body stretched impossibly. Crying out, Claire instinctively arched her spine and drew up her knees. What she felt couldn't accurately be called pleasure *or* pain, but she wondered if she'd been wrong not to tell Devon that she was a virgin.

"Dear God, I've hurt you!" Devon whispered, his movements quelled.

She met his puzzled gaze. "No, you didn't hurt me."

"You don't mean to tell me . . ." His voice trailed off. "Claire, why didn't you tell me?"

"I didn't want you to know," she said hoarsely.

"I should have known." He tried to withdraw, but Claire's fingertips grappled at his flesh and he stilled. "I would never have imposed upon you. I would never have done this," he added, averting his gaze from hers.

Confused, Claire released her hold on him, allowing his now limp body to slip from hers. Having limited experience with men, she did not understand why her virginity dismayed him, or why his arousal had suddenly vanished.

"You assumed that I was *not* a virgin," she said carefully. "And now that you have discovered I am, you are surprised? And disappointed?"

"I don't know what I thought." He rolled to his side and propped up his head on his hand. "It never occurred to me that a woman your age—"

"Wouldn't be a virgin?" Claire's tone was edgier than she'd intended, but Devon's abrupt withdrawal had wounded her feelings. Her flesh was still wet and her body still tingled with desire. But now her emotions were in flux, and once again she felt foolish and exposed.

Though she despised the old feelings of bitterness that welled up inside her, Claire couldn't resist them. Her father's prophetic warnings echoed in her head. Mary O'Roarke's silvery laughter taunted her.

Devon touched her shoulder. "Mary was not so inexperienced when I met her. I should have realized you are nothing like Mary in that regard."

Naked and vulnerable, she slapped at his hand. "Don't touch me."

"Claire, you should have told me."

"You should not have *assumed*."

He exhaled heavily. "Perhaps you are right—"

"I am bloody well right!" Sitting up, Claire grabbed at her clothes. "You read Mary O'Roarke's diary and you believed it!"

His fist pounded the carpet. "Damn it, I am bloody well tired of hearing about Mary's diary."

They dressed quickly, with their backs turned to each other. Devon opened the door, then poked at the fire while Claire sat glumly on the sofa, wondering why she couldn't get a grasp on her emotions, fearing that she was going insane. They didn't speak to one another even when sunlight peeked through the windows, and abovestairs, Millicent's bedroom door squeaked open.

* * *

"I'm afraid the lady's condition is serious." The doctor stood in the doorway, looking grim and haggard.

Claire's mouth went dry. She struggled to her feet, but fear made her dizzy. Swaying, she clutched at the side of the sofa for support. "How serious? Millicent isn't going to die, is she?"

"She might," he replied, not unkindly, but in a clipped tone that reflected his exhaustion and his obvious concern for his patient. "She needs to get to a hospital. But I do not know how we will get her there."

"I'll get her there," Devon said. "Don't worry, Claire. I've got a pair of mares who love snow."

The doctor had his doubts. "The storm hasn't let up all night, boy. The snow's been beatin' against the windows like pebbles. Do you really think you can get back to Meath in these conditions?"

"I guess I have to, don't I?"

"And in a carriage, too?" The doctor's brows inched up his forehead. "It's one thing to fetch me on the back of a horse; 'tis quite another to get your rig through these messy streets. I don't think you can do it, lad."

"You said she needed to go to hospital," Devon growled. "If her life depends on it, I'll get her there!"

A grudging look of admiration twinkled in the older man's eyes. "I'll help the ladies get her ready, then."

After the doctor left the parlor, Claire watched silently as Devon shrugged into his coat. His body was taut with determination, his expression resolute. He looked like a man marching to his own execution, but without the slightest hint of regret.

She tried to tell herself that she did not love Devon, and that she could easily live without him in her life. He had never been more than a friend to her, she reminded herself. The sexual play they'd engaged in had been pleasurable—extremely so—but there had never really been any chance for a romance to develop.

Chiding herself, she scanned Devon's backside. *Long legs, slender waist, thick dark hair.* She ought to quit wondering what *could* have been, what *might* have been, had their respective pasts been different. She ought to focus on how deeply he had insulted her. She ought to quit looking at his physique and stop remembering what his skin tasted like and what his naked body felt like beneath her fingertips. She was only torturing herself and she knew it.

Unfortunately for Claire, she couldn't shake those images from her mind. And it didn't help that Devon continued to prove himself worthy of her affection by risking his own comfort and safety for that of Claire's friends, women he had no legal or moral obligation to protect, women he looked after simply because they had once befriended Mary O'Roarke.

"What now, Claire?" he asked without looking at her.

"What do you mean?"

"What do we do now? Pretend we don't care about each other? Pretend we don't need each other?"

Guiltily, Claire averted her eyes. "Every lady in this neighborhood has needed you at one time or another."

"That is not what I am talking about."

"I'll order some tea and breakfast for you—"

"Damn the tea!" Turning, he leveled a smoldering gaze at her. "Listen to me, Claire! You need to visit your mother. When this is over, when I return and the weather lets up, I will go with you."

Had she heard him correctly? Had he lost his mind? Gasping, Claire half-sat on the side of the sofa. "You must be mad! Visit my mother? First of all, what makes you think I want to? And even if I did, what makes you think I would want to visit her with *you*?"

"I don't think you'll go without me."

"I am certain you are right!"

"But you must go, Claire."

"Who put you in charge of my life, Devon? When did it become your concern whether I ever speak to my mother again?"

"When I realized that you are afraid of me and afraid of your feelings toward me."

"I think you flatter yourself, sir! I can assure you that I am not in the least bit frightened of you!" But Claire's face suffused with heat. She supposed that lying naturally increased her body temperature.

Devon crossed the room in long strides and grasped Claire's arms. Pulling her to her feet, he gave her a gentle shake. "Oh, Claire, who are you fooling? One minute you are as cold as ice, screaming from the rooftops that you don't want a man. The next you are as hot-blooded and lusty as any woman I have ever known—"

"I suppose you have known quite a few!" In truth, it made Claire insanely jealous to think he had lain with other women.

"Never one as alluring as you," he drawled. "I have never known a woman as responsive as you, Claire. If you would only let yourself go—"

"Stop it!"

"If you would only give up those inhibitions—"

She clapped her hands over her ears. His voice, even when he was lecturing her, had a disturbingly seductive effect on her. Uncertain whether to treat Devon's remarks as compliments or slurs, Claire was flustered and confused. Her physical proximity to the man did nothing but further muddle her thoughts. His aroma filled her senses; his presence surrounded her.

"Leave me alone, Devon," she practically whimpered.

His voice softened as he pulled her snug against his chest. "Claire, you are never going to resolve your feelings until you make peace with your mother."

"How is it you know so much about me?"

"I do not presume to understand you, dear. But it doesn't take a trained physician to see that you have repressed your feminine urges for years. You feel guilty for having sexual desires. You think you are bad for having them. You think that your mother was bad for having them."

Hiding her face against Devon's shirtfront, Claire shuddered. Was she that transparent? Was her degeneracy that obvious? Embarrassed, she struggled hard to combat the tears that welled behind her eyes.

"The difference between my mother and me," Claire whispered, "is that I can control my desires."

With a chuckle, he stroked her hair. "But who wants to do that, dear? When you trust someone, you do not have to worry about controlling your desires."

Biting her lip, Claire pondered that observation. She *did* trust Devon. She trusted him more than she'd ever trusted anyone. She'd trusted him enough to let him touch her in places no one else had ever touched her. She'd trusted him enough to touch him intimately, too. Why, then, did she instinctively want to put distance between them?

"You have developed a pattern," he continued, "of luring me close to you, then pushing me away."

Was that why she wanted to sleep with him even while she plotted to move from Fontjoy Square?

Retreating, she covered her face.

"What do you want, Claire?"

She shook her head. She didn't know what she wanted.

"Why are you afraid to love me?"

Her hands dropped to her sides. As she locked gazes with Devon, a flutter of nervousness spread through her. "It is easier to *not* love you."

"Must you take the easy road, sweetling?"

"Must you take the less traveled one? Why can't we simply be friends? As we were before?"

"Ah, now that was a comfortable relationship, wasn't it?"

"Is anything the matter with a comfortable relationship?"

"Nothing at all, unless it is an invention designed to obscure a couple's deeper, more meaningful feelings."

"I do not want to delve any more deeply into my emotions than I already have, Devon."

"Then you will lose me, Claire," he said flatly. The heat in his gaze persisted, but his lips formed two tight white lines. Putting her at arm's length, he, too, took a step backward. "I haven't the patience for a counterfeit friendship. I want to love you, and I want you to love me back."

Her chest tightened. "Are you asking me to—"

"Yes, I am asking you to marry me. Marry me or leave me alone."

She stumbled to the sofa and sank onto it. Staring up, she stammered, "I cannot—"

"You're of the age of consent, Claire. You *can;* if you want to, that is. You need no one's permission."

"This is rather sudden."

"I have known you for nearly a year."

"A year during which you never once mentioned to me that you were married to Mary O'Roarke. A year during which you failed to tell me that it was you who had anonymously donated to me a house in Fontjoy Square. Do you think that is a good foundation for an honest, truthful marriage, Devon?"

"We love each other. That is enough."

"I'm sorry, sir, but it is *not* enough! How can I possibly know whether I can spend the rest of my life with you? How can I know that you won't grow weary of me and that you won't begin to hate me? The things you love about me now will be the very things you will learn to despise me for!"

"Not true!"

"You say you want me to reconcile with my mother, but within a year we'll have a squabble over who burnt the toast and you'll throw it up in my face that my mother was a whore!"

His eyes narrowed. "Is that what your father did to her? Is that what you expect of me, of all men?"

His question was like a slap in the face. "I expect nothing from you—or any other man," she countered.

"Perhaps that is the problem."

Claire opened her mouth to object, but at that instant voices sounded on the stairwell. Turning, she saw through the open door that the doctor was carrying a bundled-up Millicent down the steps. Rose trailed behind, clutching a small leather valise. It was time for Devon to go.

"Just one more question, Devon."

He paused in the center of the room. "I'll do everything I can to ensure Millicent's safety."

"I've no doubt you will risk your own neck to get her to Meath." Mustering all the courage she could, Claire lifted her chin a notch. "Why, after nearly a year, did you suddenly decide to fall in love with me?"

Exhaling, Devon gave a wry bark of laughter. "I wish I could tell you that I fell in love with you the moment I met you. I did not. I fell in love with you, Claire, the moment I gave myself permission to do so."

"And why, pray tell, did you suddenly give yourself permission?"

His shoulders stiffened. "If we are going to be honest with one another, we might as well start here. I gave myself permission because I grew tired of being lonely. You see, I know what it is to love someone and to be loved. I know what it is to have a happy marriage."

"Because you had one," Claire said numbly. This was not at all what she wanted to hear. In fact, it made her ill. Turning, she gazed at the dying embers on the hearth.

"Yes, I had a very satisfying marriage. You see, Claire, I loved Mary. And I want to love again. There is nothing wrong with that. There is nothing wrong with wanting to be loved."

"If you loved Mary that much, how can you ever love anyone else?"

"Because I want to. Because *she* wanted me to."

"But you wish she had never died. Admit it. You wish she were still alive!"

"I did not want her to die. For a long time, I thought I would die myself. But she is gone, and life goes on. My love for you, Claire, is not diminished by my love for her; rather, it is enhanced by precious memories."

"She did not want you to love *me*," Claire said dryly. "I can assure you of that."

"Perhaps not," Devon admitted. After a long pause, he said softly, "But she brought you to me. And I love you. But I will not pretend any longer that I love you as a brother loves his sister. I want you to marry me, Claire. If you cannot do that, I will find someone else to love."

By lunchtime, the storm had abated and the sun peeked through a sky of gray. Outside Lady Dolly Baltmore-Creevy's house, her longtime servant Ferghus shoveled mounds of snow from the sidewalk. The inhabitants of Fontjoy Square were slowly digging their way out from beneath a blanket of white. In Dolly's parlor, however, the mood remained somber.

"Find someone else to love?" Dolly repeated for the third time around a mouthful of dense, whiskey soaked fruitcake.

"Can you believe it? I fear I have no choice but to pack up and leave."

"Don't be ridiculous, Claire! And why didn't you tell us what was going on before now? Is that

why you were so upset when Devon locked himself
in his house and wouldn't come out?"

"I thought he was pouting because I rebuffed
him."

"He was pouting, all right, but more likely because Mary's illegitimate kid showed up on his
doorstep demanding his attention."

"A bit odd, that Aidan Sullivan, don't you
think?" Now that Claire had confessed all to her
friend, she felt free to voice her suspicion of the
redheaded interloper.

"More than a bit," Dolly said, popping a bit of
smoked trout into her mouth. For such a petite
woman, she had a huge appetite, probably because of all the exercise she did. Ever since she'd
caught the eye of the famous pugilist Dick Creevy,
she'd taken to jumping rope and tossing weighted
balls about. Nine months later, she was as wiry and
muscular as a featherweight bare-knuckler herself.
"Rose said he nearly slapped her when she refused
to tell him his real father's name."

"Does she know?"

Dolly shrugged. "She says she doesn't."

Claire fell silent a moment, thinking. She had
stolen Mary's diary from Devon and Aidan had
obviously stolen it from her. When Devon demanded that she return it to him, she'd been unable to. It was a wonder Devon wanted to marry
her. No doubt he thought she still had that diary.
He probably thought she was the very worst kind
of liar. Brushing crumbs from a lemon cookie off
her lap, she shook her head. "Well, it doesn't sig-

nify, Dolly. The immediate problem is Millicent. Do you think Devon got her to hospital safely?"

"If anyone could, he could."

The ladies finished their lunch in silence. After a servant had collected their dishes, teacups and trays, they picked up the thread of their previous conversation.

"Men!" Dolly exclaimed at one point. "They are all alike, I tell you. Boyle Baltmore wouldn't have blinked twice had I dropped dead during our marriage. He would have remarried in a fortnight and never thought of me again."

"I'm afraid Devon is not like that," replied Claire. "He is obsessed with Mary O'Roarke. He can't quit talking about her. She dominates his thoughts. Why, if it weren't for that silly diary of hers, none of us would be here."

"Then I suppose we should be grateful that she wrote it."

"I am not grateful to Mary O'Roarke. Long before she penned her memoirs, she published a much more vile and slanderous tale that nearly ruined my life."

Haltingly, Claire related the story of how Mary O'Roarke caught the Duchess of Kilgarren in bed with her father. Out of spite, the young girl had woven together a piece of gossip that destroyed mother and daughter. Not only were friendships destroyed, but the Kilgarren family was torn asunder.

"I cannot forgive her for it," Claire concluded, dashing a tear from her cheek.

"I am not certain I could, either," Dolly said quietly.

"Yet you profess to have loved the girl. Even though it was you who took the blame when she cheated on a Latin exam and was nearly expelled from boarding school."

Dolly's gaze was far away and dreamy. "Yes, but that seems like a lifetime ago, dear. Indeed, it was. Besides, I was about to be expelled from that Swiss boarding school anyway because my father had lost his money. The truth was, I preferred my friends thinking I'd been tossed out for cheating. It would have been far worse to admit that my poor papa could not pay the tuition bill."

Embarrassed, Claire twisted a linen serviette in her fingers."I am sorry, Dolly. I did not intend to dredge up unpleasant memories."

"Oh, they are not unpleasant. It took me many years to learn that there is nothing to be gained by pretending you are something you are not. When I had learned that lesson, it was much easier to look back fondly on my memories of Mary O'Roarke. I think she must have felt guilty about allowing me to take the blame for her. I suspect that is why she wanted Devon to look for me."

The notion that Mary had ever felt guilty about anything struck Claire as a novelty. "Are you suggesting that Mary wrote about the four of us in her diary because she felt guilty at having treated us so shabbily?"

" 'Tis possible." Dolly smiled wistfully. "Her diary was in the nature of a deathbed confession, I believe, not a boastful memoir. I think that after Mary grew up, she regretted many of her actions."

"I can't imagine Mary O'Roarke ever regretting anything. She was so haughty, so sure of herself, so flawless."

"By the time you met her, Claire, she had already given birth to Aidan Sullivan. Try to imagine what living that lie must have been like. I've lived many lies myself; I can tell you, it is torture to pretend you are someone you are not. Mary knew that if her father ever discovered what she'd done, he would disown her."

"I know that feeling."

"She must have been living in fear that Rose Sinclair would blab to her parents, or that her callous teenage paramour would brag to his mates." Dolly shuddered. "And aside from the fear of being found out, there was the guilt of having given away her baby. She knew that her child was being cared for by strangers. She must have wondered if he was happy and healthy. She must have worried constantly that she had failed him."

"She had, hadn't she?"

Dolly shrugged. "All of us have made mistakes, Claire. Mary O'Roarke was no different; she was not infallible. She was not a saint."

"Devon thinks she was." Bitterness burned the back of Claire's throat.

"Oh, do you really think so? He's read her diary, for heaven's sake! He knew her better than any one of us. I would wager that he knew she wasn't perfect. He loved her anyway—warts and all."

"Warts?"

"It's an expression, Claire. You don't have to be perfect to be loved. You only have to be lovable."

"And how does one do that?"

"One loves." Dolly leaned over and squeezed Claire's hand. "Simple as that."

Twelve

Claire had not been to Monto in years and she did not relish returning. But the more she mulled over her conversation with Devon, the more she realized that he was right and that she would never be able to sort out her feelings toward him, and toward men in general, until she resolved her anger toward the former countess.

As Sir Steven Nollbrook, the famous barrister, would have put it, Claire had to set the record straight. She had to confront her mother and find out why she had done what she had with Mary O'Roarke's father—*of all people!* She had to know whether she had inherited her mother's weakness, or whether there was a way to break free of the burning desires that had recently possessed her.

Few of the buildings on those narrow, roughly cobbled streets had numbers over the doors. But Claire vaguely remembered which establishment her mother belonged to. And surely it wouldn't be difficult to find the place, not if she managed to locate the general vicinity. When she stepped from her hackney cab, however, into one of the seediest quarters of Dublin where prostitution was rampant and street thievery commonplace, panic seized her.

The men who passed Claire slanted her quizzical, or even lascivious, glances. The women who met her eye looked haggard and beaten down.

After walking up and down unfamiliar streets for nearly an hour, Claire ducked inside a small, grimy-windowed pub. Clutching the neck of her coat protectively, she caught the attention of a tap girl. "Excuse me, miss. I was wondering if you could tell me where Mrs. Bunratty's establishment is."

Turning, the young girl scanned Claire from head to toe. "She's gettin' fancier ever'day, now ain't she?"

"Excuse me?"

"Mrs. Bunratty! Her gals are startin' to look like aristocrats!" The snaggle-toothed girl allowed herself a good belly laugh. "Oh, well, ye git what ye pay fer, I reckon."

"Please, just tell me where to find Mrs. Bunratty."

"I ain't workin' fer free meself, lassie."

Desperate to get out of the noisome place, Claire pressed some coins into the tap girl's palm. Memorizing the address, she hurriedly stepped outside, inhaling a deep breath of cold air. Minutes later, she stood before the unprepossessing entrance of her mother's place of occupation.

Her chest ached and her breath frosted the air.

For a moment, Claire thought of turning and fleeing. This had been a terrible idea! What made her think that confronting her mother after all these years would solve any of her problems? What made her think her mother would even want to see her?

But before she could turn and beat a hasty retreat, the red lacquered door swung open and a nattily dressed man whom Claire recognized as a well-known local politician stepped outside. Tapping the dome of his high-topped beaver hat, he nodded deferentially to Claire and bid her a good day just as if there was nothing at all unusual or eyebrow-raising about being spied exiting a brothel.

"Well, dearie," said a not unpleasant female voice, "are you going to stand outside in the cold or are you coming inside?"

Startled, Claire looked at the figure in the doorway.

She was a heavyset woman clad in a dark, exquisitely tailored but businesslike morning gown and jacket. "Well?" she repeated.

Slowly, Claire stepped across the threshold. As the door closed behind her, her eyes adjusted to the semidarkness. "Are you Mrs. Bunratty?"

The woman's eyes narrowed. "Do I know you?"

"I'm looking for someone," Claire said. "I am looking for Shannon Kilgarren."

"The duchess?"

Claire was somewhat taken aback by the use of her mother's former title. "Yes, the duchess. May I see her please?"

"Might I ask your name?"

"Claire Kilgarren."

Mrs. Bunratty frowned. "Her daughter? Well, I don't expect she'll want to see you, not after all these years! You've wasted your time, I'm afraid."

"Why don't you ask her?" Claire said crisply.

The two women stared at each other while Mrs. Bunratty apparently considered her options. The tension that hung in the air was as heavy as the velvet curtain that draped the windows and cut the daylight. Claire firmly held the other woman's gaze, reasoning that determination was more likely to achieve results in a place like this than vacillation or weakness. Her instincts served her well. After some time, Mrs. Bunratty heaved a sigh and beckoned with her fingertips. "This way."

In a parlor decorated with heavy furniture, fringed lampshades, camelback sofas upholstered in crimson velvet and thick oriental carpets, Mrs. Bunratty said, "Wait here."

Claire removed her cloak and hat, then wandered about the room nervously, pausing to examine the curios, porcelain commemorative plates with pictures of Queen Victoria and Prince Albert, gold clocks encased in glass domes, Staffordshire dogs and table coverings embroidered with ancient Celtic designs. When she heard the click of a lady's heels behind her, her fingers froze around a small statuette of Marie Antoinette.

Her mother's voice was distinctive, if not tinged with bitterness. "Pray tell me, daughter, what terrible tragedy has brought you here at last? Has your father died? Did some cur get you pregnant? Are you broke and in need of money?"

Slowly, Claire returned the figurine to its place and turned. The sight of her mother's face, still beautiful but lined with age, stole her breath. For a long time, she simply gazed at the former duchess, her mother whom she had once loved above all else, the woman whose appetite for lovemaking Claire had evidently inherited.

She wanted to throw her arms around her mother's neck and never let her go. She wanted to shake her by the shoulders and ask her how she could have thrown so much away . . . for so little.

The duchess closed the distance between them, striding elegantly across the room in a bright green satin gown that was more appropriate for a demirep's ball in London than a cold morning in Dublin. Her skin was flawless, her figure luscious. Her blond hair and blue eyes mirrored Claire's. Peering down her nose, straight and keen at the tip, she looked every bit the aristocrat she had once been.

An arm's length from her mother, Claire trembled with emotion. "How could you, Mother? What made you do such a thing? How can you look at yourself in the mirror?"

"Fifteen years later, you have come here to ask me that?"

"I should have asked you then, but I did not want to know. I only wanted to pretend that I was nothing like you. I only wanted to get as far away from you as I could."

"You succeeded in doing that, didn't you?" The duchess looked at her daughter from head to toe. "Though from the look of that suit, which is five seasons old if it is a day, I think you are a bit down on your luck, dear. If it is money you need—"

"Keep your damned money! I don't need it!" Tears welled in Claire's eyes. Sniffing, she wiped them away with the back of her glove. "I came to ask you some questions. I came because I can't quit thinking about you, and what you did to me—and to Father."

"It was your little friend Mary O'Roarke who did you in, Claire. Had she been capable of keeping her little tongue from wagging, my reputation would never have been ruined—"

"It was not all Mary O'Roarke's fault, Mother! You were caught on your knees servicing her father! It is hardly a wonder that she would despise you!"

"Dear, half of all the ladies in Dublin had slept with Lawrence O'Roarke. He was famous for his ability to . . . well, I don't suppose you are interested in that. Suffice it to say, I hardly introduced the man to a life of debauchery."

"I am not interested in who seduced whom. What I want to know is why you did it. Why did you betray Father? Tell me, *Duchess*, what did he ever do to deserve being labeled a cuckold and a fool!"

For the first time, the former duchess looked

uncomfortable, sympathetic even. Her eyes glimmered, but she did not cry. Instead, her regal, top-lofty expression turned to one of sadness. Suddenly, she looked tired . . . and old. "Oh, Claire, you were so young and naïve. You couldn't possibly have understood; I never expected you to. To be honest, as much as I have missed you, I had hoped this day would never come."

"The day has come, Mother," Claire said between clenched teeth. "I want an explanation."

Half-turning from her daughter, the duchess took a deep breath and fixed her gaze on a spot on the floor. "How long has it been since you've seen your father?"

"I have not seen him since he tossed me out. I went to work as a governess, powdering the behinds of other people's babies, running from the groping hands of lustful fathers. It has been quite a cheery existence, let me tell you."

"And are you employed with a family now?"

Claire folded her arms over her chest. She was tempted to tell her mother it was none of her business, but she supposed a certain quid pro quo was in order. She wanted information from the duchess. It was only fair to answer her mother's questions.

"No. About ten months ago my luck seemingly changed. A mysterious nameless benefactor gave me a house in Fontjoy Square. I thought for a while that Father had come around, realized how harshly he had treated me and wanted to make amends. I was insane to think that, of course."

"It wasn't your father?"

Claire shook her head. "I waited. I waited nearly six months for Father to write me a letter, confessing that he had plucked me from my prison and forgiven me. But he never did. So I went 'round to see him. To thank him. To show him that I was truly a good girl, not like my mother, but deserving of his love."

A wry smile tugged at the duchess's lips. "What did the duke have to say to that?" She held up her hand. "Wait, don't tell me. He told you that you did not exist anymore."

A sick feeling washed over Claire. "He told me that his daughter had died fifteen years before. Along with his wife."

Though Shannon Kilgarren could not have been shocked by Claire's pronouncement—indeed, she had predicted it—she flinched. "I am sorry," she said softly. "I know you loved him."

"I still do."

The duchess's jaw hardened. "Then you are a fool. The man does not love you."

"He did—before you ruined everything."

Whirling, the duchess faced Claire. Her face was no longer pretty. Flushed with anger, the woman practically hissed as she jabbed her finger in the air. "When you were little, I never expected you to understand! I held my tongue. I never said anything bad about your father. I never told you what sort of man he was. But now you are old enough to know, Claire."

Stumbling backward, Claire glanced at the door. She had come to ask her mother why she had cheated on the duke. She wasn't prepared for the duchess's vitriol. Sourly, she realized that perhaps she did not want to know the answer to the question she had asked.

"You are not going anywhere," her mother ground out. "You are going to stay right here and listen to everything I have to say."

"No. I am leaving." Claire turned on her heel.

But her mother grabbed her arm and held her fast. The two women stood so close to each other that Claire could smell her mother's expensive perfume and something else—the more subtle scent of a man's spicy cologne combined with the musky smell of sex. The duchess had been with a man this morning—already. Claire's hand flew to her mouth as she suppressed her reflex to gag.

"Your father liked to preach to anyone who would listen," the duchess seethed. "He never missed an opportunity to tell the world how righteous he was, or how evil were those men who corrupted themselves with drink or defiled themselves with immoral women. If another man looked at me, your father blamed me for it. If another man smiled at me, your father punished me."

Claire closed her eyes, but she could not block the sound of her mother's voice.

"He used to beat me, Claire. Oh, never about

my face or neck. There were never any marks where anyone could see them."

"Stop it!"

"And after a time, I rebelled. The more he punished me, the more outrageous my conduct became. I flirted with any and every man who looked at me. I did it knowing that I would get a beating at home; I didn't care, and your father enjoyed it. I thought eventually he would kill me." Hugging herself, the duchess sighed. "I suppose I hoped he would. I hated him so much, I could not bear to live with him. Death seemed a better alternative than spending the rest of my days with the Duke of Kilgarren."

An acrid taste burned the back of Claire's throat. "You were sick . . . he was sick."

"Umph. Perhaps. But at least now you know. Are you happy that you came here, Claire?"

Suppressing the nausea that threatened to choke her, Claire was unable to speak. She clutched her stomach and stood in the center of the spinning room, praying that her equilibrium would return and that her heart would not leap out of her chest. At last her nerves calmed a little. Her mother was still staring at her, waiting for an answer, some sort of explanation for Claire's presence at Mrs. Bunratty's.

"I need a place to stay, Mother."

The duchess arched her brows. "Let me guess: This has something to do with your mysterious benefactor, doesn't it?"

Biting her bottom lip, Claire nodded.

"And would his name be Devon Avondale, dear?"

Shocked, Claire gaped at her mother. "How do you know Devon?"

"I met him yesterday." A low, throaty chuckle escaped the countess's lips. "I'm afraid his interest in you is more than friendly, daughter. He wants to marry you, you know."

"That is what he says."

"And you do not believe him?"

"I do not believe he loves me."

"You're a beautiful woman, Claire. Why wouldn't he love you?"

"He loves someone else."

"Ah." The duchess smiled knowingly. "So, he is one of those. A philanderer."

"No, he is not a philanderer. Oh, Mother, 'tis so difficult to explain. He was married to Mary O'Roarke—"

The duchess shivered. "He did not tell me that."

"No, I suppose not. Mary left a diary, you see, and in it she described her encounter with me. After she died, Devon looked me up, discovered I was nearly destitute and anonymously offered to give me a home on Fontjoy Square. As I said, that was nearly ten months ago. And during that time, Devon and I became close friends. Just friends. Until recently, that is."

"When the friendship became . . . *something more?*"

"Yes." It was Claire's turn to shiver. "Against my

better judgment, I allowed him certain liberties . . ."

"Are you certain you are not pregnant?"

"Positive."

"Well, he wants to marry you, you silly duckling, so what is the problem? He appears to be well-to-do, and you say he is not a philanderer."

"A man who is so obsessed with his dead wife that he would track down the four women she wrote about in her diary and give them all homes."

The duchess wore a pensive expression. " 'Tis odd. But what difference does it make? He found you and he fell in love with you. That is the way life works, dear."

"No!" Claire stamped her foot. "He went in search of Mary's past and I happened to pop up. Every time he looks at me, he thinks of her! I am nothing more than a memento to him, a token, a souvenir of his life with Mary. He doesn't love me. He loves her, and he always will!"

"Sometimes a man can love more than one woman."

"I don't want to be second best!"

"You're only second best if you think you are." Tentatively, as if she half-expected to be rebuffed, the duchess wrapped her arms around her daughter. "Take it from someone who has learned that the hard way. Don't make the same mistakes I have made, Claire."

Frightened and confused, Claire was grateful for her mother's warmth. Dropping her head, she pressed her cheek to the duchess's shoulder. Her mother stroked her hair and patted her head, clucking her tongue the way she did when Claire was a child and had skinned her knee.

"That's what I am afraid of, Mother," Claire said, sniffing. "I'm afraid I have already repeated your mistakes."

"How so, child?"

"Oh, Mother, 'tis shameful the way I have behaved."

"Are you *certain* you are not pregnant?"

Claire's tears stained the sleeve of her mother's exquisite satin dress. Her mind flashed on the scene in Millicent's house, when Devon had entered her and discovered she was a virgin. "I do not believe that I am pregnant. In fact, I am certain of it. Fairly certain, at least, Mother."

"Oh, God," her mother replied. "What has he done to you?"

Embarrassed and embittered, struggling not to cry, Claire closed her eyes and fit deeper into her mother's protective embrace. "Oh, Mother, that is the worst part. He did nothing to me that I did not want him to do!"

The instant the door opened, Devon knew something was amiss. If the fretful expression on the face of Claire's maid hadn't alerted him to a sea change in the atmosphere, the steamer trunk in the middle of the foyer would have.

"What is going on here?" he asked, stepping

inside. As he removed his gloves, he noticed that the mirror that usually hung above the Regency-style commode had been taken off its hook. It sat on the floor now, its gilt edges covered with paper. "It looks as if someone is moving out."

The maid said nothing, merely plucked nervously at her apron.

"Would you tell your mistress I would like to talk to her?" Devon asked testily, his sense of alarm growing by the second. "I'll be in the parlor."

When Claire swept into the room, her skirts dusty and her usually perfect coiffure slightly askew, he gaped with disbelief. "What in Erin's name is going on here, Claire? It appears that you are making plans to leave Fontjoy Square."

"You're not surprised, are you?" She chafed her palms, then pulled the bell cord. "Would you care for some tea?"

He needed something to wet his parched throat, but tea wasn't it. "No." Instead, he stood at the mantel and watched at Claire calmly settled on the sofa.

When her servant arrived with the tea tray, Claire greeted the woman as if nothing was out of place. She sipped with perfect equanimity, her little finger elegantly crooked, her lips prettily puckered as Devon's body temperature soared. He didn't know whether to be angry or sad. But he could see that Claire had shut him out, withdrawn from him completely, and that fact made him feel lonelier than he'd felt since Mary died.

"What was it that you wanted to see me about?" she queried casually.

"I came to tell you that Millicent is going to be fine. She lost the babe, of course."

"I'm sorry."

Devon nodded. "As am I. But now that I am here, Claire, I am even more saddened. It appears that you are leaving. Am I correct?"

"Yes. I will be gone before next week. Packing is such an awful bore. 'Tis taking me longer than I had anticipated."

"Where will you go?"

"I am going home to Mother, as they say."

Shocked, Devon took a deep breath and held it until his lungs ached. It wasn't often that he was at a loss for words, but Claire's statement knocked him completely off balance. The implications of it frightened him. Suddenly, he understood precisely why Claire was leaving Fontjoy Square. She had discovered his visit to the duchess, and she viewed his going to Monto as yet another act of deceit and betrayal.

The thought of Claire's leaving filled him with a panicky dread. "So, you have spoken with your mother."

"I took your advice. She is quite well and looking just as beautiful as I remembered her." Claire peered coquettishly at him over the rim of her teacup. "Didn't you think so?"

"Claire, let me explain—"

"No reason to explain, dear. Mother told what you said, of course. You had good intentions. You wanted to play the peacemaker between us, bring us together, lead us to the negotiating table, so to speak. Really, Devon, you have a great future as a diplomat. Perhaps you can reconcile Great Britain with Northern Ireland as your next trick."

He tried to ignore her sarcasm, but his blood boiled. Suppressing his irritation, Devon said, "To be honest, I am surprised you visited your mother. What made you change your mind?"

She placed her cup and saucer on the table beside the sofa. "I don't mean to give you a big head, but I started thinking about what you said. And I thought that perhaps I owed it to Mother to hear her version of events. I never really spoke to her after your Mary pitched such a fit at the house party. Really, I never thought I had much to say to her."

"And now?"

"Now I realize that Mother and I have quite a bit in common, actually. But you knew that already, didn't you?"

"I don't like where this conversation is leading, Claire."

"You were the one who wanted me to talk with the countess, Devon. Well, I talked with her. I'm afraid I understand her point of view much better now. My father was an odious person who never showed her an ounce of affection. She hid his cruelty from me. She protected me from it. But meanwhile she starved for affection. And wound up confusing sex with love. Alas, I think she knows the difference now."

"Now that it's too late," he said, finishing her thought.

"Just so."

The two did not speak for a long time. Devon knew that Claire's steely exterior concealed a vortex of emotion. If he could only break through to her . . . if he could only convince her that she was not predestined to live out her mother's tragic mistakes.

His mind turned to Mary's diary. Not for the first time, he wondered why she had never mentioned Dolly, Rose, Millicent and Claire until she lay dying. He wondered why she had never told him of the existence of Aidan Sullivan. He wondered why Mary had burdened him with her confessions just before she abandoned him. Her bequest to him had been a lifetime of memories, *her memories,* and not all of them were pleasant.

When Aidan Sullivan had arrived on his doorstep, Devon experienced an anger toward Mary that he'd never felt before. He had wondered whether he ever really knew her. He had wondered why she never shared her secrets with him while she was alive. Now—as he was drawn into examining the depth of Claire's wounds and the damage that Mary's recklessness had caused her— he was angry again. How could Mary have done this to another young woman? What was Mary thinking when she spewed out her hateful gossip, destroying the duchess's marriage and ruining Claire's reputation and future?

Thinking out loud, he murmured, "Mary couldn't have known."

"Excuse me?"

Startled, he looked up. "She must not have known how strict your father was. The duchess told me that his religious beliefs were nearly fanatical. He thought a woman shouldn't enjoy sex. He believed if she did, her soul was eternally doomed."

Claire's voice dropped to a low drawl. "Oh, Mary knew all about my father, dear. She might not have known that he physically beat my mother, but she knew precisely what his reaction would be when he learned of my mother's indiscretion. You see, I had confided in Mary about my father's rigid attitudes. I thought she was my friend."

"Then why would she do such a thing?"

Claire shrugged. "We had both been carrying on a mild flirtation with the same boy. Afterwards, of course, the boy never spoke to me again. Perhaps that was what Mary had in mind all along."

"Mary would not be so petty," Devon insisted. He needed to believe that. He needed to believe that Mary O'Roarke had been kind and good and loving all her life. Otherwise, his marriage to her had been a sham.

Claire stood. She walked slowly to the mantel, her arms crossed over her chest. "You did not know the same Mary O'Roarke that I did."

The hair on his nape prickled. "I won't tolerate your maligning my wife, Claire."

"I won't be used by you, Devon. I refuse to be

an actress in this fantasy you have conjured to fill
the loss you suffered when Mary died."

Devon stiffened. Clearly, Claire was unwilling to
let go of the past, to forgive Mary O'Roarke and
her mother, to cut the emotional bindings that
prevented her from loving him. With a sigh, he
said, "What's done is done."

"On the contrary, Devon, the past is never over.
It follows us everywhere."

"And so you are willing to leave all this?" He
gestured at her surroundings. "You are willing to
leave me? Even though I have asked you to marry
me?"

She closed her eyes, and her chin wobbled. But,
after a pause, she regained her composure and
met Devon's gaze. Squaring her shoulders, she replied, "You have spent a great deal of energy attempting to understand me, and I appreciate that.
I admit, my behavior has been curious. I can
hardly pretend with you that I do not possess . . .
ah, certain desires."

The mere mention of their lovemaking made
Devon want to embrace her, but he stood rigid as
a poker. "Why would you want to deny that?"

She gave a bitter little laugh. "That is the rub,
isn't it, Devon? I was raised to think sex was bad,
and that nice girls could never enjoy it. But you
thought that talking with my mother would help
me understand the flaw in my reasoning, and help
me understand myself."

"I thought that if you could bring yourself to
forgive her—"

"Well, I have forgiven her. The problem now, dear, is not whether I can reconcile my desires with my fears and inhibitions. I have done that. I have admitted that I enjoyed making love to you. I was afraid that my desire for you would consume me, weaken me, rob me of my strength of character. My mother assured me that I was wrong to believe that."

"Then why won't you marry me? What obstacle remains?"

"The question now is whether I can reconcile my past with my future."

"Whether you can forgive Mary O'Roarke," Devon said dully. "Whether you can forgive me for failing to tell you that she was my wife. Whether you can ever look at me without remembering the pain she caused you."

"You are a very perceptive man." Claire took a step back. "And the answer to those questions, I am afraid, is a resounding *no.*"

Devon took a step forward, but Claire retreated as he approached. "I don't want you to leave, Claire."

"I must."

"We can work this out." He swallowed hard. He would do anything in his power to convince Claire that he loved her, but begging was not his style. The entreating tone in his voice offended even him.

"No, we cannot."

He would not make a fool of himself. If she was determined to go, he could not stop her. Controlling his emotions, Devon schooled his face into a mask of indifference. His fists coiled at his sides as he reined in his disappointment. He wanted to grasp Claire by the shoulders and shake some sense into her, lock her up so that she couldn't abandon him. He wanted to scream from the rooftops that she couldn't leave him, that she wasn't allowed to, that he couldn't tolerate having his heart broken again.

Instead, he nodded coolly and walked around her toward the parlor door. Experience had taught him that there were some things a man couldn't change. A man couldn't prevent his wife from dying. A man couldn't alter the past. And a man couldn't make a woman love him.

He grabbed his coat and hat but didn't bother to put them on before he stepped outside. He slammed Claire's front door shut behind him and trudged home, his heart thudding, his muscles burning with pent-up anger.

If Claire Kilgarren wanted to throw away their friendship and destroy their love, he couldn't stop her. Frankly, he was tired of trying. A man could only do so much to show a woman he loved her. If Claire refused to believe him, then their romance wasn't meant to be.

Thirteen

Because Claire could not bear to tell her friends goodbye, she slipped out of her house the next morning and took a hackney cab to Monto. She'd left behind instructions that her personal possessions and the few items of furniture that she owned be carted to Mrs. Bunratty's. The meager wardrobe that she packed in her *portmanteaux* and valises would be sufficient for at least a week, and by then, she reasoned, her belongings would have arrived at her new abode.

Not that she intended to remain at Mrs. Bunratty's for any substantial length of time. For now, it seemed a place of refuge, a place where she could reconnoiter, gather her wits and reevaluate her life. It had the drawback of being a place where no decent woman would dare set foot, and so she could not tell her friends where she was. It had the advantage of being her mother's home; after nearly fifteen years, she slowly began to reacquaint herself with the woman who had once been her dearest friend.

After a few days, Claire developed a routine of sorts. Having settled in a luxurious suite of rooms adjacent to her mother's, replete with modern plumbing, gaslit sconces and comfortable furnishings, she gave in to endless hours of introspection.

Lounging in a hot bath, her mind inevitably turned to thoughts of Devon and the erotic episode that had taken place in her own bathtub. Sleeping late in the morning, her dreams revolved around their lovemaking, and her body tingled with desire. Flipping through books of poetry, she yearned for his voice.

In short, she could not quit thinking about Devon.

But every time she thought she was going to go insane without him, she reminded herself that he had lied to her, and that his true allegiance was to Mary O'Roarke, the woman who had ruined Claire's life.

Then she looked around her and saw the duchess. Watching her mother reminded Claire that women who allowed men to take advantage of them sexually always came to no good end. But her mother was well compensated for the services she rendered. Men visited the duchess, spent a few hours in her *boudoir* and left wads of bank notes on the dresser table when they left. The duchess wasn't being taken advantage of, Claire reasoned. The duchess had turned the tables on these men. The duchess was in control of her own destiny.

One night the sound of a woman screaming for help awakened Claire from a restless sleep. Leaping out of bed, she grabbed her wrapper and ran into the corridor just in time to see a burly man sprinting for the stairs. As bedroom doors flew open, other women streamed into the hallway and raced to the room from which the blood-curdling cries emanated.

Peering over her mother's shoulder, Claire saw a sight that made the hair on the back of her neck bristle. Lying on the bed in a pool of her own blood was a young girl, naked except for a pair of silken stockings. What her customer had done to her had nothing to do with the act of love. By the time the doctor arrived, the young prostitute had already bled to death.

Of course, that upsetting scene put all the ladies at Mrs. Bunratty's on edge, including Claire's mother. Two nights later, the countess, clad in a provocative black *negligee*, sat on the edge of Claire's bed.

"I want you out of here," she said, her rouged lips pursed.

Claire's stomach, still queasy from the shock of what she had witnessed, flipped over. "But Mother, I have no place to go."

"You can't stay here. Mrs. Bunratty is charging me an enormous rate for your suite, Claire. I simply cannot afford it."

"In a few weeks, I will have secured another position as a governess," Claire argued. "I placed a notice in the newspaper today. I am certain that I will receive some inquiries—"

"I cannot wait until you receive some inquiries," her mother snapped. "Nor can you."

"I don't understand," Claire stammered. After all these years of being without her mother, it seemed unfair to be pushed out of Mrs. Bunratty's now.

The duchess scowled. "Why would you want to stay in a place like this, Claire? I thought you were trying to rid yourself of your evil impulses. I thought you were ashamed of me!"

Sitting with her back to the headboard, Claire pulled her knees to her chest. She felt like a child in her mother's presence, eager to please yet confused as to what she should do. Her mother was right; even a few weeks ago, Claire would have scoffed at the notion that she would ever set foot in a brothel. The idea of women selling their bodies to men . . . why, it was anathema to Claire's way of thinking.

Or was it?

Running the sleeve of her modest cotton nightrail beneath her damp nose, Claire tried desperately to articulate her feelings. "I don't want to go, Mother."

"This place is no good for you, Claire. You have seen what can happen to the women here when their customers are dissatisfied. That girl was my friend, and she was young enough to be *your* daughter. I don't want you around here, child. I want you to go back to Fontjoy Square."

"I cannot! Devon is there! I never want to see him again!"

Clearly puzzled, her mother stared at her through narrowed eyes. After a long moment, her shoulders slumped and she sighed wearily. "Oh, daughter, I have done you a great disservice, I can see that now. 'Twas better when you despised me and kept your distance."

"No, it was not! I don't want to be like Father, judging people, damning them, ostracizing them because they are human. Look what he did to you, Mother. He drove you here!"

"You would rather be like me? Is that what you have decided now?"

"Yes," Claire replied, her chin wobbling. Staring at her handsome mother, she thought that perhaps the duchess had not chosen such an unwise path. "At least you are in control of your emotions," she said in a quavering voice. "At least you are financially independent. You don't have someone telling you what you must do all the time. You don't have a man as your master, making your life miserable."

"Is that what you think marriage is?" A tear glistened in the older woman's eye.

Averting her gaze because it was too painful to watch her mother cry, Claire nodded.

"You would rather live in a whorehouse than be married to Devon Avondale?" her mother asked in a hoarse whisper.

"He betrayed me," Claire answered. "By lying to me about who he was and who he'd been married to. By loving the one person who ruined my life—and yours, too. By coming here against my wishes. How could I ever trust that man? Why would I want to love a man who will undoubtedly break my heart?"

"If he is a good man, Claire, you mustn't be afraid to love him."

Claire hugged her knees tightly. *If he was a good man?* Well, he had been her friend for nearly a year, and in that year he had helped Dolly, Rose and Millicent find husbands. The three women relied on him as if he were their brother, father or protector. Most recently, Devon had risked his own neck to save Millicent's life. How could Claire deny that Devon was a good man? Of course he was! Yet she could not get over feeling as if he had deceived her.

And she could not reconcile her lust for him with her long-held belief that women who liked sex were bad. She felt out of control and vulnerable. She hated the feeling that she was powerless against the strength of her own desires.

Claire dropped her head to her knees. "I can't go back," she said at last.

"All right, then." The duchess pushed off the bed. "So be it. But if you are going to remain at Mrs. Bunratty's, you are going to have to pull your weight. You know what that means, don't you?"

A streak of fear shot through Claire's body. Lifting her head, she stared incredulously at her mother through a veil of tears. "What are you talking about?"

Her mother nonchalantly lifted one shoulder. "Well, daughter, you didn't think you could stay here forever, hiding behind my skirts, so to speak, without paying your way?"

"Paying my way?"

The duchess held out her hands, gesturing at the well-appointed room, the expensive furnishings, flocked wall coverings and velvet curtains. *"Someone* has to pay for all this."

"Just give me a few more days," Claire begged, "and I will find a job, I promise."

"Your time is up," her mother said harshly.

Claire's throat constricted. She couldn't breathe. She couldn't believe what she was hearing.

"Get out now, and go back to Fontjoy Square where you belong." The duchess propped her fists on her hips. "Or service your first paying client. He is waiting downstairs. The choice is yours."

Shannon Kilgarren pulled on a concealing black wrapper and cinched it tightly about her waist. Then she marched into the parlor below-stairs, her shoulders back and her jaw firm. She had not enjoyed her conversation with Claire. In fact, it had made her stomach turn. But she had done what she thought was necessary to scare the little chit back to her senses; she knew Claire would not sell her body to a man. She knew her daughter that well. Claire would rather starve than compromise her principles. Claire was like her father that way.

Thank God the girl is not like me!

"Well?" asked Devon Avondale. "May I see her now?"

"Are you certain that is wise? Perhaps you should give her a bit more time. She's a stubborn one, my daughter."

"We are in agreement on that score," Devon said, his lips twisting in a wry smile. "But I received this missive from her. She has asked me to come. Otherwise, I would have honored her request and stayed away. I was prepared to do that when she left Fontjoy Square."

He was a handsome man, the duchess thought. And if he was half as good and kind as he appeared to be, Claire was a fool for not going back to Fontjoy Square. "Yes, I know about the letter."

She knew because she had written it.

A wave of sadness washed over Shannon Kilgarren. Her daughter, poor girl, was so afraid of her own emotions that she could not allow herself to forgive this man for wounding her. The duchess felt a deep, tragic sense of responsibility for having so thoroughly failed to show her child how to love. She knew she could never recover the years she had lost with Claire, but perhaps she could help to set things right between her and Devon.

"Well then, go on up and see her yourself, why don't you? She is waiting for you."

Devon hesitated. "There is something I want you to understand," he said, reaching for the duchess's hands. "I love your daughter very much. I would never do anything to hurt her. If she will consent to marry me, I will cherish her always.

And if you should so choose, you may come and live with us. You are welcome, you know."

The duchess chuckled. Squeezing Devon's hands, she said, "Oh, it is too late for me, Mr. Avondale, but I appreciate your sentiment. Just get my daughter out of here, will you? That would make me happy."

The glimmer in Devon's eye surprised the duchess. Why, he truly was a kindhearted man! And terribly attractive when he looked straight in a woman's eye and grinned crookedly. If she were but twenty years younger . . .

Laughing silently, Shannon Kilgarren scolded herself for the lascivious thoughts that passed through her mind. Old habits died hard. It had been years, decades even, since a man wanted her for anything other than sex. Shannon had not been joking when she told Devon that it was too late for her to live in polite society. Her sexual desires were hopelessly commingled with her need for human affection, approval, even her need for financial security. She wouldn't even know how to make conversation with a nice man like Devon— not without peppering her banter with provocative, flirty talk, that is.

She was glad that her daughter had not followed in her footsteps. But the duchess also knew that Claire had built an almost impenetrable wall around her heart in order to protect herself. And she hoped that Devon Avondale possessed the necessary weaponry to destroy that wall.

Wistfully, she watched him leave the parlor and ascend the stairs that led to Claire's suite of rooms.

When he had gone, the duchess collapsed onto a small settee, covered her face with her hands and sobbed. Which of them was more pathetic, she wondered—she for having so little self-respect that she would sell her body to a man? Or Claire, for having so much pride that she would rather be alone than admit her vulnerabilities?

Following the directions given to him by the duchess, Devon turned right at the second landing and walked down the dimly lit hallway until he came to the third door on the right. Inhaling deeply, he rapped on Claire's bedroom door.

After a moment, he heard her call, "Come in."

Stepping inside, he shut the door gently behind him. His eyes adjusted slowly to the shadowy room. A single taper flickered on Claire's bedside table. She sat on the edge of the bed, her back half-turned to him, her shoulders hunched, her blond hair hanging loosely about her face. Clutching the throat of her white linen robe, she shivered uncontrollably.

Devon crossed the room, compelled by the need to gather her up in his arms. But when he stood a pace away from her, he froze. He had hardly expected a warm welcome, but Claire's posture was more forbidding than he could have imagined. She did not even look up, but remained on the side of the bed, her knees drawn up protectively toward her chest, her physical language telling him to keep his distance.

A lump formed in his throat. Standing in the semi-darkness, he felt powerless to assuage Claire's wounded feelings. Uncertain what to do, he touched her shoulder.

She flinched.

He drew back, stung.

Outside a bitter wind battered the windows of Mrs. Bunratty's establishment. Down the hall, a woman's high-pitched voice mingled with a man's raucous snort of laughter. Belowstairs, someone banged out an incongruously jolly tune on a piano. But inside Claire's bedroom, the silence was oppressive.

She turned, facing her headboard, refusing to look at the visitor standing beside her bed. "I know what my mother wants me to do, what she expects me to do," Claire said softly.

Devon opened his mouth to answer, but Claire continued haltingly. "My choices are limited, I suppose. If I want to stay here, I must obey Mrs. Bunratty's rules and earn my keep."

She sniffled before going on. "Otherwise, I must return to my former home. Indeed, I would like to go there, but for a certain man who would almost surely break my heart . . ."

Understanding struck Devon like a thunderbolt. Claire had not written him a letter asking him to come and visit her. The duchess, shrewd old tabby that she was, had orchestrated this encounter.

Claire thought she was speaking to a customer.

Another one of the duchess's tricks, no doubt! But the realization that Claire had chosen to entertain one of Mrs. Bunratty's clients rather than return to Fontjoy Square rattled Devon's nerves.

Clearing his throat, he fought to suppress his own hurt and anger. What had he done to wound Claire Kilgarren so deeply that she would completely forsake her principles and choose a life of prostitution over a life of loving him? What in the hell could he do now to rectify this situation?

She wiped her tears away with her sleeve. "I must be honest with you, sir. I do not enjoy sex."

It was difficult for Devon to maintain his composure at hearing that. Claire loved sex more than any woman he'd ever known! Why couldn't she just admit it, and forget all about her past, her mother and the ruinous gossip Mary O'Roarke had instigated? Why couldn't she forgive him for failing to disclose his identity this past year? Why couldn't she just trust him?

He supposed it wasn't as simple as that. With a sigh, he recalled how Mary had once told him that women and men actually reasoned differently. A woman would think through a thousand permutations of a problem before solving it; a man would take whatever action was necessary and never give it a second thought.

He held his breath as Claire slowly stood up, her back still to him. Her fingers moved at her throat, and her linen wrapper slid off her shoulders.

"Forgive me if I do not look at you, sir."

Releasing a sigh, Devon's gaze took in the sight of her bare shoulders, the silhouette of her slender hips beneath the thin gauze of her nightrail. The urge to touch Claire, to hold her body against his, assailed him. The smell of her freshly washed hair lured him closer. Taking a step nearer to her, he breathed in the scent of her body and, despite his determination to control himself, moaned with desire.

Her body shuddered. "I should tell you also, sir . . . that I am not an experienced lover . . ." Her voice trailed. "I really do not even like men very much."

A low chuckle escaped Devon's throat. What an inartful liar his little Claire was! In this setting, she seemed eager to announce her lack of sexual prowess. Which struck him as odd, since she had concealed from him the fact that she was a virgin.

She gasped. "Why are you laughing?

He decided to play along. Laying his hands on her shoulders, he stood behind her, pressing his body against hers, nuzzling the crook of her neck. When her body stiffened, he wrapped his arms around her middle and kissed her.

She drew in a jagged breath. "Please, sir, I would appreciate your getting on with it. There is no need—"

"No need for kisses?" Devon drawled.

Pivoting in his embrace, she pressed her palms to his chest. "Devon? What are you doing here?"

"I came to take you home, Claire."

"This is my home," she protested. "For now anyway. How dare you—"

"I did not intend to startle you. But you did not give me a chance to announce myself."

"I thought you were one of Mrs. Bunratty's customers!"

"And you were willing to sleep with him rather than return to Fontjoy Square?"

"Yes." Anger shone in her eyes. Claire pushed against Devon's chest, but he refused to let her go.

Grasping her arms, he gave her a little shake. "Think about what you are saying! You cannot possibly want to remain here!"

"I will not be told what to do!"

"You are that afraid of losing yourself to me? You are that afraid of loving someone?"

"I do not want to wind up some simpering fool, devoted to a man who will undoubtedly hurt me. And I will not be a prisoner of my own desires!"

"What makes you think I will hurt you?"

"You already have!"

"And why do your desires imprison rather than liberate you?"

Claire gave a little snort of derision. "You can't understand, Devon, because you are a man. So just leave me be and get on with your life, will you? And I will get along with mine, thank you!"

"I cannot accept that, woman!" Suddenly, Devon was angry, too. He was doing everything he could to convince Claire that he loved her, and she was unwilling to trust him even the slightest bit. "I am not asking you to take a leap of faith, Claire, just a tiny baby step. Just give me a chance! Just come back home with me and give me a chance!"

Closing her eyes, she shook her head. For a long time, Devon thought she wasn't going to say another word. He thought he had never seen anyone so unhappy. Tension rolled off Claire's body; her expression was taut with confusion. Her eyes were puffy and her cheeks were streaked with tears.

And nothing he could do would console her.

Risking everything, he pulled her into his embrace and held her snugly against him. Her body shivered and trembled in his arms. Her muffled sobs strained his own composure. With his chin on the top of her head, he hugged her as tightly as she would allow. He wanted to murder the man who had caused Claire to so distrust men in general. And not for the first time, he felt a surge of anger toward Mary O'Roarke, too. How his beloved wife could have wounded such an innocent, guileless child, he would never understand.

At length, he tipped up her chin. "Are you all right? Need a shot of whiskey? A hot toddy? A hot bath?"

Tiny beads of wetness sparkled on her lashes. "I would like to lie down, if you don't mind."

He tucked her into bed as he would have done a child, plumping the pillow, tucking the covers around her and smoothing the counterpane. She looked small and frightened and fragile. He wanted to protect her . . . but he wanted to love her, too, fully and wholly, the way a man was meant to love a woman.

"Do you want me to leave now, Claire?"

Her lips curved upward. He thought she was going to say, "No." Devon's heart thudded. Surely she would want him to stay with her.

Instead, she squeezed his fingers and said quietly, "I think it is best if you leave now, Devon. Please try and understand. I simply cannot marry you, and there is no use in our torturing ourselves about it any longer. I will send for my things within the week. I am grateful for what you have done for me, but it is best that I not return to Fontjoy Square. Tell the others good-bye for me, will you?"

Slowly, too shocked to reply, too shaken to argue, Devon retreated. He walked out of Claire's room confused, saddened and angered. He had been a fool to believe that Claire had written that letter. The duchess had tricked him and her daughter had rejected him.

Leaping into his carriage, Devon muttered an oath. He could not solve Claire's problems, he could not erase or alter her past and he could not make her love him. He would do well to quit thinking about her and go on with his life.

Lady Claire Kilgarren was truly on her own now. He wished her well, but she was no longer a part of his life.

* * *

A half block from Mrs. Bunratty's, his back pressed against the door of a pub, stood the boy who called himself Aidan Sullivan. Red-faced and white-lipped, he pulled his heavy coat around his middle and shivered against the cold night air. Despite his discomfort, a tiny grin flickered on his lips. He didn't flatter himself by thinking that his appearance in Fontjoy Square had precipitated this turmoil, but he was fairly certain his pilfering of Mary O'Roarke's diary had complicated matters between Devon Avondale and the beautiful Claire Kilgarren. He considered himself something of an expert at driving wedges between people. And, of course, for a price he could pull those wedges out.

He rubbed his hands together to warm them. Devon's expression when he'd left Mrs. Bunratty's was grim, to say the least. No doubt he was displeased that his lady love had fled her home and ensconced herself in a house of prostitution. No doubt he would do or pay anything to get her back.

When Avondale's carriage had rumbled away, Sullivan emerged from the shadows and, despite the chill that pervaded his bones, strolled casually past Mrs. Bunratty's front door. When he reached the corner, he turned and strolled back. The streets were relatively empty and no constables were in sight. Business at Mrs. Bunratty's was probably slow due to the cold weather. Men were always welcome at Mrs. Bunratty's any time of the night or day, but when business was dwindling, the ladies were particularly accommodating. Concluding that the time was right, Sullivan knocked on the front door.

Then, without waiting for an answer, he stepped inside.

Claire started nervously at the sound of someone rapping on her door. Reaching for the lamp on her bedside table, she called out, "Who is it?"

A Cockney-accented voice replied, "They's a caller down below, mum. Says you'll be wantin' to see him no matter how late the hour is. Want me to send the young feller up?"

Tossing off her covers, Claire padded across the floor and opened her door. Peering into the wizened face of Mrs. Bunratty's maid, she asked, "Who is it? I am not expecting anyone."

"Says his name is Sullivan. Says you'll want to see him, mum. Says he has somethin' fer ye."

It had to be the diary! Claire's pulse skittered as she attempted to process this unexpected turn of events. Why was Aidan Sullivan returning Mary O'Roarke's diary to her? And why had he chosen tonight to do so?

"I'll meet him in the parlor," she said, closing the door. Hurriedly, she tossed off her nightrail, pulled on a pair of warm woolen stockings and threw on a sturdy gown. Aidan's midnight visit was strange, to say the least, but the promise of getting Mary's diary back in her hands outweighed her disdain for the boy's bad manners.

The house was quiet as she descended the stairs. Cold weather was bad for business, Mrs. Bunratty had observed earlier that day. Most of the girls were asleep in their beds—alone. The duchess had not returned to Claire's room since their unpleasant exchange earlier that evening. The parlor was empty except for the young redheaded man who stood beside the well-stocked sideboard, crystal snifter in one hand, leather-bound diary in the other.

As he turned, he scanned Claire's figure, a peculiar glint in his eye. "Thank you for seeing me, Claire."

She rankled at his use of her Christian name, but rather than show her irritation, she extended her hand politely. "I am usually asleep at this hour, Mr. Sullivan. But I understand you have something for me."

Arching his brows, he held out the diary.

As Claire fingertips touched it, he snatched it back. "Not so fast, dearie."

Biting back a sharp response, Claire met Sullivan's gaze. "Is it money you want?"

He chuckled. "Now you are catching on."

"Then I am afraid you will be disappointed. I have none."

He swallowed his whiskey, grimaced, then chuckled malevolently. "No, but your friend Mr. Avondale does."

"What?" Stunned and bewildered, Claire took a step backward. "What does he have to do with this?"

"He is clearly besotted with you."

" 'Tis none of your business how Mr. Avondale feels about me."

"Ah, but it is, Claire. You don't mind if I call you Claire, do you? I feel like I know you so well." His gaze roved the walls, fixing on a huge portrait of a plump naked woman surrounded by cherubs. "But then, I am sure I am not the only man who feels he knows you."

Heat suffused Claire's face. "I am afraid you misunderstand, Mr. Sullivan. I do not *work* here."

"Not yet, perhaps. But I do not believe Mrs. Bunratty will allow you to stay much longer unless you do."

"Don't concern yourself with my circumstances. How much do you want for that book?"

He stared pointedly at her breasts, and then her hips. Licking his lips, he took a step closer to her. His breath was stale, tinged with the odor of whiskey; his cheeks were unshaven and his hair scruffy. Claire's nose wrinkled as he lightly touched her face.

"Perhaps I will be your first customer, milady. Please me, and in return I will give you Mary O'Roarke's diary."

She batted his hand away. "Cur! Idiot! I wouldn't let you touch me if you were the last man on earth and if you promised to pay me a pot of gold!"

The slap came so quickly that Claire hardly knew what hit her. The cold stinging sensation that robbed her of her breath also deprived her of her ability to stand. Her knees crumpled and the floor flew up to meet her. The room went black. The last thing Claire heard before she fell to the carpet was Aidan Sullivan's cruel laughter.

Fourteen

Rose and Dolly, seated side by side on a sofa in Devon's study, exchanged worried looks. Across from them, in his favorite wingback chair, sat Devson Avondale, his expression stern, his jaw unshaven. He had the air about him of an angry pirate; his long legs were languidly crossed and his arms were casually resting on the arms of his chair. But his black eyes were as threatening as a skull-and-crossbones pennant flapping in the breeze.

"Well, Devon, what do you propose to do?"

"About what?"

Rose said testily, "You know about what!"

Dolly laid a restraining hand on her friend's arm and said more patiently, "About Claire. Her servants told ours that she has packed her things and does not intend to return."

"I cannot order the woman to come back here. She is not a child. She can do as she pleases."

"No, but you could at least act as if you cared!" snapped Dolly.

Devon pinched the bridge of his nose. "Why should I care? She has made it quite plain to me that she does not want me anywhere around her. She has made her choice. There is nothing I can do."

Dolly let out a little huff of disgust. "Men!"

It was Rose's turn to assert a calming influence. "Now, Devon. You must know something about where Claire has gone."

"The servants have invented an outlandish story," inserted Dolly. "If one would believe what they say, she has gone to a house of ill repute."

"A very well-known one," added Rose. "In Monto. Just around the corner from the Dorcas Society. I know Mrs. Bunratty well—by reputation, of course." Rose touched her throat. "I'm afraid my late husband knew it even better than I."

Dolly felt a flutter in her stomach. She knew Mrs. Bunratty, too, far better than Rose, she surmised. After all, she had once masqueraded as a prostitute in order to lure her husband Dick Creevy to her. Dolly knew exactly what went on in places like Mrs. Bunratty's. "I cannot picture Claire in a place like that," she murmured.

"There's a lot about Claire that would surprise you if you only knew it," grumbled Devon.

"And what is that supposed to mean?" the ladies asked in unison.

"Nothing!" Devon rose to his full height. "I don't want to discuss it any more!"

"So you do know where she is," Dolly insisted. "Is it true, Devon? Is she at Mrs. Bunratty's?"

"I'm sure I don't know," Devon said, rather unconvincingly in Dolly's opinion.

"If you don't want to discuss Claire's whereabouts, then allow me to change the subject," Rose inserted. "I've been thinking about that strange young man, Aidan Sullivan. What he told you doesn't add up, Devon."

"Nothing about that little upstart adds up, Rose. I wish I had never laid eyes on him!"

Rose stood, plucking Devon's shirtsleeve to get his attention. "Now, listen, Devon, this could very well be important. The boy told you he was from the north."

"What has that to do with anything? I don't give a rat's ass where he is from!"

With her balled-up fist, Rose gave Devon a jab in the arm. "Enough of that!"

Dolly had to feign a coughing spell to keep from laughing. Devon's mood was irrepressibly black, and both women sympathized with him, but even Rose's long-suffering and maternal patience had its limits.

"I'm sorry," he said grumpily, staring absently at the fire. "I do not recall everything the boy said to me, but I remember that he called his papa a drunkard. Said he moved around a bit as a child. My overall impression was that he did not adore his adoptive parents."

"Ingrate," remarked Dolly.

"Perhaps he deserved better," observed Devon. "After all, his mother would have thrown him in the Liffey had it not been for Rose."

Rose clapped her palms together. "Enough of that. My point is, I have looked up the records at the Dorcas Society. Mary O'Roarke's baby was adopted by a Dublin couple who later moved to Scotland when the father inherited his father's pharmacy. Either the adoption records are false or Aidan Sullivan is telling a lie about his parents."

"Why would he lie?" asked Dolly.

"That's what I would like to know," Rose replied pensively.

"I don't see that it matters." Devon clasped his hands behind his back and rocked impatiently on the balls of his feet. "I don't mean to be rude, ladies, but I would like to be alone. Would you permit me to see you to the door?"

Dolly sprang to her feet beside Rose.

"We know the way." Dolly peered down her nose at Devon. Why he was being so uncooperative was a mystery to her, but she did not believe for a moment that he was disinterested in Claire's fate or Aidan Sullivan's clankers.

It was too cold for the women to continue their conversation on the street, so they hurried to Rose's house where a cheery fire crackled on the hearth in the parlor.

"What do you make of that?" asked Dolly, standing with her back to the fire and her skirts hiked up.

Rose withdrew a piece of paper from a cubbyhole in her secretary's desk. Seated on the sofa, she scratched out a few notes to herself, then looked up at Dolly. " 'Tis always easier for me to figure things out if I write them down."

"Well, what have you written, Inspector?"

Rose nibbled on the end of her pen. "There is something troubling about all this, Dolly. Aidan's appearance, for example."

"It does seem odd that after all these years, he would suddenly decide to search for his natural mother."

"Of course, he has a ready explanation for that. He says his parents recently died, and before they did, they confessed to him that he was adopted. That's when he looked up the Dorcas Society and was given Mary O'Roarke's old letter."

"But he told Devon that he came from the north."

"And the records show clearly that he was adopted by Dubliners who later moved to Scotland."

"Is it possible that they moved *back* to Ireland and located in the north?" Dolly queried.

Rose shrugged. "Anything is possible." After a moment, she said, "Then there is Aidan Sullivan's curious visit to me."

Dolly's ears pricked. "He visited you, too?"

"Yes, and he wanted me to tell him his father's name. I wouldn't do it, of course. I have no intentions of doing so."

"Perhaps the boy deserves to know, Rose," Dolly suggested quietly. "It disturbs me to know that some irresponsible Romeo would be able to shirk his responsibility to this boy forever. Mary had to live with the consequences of their summer affair; why shouldn't he?"

"You make a good point." With a sigh, Rose jotted down another note on her paper. "Do I understand that Mr. Sullivan paid a visit to your house also?"

"I wasn't going to mention it to anyone." Dolly dropped her skirts. "My backside is toasty enough." Throwing herself onto the sofa, she pulled her feet under her and sat like a young girl.

"What did he want from you?"

"Money," Dolly replied bluntly. "He told me a very sad story about how his lungs were scarred from working in the coal mines in Birmingham."

"Birmingham?" Rose's brows shot up. "Well, that lad does travel about, doesn't he?"

"He could have, Rose. Perhaps he worked there one summer. It wouldn't be completely at odds with the rest of his story."

"Go on with yours," Rose urged her.

"At any rate, he said he hadn't had steady work in ages. That he spent his last penny in order to get to Dublin and track down his natural mother. That he had counted on her to see him through this winter, but that he'd been sorely disappointed to learn that she had died. And, of course, that Mr. Avondale was none too eager to pad his dead wife's bastard son's pockets."

"What man would be? Did you give him any money?"

"A couple punt, that's all."

The women fell silent, both of them mulling over the discrepancies in Aidan Sullivan's stories.

"What do you make of it?" Dolly asked again.

"I don't know," Rose replied slowly. Ducking her head, she scribbled on her paper again. When she looked up at Dolly, her expression was worried. "You don't think Aidan Sullivan's *appearance* in Fontjoy Square has anything to do with Claire Kilgarren's *disappearance,* do you?"

"I think Claire and Devon had a lover's quarrel and she packed up her bags and left," replied Dolly.

"Then why in the name of God do her servants believe she has taken up with that obnoxious Mrs. Bunratty?"

Dolly shivered. "I don't know, but if she did, Devon was right: There is much we don't know about Lady Claire Kilgarren."

"Mr. Avondale?" The butler cleared his throat. "Mr. Avondale, sir? A porter just arrived . . . said this was an urgent message."

"Can't you see I am sleeping?" Groggy from too much scotch whiskey, Devon waved his butler away. He'd been slouched in his armchair since Dolly and Rose departed, and given the foul mood that he was in, he meant to remain there. The last thing he needed was a visitor. "Tell those meddling ladies to go away. I don't want to talk about Claire anymore."

"I'm sorry to disturb you, sir, but you'd better have a look, see."

Blinking the fog from his eyes, Devon focused on the vellum envelope his butler held out to him. "Christ on a raft," he bleated. "I don't want that bloody thing. Another entreaty from those worrisome women! They want me to go to Mrs. Bunratty's, I suppose, and beg their good friend Claire to come back to Fontjoy Square. Well, I won't do it, I tell you! I'm through with making a fool of myself."

"But, sir, I think you should read this. With all due respect, sir, I've read it already. Didn't want to disturb you unless it was absolutely necessary. It appears to be an important message, sir."

"Millicent hasn't taken a turn for the worse—"

"Oh, no, sir!" The butler thrust the envelope at Devon.

Reluctantly, Devon turned the cream-colored envelope over in his hands, studying the unfamiliar and nearly illegible print. Whoever had penned this note was not a practiced writer. Clumsily, he tore it open and removed a single sheet of paper. He got a whiff of floral perfume as he unfolded the note.

He scanned the message with a growing sense of dread. "Light that lamp," he instructed his butler gruffly. His heart thundered. Holding the paper close to the light, he read the words aloud.

" *I have your precious Claire. If you want her back, come to County Westmeath, just south of Mullingar, where the Belvedere House stands just off the road to*

Kilbeggan. I'll meet you at the Jealous Wall at midnight tonight, and there you will find your little treasures, both of them. Bring 5,000 punt and you can have them.' "

"Who would do such a thing?" the butler asked, his face ashen.

Devon strode to the fireplace, crumpled the note and started to toss it onto the flames. Thinking better of destroying the evidence of the duchess's misdeeds, however, he proceeded instead to the sideboard. Finding his decanter empty, he opened the cupboard beneath, deposited the wadded up ransom note and found a new bottle of scotch. Then he poured himself another stiff drink, threw his head back and shuddered as the liquor scalded its way down his throat.

"Claire's mother sent the note."

"Excuse me, sir?" The butler was evidently aghast at his employer's indifference to the ransom note.

"I wouldn't give it a second thought," Devon assured his faithful retainer. " 'Tis nothing but a ploy, a ruse . . . a joke meant to draw me out. But I won't be made a fool of again! Shannon Kilgarren will have to find someone else to take her daughter off her hands!"

"If it is a joke, sir, then it is in very bad taste, if I may say so meself."

"You may, and it is."

"Are you certain it is a joke, sir?"

Devon, glass in hand, returned to his favorite chair. "Turn off the light, will you, and leave me alone. Yes, I am certain it is a joke. The Kilgarren women have a strange sense of humor, I'm afraid."

When the old man had doddered out of the darkened room, Devon drained his glass. If Claire and her mother thought they could lead him around like a bull with a ring in his nose, they were wrong.

Without warning, his anger exploded. Bitterly, Devon threw up his arm and sent his crystal glass smashing onto the marble hearth.

His pulse faltered, then picked up again and raced violently. The brutishness of his action shocked even him. Disgusted, Devon closed his eyes and tried desperately not to cry or lose control of his emotions. He tried to convince himself that he could easily cease loving Claire. All he had to do was focus on the negative aspects of her personality and forget how sweet her lips were and how luscious her body was.

In his mind, he attributed to her all sorts of unseemly qualities: She was fickle, unpredictable, repressed, perhaps even hypocritical in her views regarding sex. She did not know what she wanted; in her confusion, she had a tendency to become defensive, acerbic and petulant. A grim chuckle escaped Devon's throat. Why, if he tried hard enough, he might even be able to convince himself that Claire was hopelessly flawed, helplessly out of touch with her own emotions.

He tried. He tried to forget how vulnerable she was, and how responsive she could be, and how utterly sexual she was when he held her in his arms. He tried to forget the powerful emotions he'd felt when he made love to her, and how frightened he was when he thought he had hurt her. He tried to forget the silkiness of her skin, the creaminess of her breasts and the gentle curve of her hips.

But Devon could not banish from his mind the notion that he loved Claire more than anything else in his life. He loved her, *warts and all*. He loved every insecure, frightened little inch of her. He loved her laughter, her wit and intelligence, the way she tossed her head. No other woman would do for Devon. He wanted Claire Kilgarren back in Fontjoy Square and back in his arms. He wanted her so badly he thought he would go insane.

But he would not make a fool of himself again. Begging was not Devon Avondale's style.

Exhausted, he pushed deeper into his chair. Crossing his arms over his chest, Devon prayed for the dreamless sleep that too much liquor brought, the blackness that would obliterate his pain if only for a little while.

When he awoke hours later, his head throbbed and his gut ached. He grimaced at the sunlight that squinted through his windows. A sour taste coated his tongue. Unsteadily, he crossed the room, heading toward the sideboard.

"Sir?" The butler entered the room gingerly, as if he was well aware that his footsteps might exacerbate his employer's alcohol-induced headache.

"Sorry to bother you, but there's another porter at the door. With another note."

"Burn it!"

The butler took a deep breath, stood steadfast beside Devon's chair and held out the note. "I was afraid you would say that, sir. And so I took the liberty of reading this one, too. It is from the same individual who wrote you last night."

"I suppose she was surprised that I did not show up at Belvedere House." Devon felt a twinge of guilt, but not enough to outweigh his determination not to make an idiot of himself over Claire.

"Yes, sir. But you've been given another chance, as it were. The writer of the note now says he will return Lady Claire Kilgarren to you if you appear at the Jealous Wall tonight at eight o'clock. With ten thousands pounds, I am afraid."

Devon gave a harsh bark of laughter. "Ho! The price has gone up now, has it? Well, I have to admit that the countess is more brazen than I gave her credit for. That old gal is determined to unload her daughter on me! But, she won't do it, I tell you!"

"Are you certain you know the identity of the kidnapper, sir?"

"Are you questioning my judgment?" Devon growled.

"No, sir . . ." The butler's face reddened. "It's just that everyone here is so fond of the lady. We wouldn't want anything untoward to happen to her."

Devon waved the man away. "Claire has not been kidnapped, I promise you. Now go away. And this time don't bother me if any more porters show up at the door with any more messages! Do you understand?"

"Yes, sir." Grim-faced, the butler turned. "I think I do understand."

At the Cork and Clover Inn, just north of Mullingar, Claire huddled on a rickety chair in the corner of the tiny room rented the night before by Aidan Sullivan. Despite the fire burning in the hearth, she shivered so hard her teeth clattered. Her jaw and head ached from the blow Aidan Sullivan had inflicted on her. She'd been on the verge of nausea since she'd awakened on the floor of a carriage as it jolted along country roads and realized what had happened to her. Every time Aidan looked at her, her stomach flip-flopped.

The knock at the door had startled both of them. Leaping up, Claire meant to dash toward freedom if the unexpected visitor was the innkeeper or his wife, wanting payment for the room. But Aidan crossed the floor swiftly and batted her aside with his arm. Stumbling, Claire fell onto the bed. Pinning her shoulders to the thin, straw-stuffed mattress, Aidan hovered over her, a disturbing glint in his eye.

He touched her hair and said, "Want some bed play, then, is that it, lassie?"

Cowering, she shook her head and tried to quell the reflexive urge to spit at him. Aidan's sour breath made her ill.

A husky male whisper sounded on the other side of the door. "Open up, Mac!"

Reluctantly, the redheaded man straightened, pulling Claire to her feet with him. "You'd best sit in that chair. My friend might get the wrong idea if you are sprawled out on the bed when I let him in."

Quickly, Claire returned to her chair and wrapped her arms protectively about her body.

The man Aidan admitted to the room was burly, snaggle-toothed and poorly dressed. "I want me money, Mac."

"You'll get paid when I do." Aidan removed a flask from his cloth satchel and took a quick swig. "Here, have some."

The burly man slanted a suspicious glance at Claire, then reached for the whiskey. After taking a long pull, he sighed, belched and returned the flask. "I've done what ye asked me. You never said me pay was dependent on whether the gent showed up to get her."

"Then how do I know you delivered the messages? He wasn't at the Jealous Wall this morning, and I don't yet know whether he'll be there tonight! You might have thrown the notes in the Liffey for all I know. 'Tis a bit difficult to believe that the fine Mr. Avondale would actually allow his lady friend to languish a moment in the company of a rogue like me."

"Maybe he doesn't know it's you who snatched his woman," the man argued.

"Well, I couldn't bloody well sign me own name,

now could I? Or even Aidan Sullivan's name, for that matter! Every constable in Ireland's going to be lookin' for me, so there's no point in signin' me name to me crime!" Aidan bellowed.

Pacing the length of the tiny room, he took another generous drink from his flask. His anger infected the room, filling it with tension.

"Besides, I think I pretty well described the situation when I told him I would return his treasures to him if he paid me the money!"

"Maybe he don't care about his little treasures. Didn't you tell me he refused to pay you for the diary?"

Aidan's nostrils flared and his face turned scarlet. "But he'd pay to get his lady back. I know it! I would have thrown in the diary for good measure, just to show that there are no hard feelings. Don't you understand anything, you moron? I can be a gentleman, too, you know!"

The burly man threw back his head and guffawed. "Now ain't that a good one? My pal Mac . . . a gentleman, no less, because he's willing to return the woman he made off with, and throw in a worthless diary in exchange for ten thousand punt."

Slowly, Claire began to comprehend the situation. Sullivan had kidnapped her in order to extract money from Devon Avondale. No less than two ransom notes had been delivered to Devon. But Devon had yet to appear at the designated rendezvous with the cash. Clearly, he wasn't interested in rescuing her from her abductor.

Her heart sank like a stone. Aidan—or Mac, as he was known to his brigand friend—continued to rail about Devon's failure to respond as he'd anticipated. But his words faded to the back of Claire's mind as it dawned on her how utterly alone she was. It actually made her chest hurt to realize that Devon had totally ignored her plight and turned his back on her when she needed him the most. If he hadn't responded to Aidan's first message, he would not respond to the second one.

But what else could she expect from a man who cloaked himself in secrets? What else could she expect from a stranger? And what else could she expect from a man whom she had rejected?

Struck by the irony of her situation, Claire battled the urge to cry. She had sent Devon away because she was afraid of being controlled by him, or rather by her desire for him. And here she was, in the clutches of an odious villain, desperately wishing that Devon would gallop up on a white horse and rescue her.

Well, he wasn't going to rescue her; that was abundantly clear. And, despite the fact that she had just days before told him in no uncertain terms to leave her alone, she felt betrayed by him once more.

Time stood still. While Aidan stalked from one end of the room to another, Claire's thoughts focused on Devon. She tried to picture his reaction when he opened Aidan's ransom note. Had he been saddened? Or had he crumpled up the note and tossed it in the fire with disdain and indifference?

A tiny moan escaped her lips, but no one heard it above Aidan's yelling. He grew more agitated by the minute, and more frightening to both Claire and the potato-faced man who stood in the middle of the floor shuffling his feet. Unable to ignore him, Claire suddenly grasped the enormity of her peril. If Devon refused to pay her ransom, Aidan had no use for her. If he left her alive, she would tell the constables who he was. In order to protect himself, he would have to kill her.

Blackness descended on her. In what she thought were her last moments on earth, Claire reflected on her life and concluded that she single-handedly had ruined it. She had spent years nurturing a grudge against Mary O'Roarke and blaming her mother for everything. She had wasted so much time and energy being ashamed of what and who her mother was. And she had frittered away her youth and given up the possibility of having a husband and family because she was too afraid of her sexual desires, too afraid of being controlled by a man, to allow herself to love.

What a fool she was!

But it was too late now. Now she was Aidan Sullivan's captive, and the man she loved wasn't going to rescue her.

If she wanted to live, she would have to rescue herself.

"Ten thousand?" Aidan shrieked, rounding on his accomplice.

Mr. Potato Face's mouth gaped.

Claire's skin prickled and her heart thudded. The air pressure in the tiny room could have crushed a diver's bell.

"I asked for five thousand," Aidan said menacingly.

"That's what I meant to say, five thousand. Just a slip of the tongue, Mac."

Aidan's eyes squinted and he spoke in a whisper. "You changed the numbers, didn't you? Thought you'd collect the money and keep the extra for yourself, didn't you?"

Gulping, the bigger man took a step back. "We're in this together, Mac."

"Like hell we are!" Aidan, his arms outstretched, his fingers grappling the air, suddenly rushed at his compatriot. What he lacked in size and strength, he made up for in sheer bravado, Claire noted bitterly.

The bigger man grabbed Aidan in a bear hug, and for an excruciatingly long moment, the two carried on a grotesquely brutal dance. Aidan snorted, spat and flailed his arms while Mr. Potato Face held him in a viselike grip.

Desperate to escape, and aware that this might be her only chance to do so, Claire slid to the edge of her chair. If the men moved away from the door just a bit . . .

"Let go of me, you ass!" Aidan kicked at his

tormentor's shin and stomped on his big feet. "Let go of me or else!"

"Promise me you won't be mad." In his effort to avoid Aidan's boots, the big man pushed his captive across the floor and away from the door.

"Let me go, damn it!" Aidan growled like a vicious dog.

"Promise?"

"I promise."

The men stood stock still, Aidan frozen in the giant's grasp with his face turned away from Claire.

Seeing her chance, Claire bolted from the chair and lunged at the door.

Then a series of events unfolded so rapidly that to Claire they seemed a blur.

The iron bolt slid back easily and the door swung open.

A gunshot split the air, and behind her a heavy thud sounded.

Aidan shouted, "Come back here, you ignorant wench!"

She glanced over her shoulder and saw Mr. Potato Face lying on the floor on his back, a pool of blood spreading beneath him.

Fear weighted her limbs, and her moment's hesitation gave Aidan the time he needed to burst through the open door, grab her by the arm and yank her back into the room.

Inside, she ran to the corner, threw open a window and screamed as loudly as she could. "Someone help me!"

But her cries were cut short by the rough, cal-
lused hand of Aidan Sullivan.

"Shut up or I'll put a bullet in your brain."
Clapping his palm over her mouth, he dragged
Claire away from the window and tossed her onto
the bed, where she scrambled up to the headboard, cowering beneath his malicious gaze.

The very sight of him, bending over her while
he brandished his pistol at her, made her throat
burn with acid. "Now, they's bound to be a curious
innkeeper runnin' up here in a little while. And
I want you to be a good girl and go along with my
story. That fool on the floor tried to rob me and
have his way with you, and I shot him. Plain and
simple. Country folk don't blame a man for de-
fending what's his."

"And why would I tell a lie like that?" As soon
as the innkeeper came, Claire intended to tell him
she'd been kidnapped!

"Because if you don't, I'll shoot the innkeeper,
too. And then I'll hop out that window, drive to
the Jealous Wall as fast as I can and put another
bullet through Mr. Avondale's brain if he even
shows up with the blunt, that is." Aidan giggled
demonically. "I won't be taken alive, you know
that, don't you? So unless you want the blood of
two innocent men on your hands, you'd better do
as I say."

Confused and scared out of her wits, Claire nodded silently. Within seconds, the innkeeper
rushed into the room, spied the man on the floor
and gasped. Stumbling backward, his fist at his

mouth, he stared slack-jawed first at the corpse and then at Aidan, who had tucked his pistol out of sight in the back of his trousers.

"You shot him!" the man cried. "What for?"

"He broke in while my wife and I were napping." Aidan ran his hand through his curly hair. His voice quavered when he spoke, sounding as nervous as he looked. "When I awoke, he was standing over the bed, on my wife's side. No telling what he intended to do to her. Are you all right, sweetling?"

Claire nodded again.

"There was a scuffle," Aidan continued. "Well, I guess you can see that. I had no choice. My money purse is empty; no doubt my money is in this criminal's pockets."

Gingerly stepping away from the widening pool of blood, the innkeeper wiped his fingers on his apronfront and sniffed. "Well, its good riddance to that rubbish, then, ain't it? Want me to send for the sheriff?"

"No need. Just throw him in the nearest ditch, that's my advice." When the innkeeper wasn't looking, Aidan gave Claire a knowing wink. "Come on now, help me get this animal out of here. If you'll take the head, I'll get his feet. Darling, you stay put. I'll be back in a trice!"

Huffing and puffing, the two men managed to half-lift and half-drag Mr. Potato Face's lifeless body from the room. The corpse bumped noisily down the steps; then there was a brief moment of silence before Aidan bounded back into the room, his face cracked by a toothy grin.

"He bought my story, sweetling, hook, line and sinker."

"You are an amazing actor," Claire replied calmly. Her fear had receded. Now that she had decided no one was coming to rescue her, she would have to save herself. And she would need her wits about her in order to do that.

Aidan's inappropriate jollity sickened her, but she tamped down the urge to leap on him and scratch his eyes out. As he moved about the room, stuffing his meager belongings into his satchel, she studied him as a scientist might study a mutant plant.

"Where are you going?" she asked at length.

"I'm going to the Jealous Wall to meet Mr. Avondale."

"I thought you said he wasn't coming."

"Well, he's been given another chance. If he is foolish enough to ignore my missive, why then, I shall have to take other measures to get my money from him."

"What money? Why does he owe you anything?"

" 'Tis society that owes me, dear. Oh, you wouldn't understand, but you see, I wasn't born with a silver spoon in me mouth like you were. I've had to claw my own way up, and make a living as best I can. And this is how I make me livin'."

"Kidnapping people?"

Standing at the edge of the bed, Aidan shrugged. "Impersonating long-lost or illegitimate sons.

You'd be amazed by how guilty some people feel! It's easy, lassie! I keep me eyes and ears open for an opportunity, like the one I got when I learned that a lad named Aidan Sullivan died in Edinburgh. I was working in hospital there, changing the kid's bedsheets when his folks started talkin'—like I wasn't even there, like I was invisible or somethin'."

"Mary O'Roarke's son is . . . dead?" The puzzle pieces began to fall into place. As Claire realized how evil-minded her captor was, her determination to survive her ordeal grew stronger.

"Died of a lung disease." Mac clucked his tongue. "Like mother, like son, as the saying goes. Anyhow, before he croaked, I learned all about the circumstances of his birth. He wasn't the old folks' natural son, see. He'd been adopted through the Dorcas Society in Dublin. And the only thing the old folks knew about the chit what gave birth to him was that she was from a good family and scared to death someone would find out what she'd done."

"So you saw an opportunity to profit from Mary O'Roarke's fear?"

"Aye, lassie, now you're catching on." The young man seemed pleased with his criminal enterprise. Gesturing toward the bloody spot on the floor, he continued, "Like I said, it was easy enough to send Brutus there into the office in Monto. He got the file and the silly letter that Mary O'Roarke had written to her son many years before. Tracking her down was child's play."

"You didn't know she was dead, though." Claire

didn't attempt to hide her contempt for Mac. "You must have been a wee bit disappointed to learn that she died nearly six years ago."

"You're right about that! Just think what she might have paid Aidan Sullivan to disappear if she had been alive!"

"Why didn't you just leave when you discovered she was dead?"

"I had a lot of time invested in this caper, see. So I decided to keep a presence in the neighborhood, get a feel for the lay of the land, so to speak. And then I realized there was another way I could make money. Mr. Avondale is somewhat obsessed with his dead wife's diary, you know."

"I know."

Aidan stood beside the bed, suddenly sober, his arms crossed over his chest. A hard glint shone in his eyes. "I have to admit, I thought he would pay a handsome price for that book. Apparently, the man is far more niggardly than I had predicted he would be."

"Then what makes you think there is even a chance he will show up at the Jealous Wall?"

"Curiosity, if nothing else, lassie. He's not the sort of man who enjoys being bested by a lowlife punk like me."

"If you're not Aidan Sullivan, then who are you?"

A slow wolfish grin dominated his face. "Just a poor sailor boy who got tired of the water, girlie. That's all you need to know. Now it's time for me to leave."

The relief that poured through Claire's veins was temporary. From his satchel, Mac extracted a coil of rope. When she realized what he intended to do, Claire leaped off the bed and sprang for the door. But, again, her captor was faster and stronger. Mac grabbed her from behind and slammed her against the door, knocking the breath out of her.

He whirled her around to face him. Eyes glittering, he drew back his arm, palm open.

Instinctively, Claire turned her head, shrinking from the blow.

She awoke, blinking into the glow of a gas lamp on the bedside table. Her eyes were scratchy and her head throbbed. Painfully, she moved her head from side to side. Her thoughts were muddled and her memory of where she was, how she came to be there and what had happened to her was fuzzy.

The memory of her abduction and her struggle with Mac slowly returned to her. Her breathing came in shallow gulps. A filthy, foul-tasting rag filled her mouth, causing her to gag. She couldn't scream because no one would hear her, and she couldn't cry because of the danger of choking.

Panic seized her as she realized that she was flat on her back, her wrists and ankles bound by rope to the posts of the bed. The pungent smell of the straw mattress prickled her nostrils. Her limbs ached and her gut twisted. Mac had tied her up and left her at the inn in order to meet Devon Avondale at the Jealous Wall.

That could only mean one thing: that Mac did not intend to exchange Claire for money.

Instead, he meant to rob Devon—*and probably kill him.*

Fear and guilt sharpened Claire's senses. She should have told the innkeeper she had been kidnapped. Her silence had not saved Devon but rather had put him in jeopardy.

Marshaling her strength, Claire forced herself to calm down, breathe regularly and assess her situation. She wriggled her wrists, cringing at the sting of the rope against her sensitive skin. Mac had bound her tightly to the headboard, and her struggle against her restraints only left her with cuffs of raw skin.

After a while, she tried to move her legs. Her left ankle was firmly lashed to the bedpost, but the binding on her right ankle was loose. With her eyes closed, Claire concentrated on the sensation of the ropes as she rotated her foot, eventually sliding it free of the restraint.

With her right foot free, she relaxed for a moment, her gaze now scanning the room desperately. Beads of perspiration dotted her upper lip. She still couldn't untie her wrist restraints, and there was very little that she could reach with her toes. Her hopes of escaping were dashed. Her head fell back on the hard bed. She had struggled free of one ankle restraint, but she was still a prisoner in the tiny room at the inn.

And if Devon Avondale was going to meet Aidan Sullivan at the Jealous Wall—a possibility that even

Claire in her cynicism could not rule out—he was hurtling toward certain death.

Not only was he her best friend, but *she loved him more than she had ever dreamed she could love a man.*

Claire would save Devon from the fiendishness of Mac—or she would die trying.

Fifteen

A female voice, distinct in its refinement, interrupted his journey. "Going back for a bit of the hair of the dog that bit you?"

Wheeling, Devon took a long look at Lady Shannon, the former Duchess of Kilgarren. "What in the devil are you doing here at this bloody hour?"

"Darling, it is well past noon." She walked confidently into the study, her pale blue gaze fixed on Devon. If it had not been for the subtle net of wrinkles at the corners of her eyes and the inappropriate brightness of her morning gown, she could have passed for Claire's twin sister.

Devon turned his back on her and reached for a fresh glass.

"Tossing glasses on the hearth, I see," she mused behind him. "And I doubt you were dancing a jig when you did it. Something must be troubling you."

"Yes, something is troubling me!" He rounded on her. "You! Get out of here! You won't trick me again! I know you wrote that letter!"

Her swaggering smirk faltered. "I fear that Claire will never forgive me for that."

After a length, he asked, "Why have you come here?"

"To tell her that I am sorry, of course."

Devon let out a mean bark of laughter. "She isn't here, my lady, and you know it!"

"What do you mean, she isn't here?"

"You are quite an actress," Devon growled. "If I didn't know better, I would think you really don't know where your daughter is."

"She is not at home," the duchess said slowly. "Are you telling me you don't know where she is?"

Something in the woman's voice made the hair on Devon's neck bristle. "You admit you wrote the letter, don't you?"

She nodded. "It was a pathetic attempt to lure you to Mrs. Bunratty's. I thought that if you saw her . . . and if she saw you—"

"I mean the second letter. The ransom note. The letter in which you attempted to lure me to County Westmeath."

"I don't know what you are talking about."

For the first time Devon experienced a nauseating wave of apprehension. "I got a letter stating that Claire would be returned to me in exchange for five thousand punt. Then I got another, stating the price had been raised to ten thousand."

"And you thought I sent it?" The duchess's eyes widened.

Instantly, Devon could see that he had been

wrong. No matter how skillful an actress the duchess was, there was no way she could pretend to be as frightened as she looked. "Oh, my God." His glass fell to the floor.

"Someone has abducted Claire!" The duchess had turned pale; her entire body trembled. "But why?"

Ignoring her question, he demanded, "How long has she been missing?"

"Since yesterday. I just assumed she had come back to you."

"And when I got the notes, I thought you had written them." Devon glanced at the fire. "Damn it! I should have paid closer attention to the words of the first letter. The writer said he would return my treasures to me when I gave him the money."

"Treasures? There is someone other than Claire whom the kidnapper is holding from you?" the duchess asked incredulously.

Devon supposed she had every right to doubt him. At the moment, he felt like kicking himself for failing to pay closer attention to the abductor's note. "Someone or *something*."

"Do you know what it is?"

He slammed one fist into his open hand. "Mary's diary."

"Oh, that wretched diary! I am sick of hearing about it!" Claire's mother pinned an accusing stare on Devon. "Well, Mr. Avondale, it seems to me that you have gotten my daughter into a dangerous situation. What are you going to do to get her out of it?"

"I'm going to take ten thousand pounds to the appointed meeting spot and get Claire back. And if Aidan Sullivan lays a finger on Claire, I'm going to pound the little bugger to a pulp. I don't care if he *is* Mary O'Roarke's son."

"I'll go with you."

"No you won't. I won't have another woman put in harm's way on my account."

"Where are you to meet this man?"

"I won't tell you. You would only try to follow me."

"You have no right to withhold that information from me!"

Ignoring the duchess's protests, Devon stalked out of the room. Half the day was gone and he had a long journey to make.

In his bedchamber, Devon snatched clothes from his free-standing closet and pulled on his heavy boots. He gave instructions for his carriage to be brought around. He scratched out a note to Dick Creevy, briefly explaining that Claire had been kidnapped by Aidan Sullivan and that he was going to retrieve her. If anything happened to him, at least Creevy would be able to point his finger at the correct man.

"If I do not return by midnight tonight, deliver this to Dick Creevy." He entrusted the note to his butler. "But not a moment before, do you understand? I don't want my neighbors to turn into a vigilante mob. There's been enough drama around here lately!"

Then Devon reached beneath his mattress, re-

moved his pistol and tucked it inside the waistband of his trousers. He wasn't taking any chances
with Aidan Sullivan. No matter the boy's relation
to Mary, Devon wouldn't allow him to hurt Claire
Kilgarren.

Deflated by his refusal to take her with him,
Shannon Kilgarren sat on the sofa in Devon Avondale's study. The bustle and noise associated with
his departure faded as soon as the front door
closed behind him. It was almost as if a collective
sigh went up from his servants.

She thought of returning to Mrs. Bunratty's but
couldn't force herself to do so. She had lived without her daughter for years; now she had found
her and lost her again. Whenever Devon returned
to Fontjoy Square with Claire, the duchess intended to be there.

In the late afternoon, Avondale's maid, obviously preoccupied and oblivious to the duchess's
presence, stumbled into the study with a dusting
feather in her hands. After giving the sideboard a
rather cursory swipe, she picked up a decanter
and poured herself a drink. Sighing loudly, she
slowly turned, caught a glimpse of the woman on
the sofa and started as if she'd seen a ghost.

"Oh, me lord! Who are you?"

"Lady Shannon Kilgarren."

"Lady Claire Kilgarren's mum?" The red-
haired, ruddy-complexioned woman stared in fascination. With drink in hand, she crossed the

room and stood beside the sofa. "Well, what are ye doin' 'ere, if ye don't mind me askin'?"

Grateful for the company, and sensing that this woman might be a rich source of useful information, the duchess gestured at the drink and said, "Get me one of those, will you, and I will tell you all about it."

Devon's carriage rumbled northward at a dangerous speed. The roads, still patchy with ice from the recent storm, were slick in some places, rutted in others, but treacherous all the way. In good weather, the trip would have taken less than three hours. But it was nearly eight o'clock by the time Devon arrived at Belvedere House.

A lone horse was hobbled at the edge of the gardens, but in the dim light cast by his carriage lamps, Devon saw no one else in the vicinity. Grateful that it was a clear night, he leaped from his rig and paused at the edge of the road.

His driver, a gruff old man who had been in his employ for decades, cast a suspicious eye in the direction of the Palladian villa. Surrounded by gardens and overlooking Lough Ennel, the eighteenth-century structure loomed eerily against the star-studded sky. Beyond it, a series of terraces, framed by urns and yews, descended to the lake. Adjacent to the rolling parkland was the Jealous Wall, built by the envious Earl of Belvedere in 1755 to block the view of his brother's more magnificent mansion.

"I dunno, sir; I have a bad feelin' about this."

Truth be told, so did Devon. If Aidan Sullivan had arrived on horseback, where was Claire? He supposed she could have shared a saddle with him, but in this weather it would have been difficult.

He had no choice, though. He couldn't walk away from this rendezvous because he had a *bad feeling*. Claire's life was at stake, and he wasn't about to abandon her to a devil like Aidan Sullivan.

"Stay here," he instructed his driver. "But if Aidan Sullivan returns to his horse without me, turn this rig around and drive as fast as you can to the nearest town. Mullingar, I think it is. Find a sheriff and tell him what has happened—"

"I ain't gonna leave you, sir!"

"You can't help me by getting yourself killed," Devon said firmly. "Now do as I say. Keep a sharp eye out. And, God willing, I will be back shortly. If I return with Sullivan and Claire in my company, then we will give that little bastard the real money."

In his left hand, Devon clutched a leather valise stuffed with wads of newspaper. Unbuttoning his heavy coat with his right hand, he felt the butt of the pistol tucked inside his trousers. Alert to every snap of every twig beneath his boots, he cautiously strode across the grounds toward the high stone wall that once blocked the green-eyed earl's view of his brother's property. Wind whipped at his legs and blistered his face. An owl hooted in the distance. A sense of foreboding stole over him as his vision adjusted to the shadowy landscape. In this setting, Aidan could sneak up on him easily.

He stood in the middle of a grassy courtyard surrounded by the crumbling, lacelike remains of the wall. "Aidan Sullivan! If you are here, come out of the shadows! I have your money!"

The crunch of gravel sounded behind him.

Turning, Devon withdrew his pistol and pointed it at Aidan Sullivan as the man emerged from the darkness, his lips curled in a cocky smirk.

"Don't shoot me," Aidan said in an oily voice. He lifted his hands in the air. "As you can see, I am unarmed."

"Where is Claire?"

"In a safe place. Where is my money?" The boy's gaze darted to the valise in Devon's hand.

Devon swallowed hard, tamping back the impulse to shoot the redheaded villain. "That wasn't the agreement, Aidan. You said if I brought the money here, you would give Claire to me."

"And the diary."

"Damn the diary!" Even Devon was struck by the ferocity of his anger. The diary was a relic of the past; Claire represented his future. At the moment, he could not have cared less about that book. "Where is Claire?"

"I left her at the inn, my friend. If you have the money, you can give it to me now, and I will tell you exactly where she is."

White spots danced in front of Devon's eyes. With his blood boiling and his heart hammering, he feared he would lose control and kill Aidan before he discovered Claire's whereabouts. Clamping his jaws together, he battled his frustration and fury. In a strangely quiet voice, he replied, "You won't get the money until you tell me where Claire is."

With lightning swiftness, Aidan produced a pistol and fired off a shot.

Stumbling back, Devon felt as if a red-hot poker had been thrust into his left shoulder. His fingers relaxed and the valise fell to the ground. But then his own pistol glinted in the starlight, and another shot cracked the still country air.

Aidan took an awkward step forward, his gaze fixed on the valise. Then his eyes widened in surprise, his mouth formed an oval and his coat fell open. A splotch of crimson blossomed on his shirtfront, just beneath his collarbone. Sputtering incoherently, still grasping at the valise, he collapsed.

"You've shot me, damme! I can't believe it!"

Devon had no sympathy for the man. Grabbing him roughly by the lapels of his coat, he held the pistol to his temple and said, "Where is Claire? Tell me, and I will see to it that you get to hospital. Keep your secret and I'll send you to the grave with it."

"Get me a doctor," Aidan rasped, "and then I'll tell you."

The hammer clicked. Devon cocked his pistol and pressed the snout of it to Aidan Sullivan's temple. "We are finished negotiating, lad. Tell me where she is."

"At the Cork and Clover, just north of here," the young man said.

"Thank you." As Devon released him, Aidan fell to the ground.

"You're not going to leave me here, are you?"

"I think I will leave my driver here. And I will borrow your horse, if you don't mind. If I find Lady Claire Kilgarren safe and sound at the Cork and Clover, as you say, then I will return. If not, *my friend,* you are going to die a very slow death."

Devon's thirst for revenge urged him to shoot the boy dead now, but his more refined sense of justice would not allow him to do it. Without an ounce of concern for Aidan's welfare, he yanked him off the ground and half-dragged him back to the carriage. There he tossed him onto the floor of the compartment and slammed shut the door.

Devon's driver bristled at the change in plans. "Why do I have to be his prison guard? If it was me, I'd have killed him on the spot if he hadn't produced the lady as promised. And judging by the looks of him, you damn near killed him anyway. Finish him off, I say!"

"I don't think the bullet hit anything vital," Devon countered. "And if we kill him, we may never learn the true story behind this nefarious escapade."

Throwing himself onto the back of Aidan's horse, he gave his driver a curt salute. "Now, do as I say and I will return in a trice. That I promise."

The road between Belvedere House and Mullingar was pitch black and treacherous. Only one rider, unrecognizable in the dark, passed Devon as he galloped northward toward the inn. The horse Devon rode was foaming at the mouth by the time he pounded into the courtyard of the Cork and Clover. A tiny boy, no older than ten years old, scampered out of the inn, took Devon's reins and promised to stable and water his mount in exchange for a couple of pennies.

At the scarred wooden bar in the pub downstairs, Devon removed his gloves and signaled a tap girl.

"I'd like a word with the innkeeper, please."

A few moments later, a big-bellied man wearing an apron emerged from the kitchen, wiping his hands on an apronfront that looked as if he'd worn it while slaughtering a cow.

"Lookin' for a room, sir?"

"Not exactly." Scanning the tiny tavern, Devon leaned across the bar and lowered his voice. "It's a lady I'm looking for."

The innkeeper's brows shot up. "Oh! Well, I think I can help you, then. Tessie here is always willing, and quite reasonable in her asking price—"

The tap girl giggled and blushed.

"No, no, you misunderstand. I'm looking for a

particular lady, a very proper woman with blond hair and blue eyes named Lady Claire Kilgarren."

"No ladies of that sort here, sir."

"Are you certain?"

The innkeeper nodded.

"She might have been wearing a blue suit. And she would have been in the company of a red-headed man named Aidan Sullivan. A despicable rogue, if you want to know. He tried to kill me tonight." Devon jerked his head, indicating the tear in his coat and the black stain of blood on his shoulder.

"Good God, man, are ye hurt badly? They's a butcher in the kitchen who can—"

" 'Tis a nick, that's all. Hardly even hurts," Devon lied. In fact, his shoulder burned insanely, but the wound wasn't deep and the bullet had not caused any permanent damage. The pain he felt was inconsequential compared to his concern for Claire's safety. "Now, think back. Have you seen any such couple in the inn? They might have been acting strangely. The woman was held against her will, you see. 'Tis very important that you tell me everything you can remember!"

The man scratched his head. "Can't say as I remember anyone like that. But maybe . . . well, there was *one* young gent with red hair what rented a room with his wife. She had blond hair—"

"Yes, yes?" Devon pressed a wad of currency into the innkeeper's chubby palm.

"They've already gone, sir. The young man left earlier this evening, and I can't say I'm sorry to

see him go. Odd sort, he was. Left his wife behind
tied to the bed, he did! And his jealous folly damn
near caused my establishment to burn to the
ground."

"He left the lady tied up?" Devon's pulse galloped. "Where is she now?"

"She left just about an hour ago. Just after the
fire broke out in her room. Lucky for her, my boy
spied the flames from the courtyard where he was
tending to a guest's horse. He sounded the alarm
and I doused the fire with a pitcher of water. Once
the lady was untied, she leaped off the bed and
flew down the steps like the devil was in behind
her—"

"You let her go? Just like that?"

"I didn't have no reason to hold her, sir."

"Where did she go?"

"How would I know?"

"How did she travel? Did she have a carriage at
her disposal?"

"Sir, I didn't question her. She just left, see.
That's all I can tell you!"

Devon drew in a deep breath. His chest ached
and his fingers closed in fists at his sides. But before he could question the innkeeper further, a
frightened-looking stable boy rushed into the tavern and stood beside the bar. Looking up at his
rotund elder, his face smudged with dirt, his chin
wobbling, he chirped, "Father, someone has stolen your mare!"

The innkeeper grabbed the child by the shoulders and shook him. "Stolen old Mollie? The best

gray in my stables? And what the hell were you doing, lad? Sleeping?"

Crossing the room, Devon heard the sound of a heavy slap laid across the boy's cheek. The child whimpered his apologies and rushed from the tavern, brushing past Devon. Devon would have liked to turn around and teach the innkeeper a lesson or two about mistreating his child, but this was no time to exercise his reformist principles. If Claire had left the inn on a stolen horse, then she was on the road, either to Dublin or to . . .

Jolted into action, Devon plunged into the courtyard. Knowing Claire as he did, she had predicted Aidan Sullivan's trickery. If the man left her at the inn, then he never intended to exchange her for the ransom money. Instead, he meant to kill Devon and rob him of the ten thousand punt in his valise. God only knew what he would have done to Claire after that.

And Claire would never have allowed Sullivan to ambush Devon. Somehow she had escaped, stolen a horse and rode off toward Belvedere House.

Swearing colorfully, Devon grabbed the reins from the stable boy. Tossing a few coins in the lad's direction, he swung himself into the saddle and dug his heels into the horse's sides. He knew exactly where Claire had gone, and he wouldn't rest until he found her.

Icy wind tore at him as his horse headed northward again. Leaning forward, urging his animal to run even faster, Devon squinted into the blackness. One misstep on the horse's part would mean disaster on roads as pocked and muddy as these. But his own safety was not a consideration. Devon would not rest until he held Claire in his arms.

The thought that she might rebuff him, that she might tell him to go away, rode with him. Devon understood that Claire's father had instilled in her a fear of men, a self-loathing that inhibited her and prevented her from giving herself to any man. Her strict, judgmental father had taught her that only bad women liked sex.

And so she had long suppressed her physical needs because she feared the vulnerability that her sexual desire generated. She feared being like her mother. She feared being dominated by a man who might judge her, or worse . . . leave her.

Her fears, Devon supposed, were understandable, perhaps even a normal response to the repression of her upbringing. But those fears would not go away simply because Devon wanted them to, or because he loved Claire. Only Claire could make the decision to overcome her fears and trust him. Only Claire could make the decision to love a man, and allow herself to be loved.

Unfortunately, the fact that Devon had concealed his true identity from Claire for nearly a year lessened the chance that she would ever trust him. And her suspicions regarding his good faith were heightened by her hostility toward Mary O'Roarke.

Oh, Mary, what were you thinking? Why did you persecute this little girl so? Even if you did discover the duchess was having an affair with your father, why destroy the reputations of two women?

His horse's hooves slipped as the beast rounded a sharp curve. Whuffling and snorting, the horse stumbled. Panic stabbed Devon's heart. He couldn't afford to make a mistake. He had to find Claire, if only to assure himself that she was all right. He knew she might never accept him as her husband, but that didn't affect his love for her. Mary O'Roarke had been the love of his life . . . until he fell in love with Lady Claire Kilgarren, and he did not intend to abandon his love just because she wouldn't marry him.

The horse righted itself and found its gait once more. Relieved, Devon pressed forward. Though his journey took less than hour, it seemed an eternity. At first, he wasn't aware that his lips were moving and his thoughts were sounding on the wind. But as drew back on his horse's reins, he heard his own voice whispering a prayer to Mary O'Roarke.

"Please, Mary, if you are listening to me. Please, don't let anything bad happen to Claire."

He didn't understand why Mary had ruined Claire's reputation those many years ago, or why she had written about Claire in her diary. Perhaps the clue was to be found in his dead wife's entries. He was reminded of a short one at the end, a brief soliloquy that seemed to have no relation to the stories of the four women who lived in Fontjoy Square. Devon had never paid much attention to that particular passage. Now, he wished he had memorized it as he had other recollections. Because he knew in his heart that Mary was sorry for what she had done.

mentioned it at the next other recollections. Beside an interesting that may what was very for what she is done.

Sixteen

Leaping from his horse, Devon knew instantly
that something was amiss. His driver was nowhere
to be seen, and the lamps on the side of his carriage had been extinguished. The unnatural quiet
and the almost total darkness of the tableau were
sinister omens.

Stealthily, Devon crept to his rig. With his pistol
clutched in his hand, he grabbed the brass handle,
cranked it and pulled open the door.

The interior of the cab was dark, but he made
out two silhouettes, one a heavy, lumpish figure
slumped against the squabs, the other a petite feminine shape perched primly on the leather bench.
Hurriedly, Devon tucked his pistol in his trousers,
threw off his gloves and lit the carriage lamps. As
light seeped over the scene, he crouched in the
doorway of the rig, his gaze focused on Claire.

Her hands were clasped in her lap and tied together at the wrists. Her feet were bound with rope,
and a dirty kerchief was stuffed in her mouth.

"Dear God," Devon muttered, stepping inside

the cab to release her. His blood roared in hi
veins, deafening him, dulling his senses. Reaching
for Claire, he met her wide-eyed stare.

She shook her head and stamped her feet, fix
ing her gaze at a point over his shoulder and jerk
ing her chin upward.

Too late, Devon realized that she was trying to
warn him. The blow at the base of his neck sen
him sprawling on the carriage floor. Dazed, he
pushed to his knees, only to be kicked in the rib
so hard that a dazzling show of colors burst before
his eyes. Pain gripped his entire body, robbing him
of his breath. Just before the black sea of sense
lessness rolled over him, Aidan Sullivan's obnox
ious voice curled around him.

They sat in the chilly compartment, the three
of them, tied up like prisoners of war, awaiting
their fate with grim resolution. At least Aidan had
removed their gags, and the hapless driver had
begun to moan and flicker his eyelashes. Devon
had regained consciousness, too, though blood
ran from his hairline to his collar and soaked the
shoulder of his coat. Seated opposite him, Claire
could only wonder how she might ever have lived
without him. In the past few hours, she had real
ized how important he was to her, how much she
needed him—and how liberating it was to admi
that need.

True independence, she had discovered, wa
found in loving a man, not in hiding from him.

"Are you angry with me?" she whispered.

Devon glanced at the ceiling through which Aidan could be heard settling into the driver's perch, slapping the ribbons on the horse's rumps and urging them to go. "Why would I be angry with you, Claire? I love you, you know."

Her throat constricted. "I love you, too," she managed. " 'Tis all my fault that we are here . . . had I never run off to Mrs. Bunratty's . . ."

He made a hushing sound. "Ah, lassie, we all of us make mistakes. And very few of those mistakes cannot be corrected. It is when we fail to learn from our mistakes that we are to blame."

Her neck jerked as the carriage jolted into motion. "He means to kill us on the side of the road, doesn't he? He'll say highwaymen overtook us and killed everyone but him. He's got a wound to prove his story, and there won't be anyone to contradict it."

"Based on what I have seen, I would say he is capable of just such a dastardly deed." Devon's eyes were heavy-lidded and his speech slurred.

"Well, then, we haven't much time, Devon. I love you, and I want to marry you."

His brows lifted sluggishly. "Marry me? What has changed your mind, Claire? Not that I'm unhappy to hear it."

She wanted to touch him so badly, she ached. But her hands were lashed tightly together and her feet were bound. She couldn't even kiss him, or smooth his hair, or breathe in his scent. *So near, yet so far,* she thought wryly.

" 'Tis hard to say," she admitted quietly. Her body slid down the length of the cushions as the carriage turned, rumbled onto the road and picked up speed. "I realized that I needed you. Not to rescue me or to save me, but to love me and share your life with me."

He gave a deep, throaty chuckle. "Pray tell me, lassie, when did you realize this?"

"Too late, I fear," she answered as a tear slipped out of the corner of her eye. Unable to dash it away, she turned her head. "Too late."

It is not too late!

Despite his struggles, Devon could not free himself from the restraints that bound his wrists and ankles. The scenario described by Claire was entirely plausible, and as the minutes ticked by, the likelihood of their escape diminished. Furious at himself for allowing Aidan to ambush him, Devon clenched his jaw and tried to ignore his torn shoulder and pounding head.

Devon chuckled grimly at the injustice of their situation. At last Claire had cast aside her fears, and now they were entrapped by a murderous rogue. How could he have come so close to finding happiness, only to lose it again?

He had to do something, but what? Frustration coursed through his bloodstream like a deadly sickness. If he could not save them both, at least he would save Claire. He could not allow her to come to such an untimely end. It was bad enough that he had lost his precious Mary to a dreadful disease that the doctors couldn't cure. Devon would not tolerate the waste of Claire's life, too.

But time was running out.

Abruptly, the carriage came to a halt. Peering out the window, Devon saw nothing but blackness, but as the rig hadn't veered off the bumpy path, he suspected it had stopped in the middle of the road. Overhead, Aidan scrambled off the driver's seat and landed on the muddy turf with a sloppy thud.

Devon's head jerked and his muscles tensed as the carriage door flew open, flooding the cab with light.

"Well, girls and boys, 'tis time for some fun!" With a ghoulish cackle, Aidan stood on the running board, leering into the cabin and brandishing his pistol. "Who wants to be first?"

"Let the lady go," Devon said. "You have no reason to harm her."

"She has seen me, old man! That is reason enough. I plan to be on a boat to Scotland 'ere morning. You don't think I want to leave behind any witnesses, do ye? God knows, I might want to return to this godforsaken land of fairies and leprechauns some day!"

"I won't tell anyone," Claire promised. "Besides, I don't know your real name. I only know you as Aidan Sullivan."

Devon's ears pricked up. "If you are not Aidan Sullivan, then who in the bloody hell are you?"

"Ha, you hadn't figured that out yet?" Aidan

threw back his head and roared with laughter. "Well, I might let your lady friend tell you, but there doesn't seem to be time, now. Suffice it to say that your dead wife's bastard son bought the farm himself in Edinburgh not long ago."

"You mean you were only pretending to be Mary's son?"

"That's right!"

Devon quickly figured out the scam. "You meant to extort money from her in exchange for your going away. You thought she would be eager to pay her illegitimate child to disappear and never bother her again."

"Precisely."

Devon snorted. "Had Mary been alive, I'm certain you would have been disappointed, Mr. . . . whoever you are."

"You can call me Mac." The redheaded youth's features twisted in a cruel, ugly mask. Lifting his arm, he leveled the pistol, aiming first at Devon's head, then at Claire's. "Goodness me, I can't decide who to shoot first."

"Shoot me, I told you. And there won't be any need to do away with Claire. She hasn't seen a thing, and believe me, she will keep her mouth shut."

Giggling, Mac hovered in the open doorway of the cab, taunting his prisoners by waving his weapon wildly. Doubled over with laughter, he did not hear horses' hooves sounding in the distance.

Claire and Devon exchanged glances. An intimacy passed between them, a powerfully charged understanding that if they combined their wits and resources, they might—*together*—survive. They had only to distract the boy so that he would not detect the splashing rumble of the approaching horses.

"If it's money you want, I've got plenty," Devon said, cold sweat bathing his body.

"More than ten thousand punt?" Mac's eyes rounded and his pistol pointed at the ceiling. "Really?"

"Really," Claire inserted. "He is telling the truth, I swear it."

"How fast could you get it?"

"I could go to the bank straightaway, as soon as we get to Dublin."

Greed sparkled in the young man's eyes. "How do I know you won't try to escape between here and there?"

"You've got me tied up, you ass—"

Mac's gun flew up, the snout aimed at Devon's face.

"Oh, Devon!" Claire cried. "Tell him where you buried that gold you brought back from the war. It's our only hope, isn't it? Perhaps he'll release us in exchange. If you won't tell him where it is hidden, I will!"

Impressed by Claire's cleverness, Devon went along with the act. "Didn't I tell you to keep your mouth shut about the gold?"

A look of confusion marred Mac's features. "Gold? What gold? Where is it? Come on, the lady's right! This ain't no time for secrets!"

"I know where it is!"

"Claire, keep your mouth shut," Devon hissed.

Mac leaned inside the compartment, his lips glistening, his nose twitching. It was almost as if he could smell and taste the riches in his future. He was so absorbed in extracting a fictitious treasure map from Devon that he failed to notice the plod and rustle of the horses that drew to a halt at the edge of the road.

Pressing his pistol to Devon's forehead, he said, "Tell me where you stashed your fortune, Mr. Avondale, or you won't live to see the sun come up. The lady's correct; it's your only chance."

"Never."

"Shall I count to three?" the young man said in a childish, singsong voice. "One. Two."

"Bugger off!" Devon said, interrupting.

"Are you crazy?" Mac yelled. "This is no time for greed, man! Tell me where the money is!"

Tension filled the carriage. The crazed look in Mac's eyes was frightening; He hadn't shot anyone because he sensed he was on the trail of a cache of gold. He had lowered his guard, but he could lose his patience at any moment. He was still dangerous.

Over the youth's shoulder, Devon spied a movement in the shadows. As the shapes of two horsemen materialized in the lamplight, Devon screwed up his courage, grinned and shook his head.

"Go to hell, Mac."

Mac drew back his arm, whipped his pistol

across Devon's face and screamed at the top of his lungs. "Tell me where the gold is, you son of a—"

Outside the carriage, a horse snickered, and it wasn't one of the mares harnessed to the rig. Mac went still, his features frozen in a rictus of surprise and fear. Understanding came to him swiftly. Turning, he saw the outline of two men aiming pistols at him.

Dick Creevy said calmly, "Put that gun down or I will shoot you."

Devon looked at Claire. Their fate hung in the balance. "I love you," he told her.

She smiled.

Gunfire erupted.

Two shots were fired in rapid succession, one from Mac's pistol and one from Creevy's. Devon's heart skipped a beat as Mac stood resolutely in the doorway. Silence reverberated in the tiny compartment; the silence outside was even more ominous.

Holding his breath, Devon was certain that Creevy had taken a bullet and was lying on the ground, dying or dead already. Then—ever so fluidly—like a diver teetering on the edge of a sheer cliff, Mac shuddered, wavered and pitched headfirst out of the carriage—facedown on the muddy road to Mullingar.

Two weeks later, Millicent Hyde-Wolferton entered Devon Avondale's grand dining room on the arm of her husband Alec, the famous war veteran who had once been a spy for the British government. She walked in carefully minced steps, her body still sore from its ordeal, her mood still depressed. An hour earlier, she had informed her husband, recently returned from London, that she wasn't up to attending Claire and Devon's wedding celebration. But at the last minute, she realized she couldn't miss her friends' nuptial party. Devon had saved her life, after all, and she yearned to return to her former high spirits.

As the rest of those gathered took their seats around the long cherry wood dining table, Millicent inhaled deeply. It was good to be with friends. She was glad she had come. As she caught the pretty violet gaze of her dearest friend, Rose Sinclair-Nollbrook, she smiled for the first time in weeks.

Rose, who for a week had sat nights with Millicent at hospital while caring for her own children during the day, smiled radiantly as her husband pushed in her chair and bent to nuzzle her neck.

It was a rare occasion, with all the husbands of Fontjoy Square in attendance. Liveried servants poured champagne into elegant Waterford flutes as Dolly and Dick Creevy took their places opposite one another. Then Devon Avondale stood and raised his glass to Claire, his beautiful wife, who was seated at the far end of the table.

It was a moment that would sparkle forever in Millicent's memory. In the last year, living at Fontjoy Square, she had fallen in love, learned to forgive, reconciled with her father and acquired a family. Though she had lost the baby that she and Alec so wished for, she had hopes that they might create another. As soon as her body healed, she knew that she and Alec would try.

Rose surveyed the glittering table with a maternal pride that made her heart swell. Millicent, her dear little neighbor, was going to be all right. In the last year, it seemed to Rose that the world had become a cozy place. Her dreams of having children were fulfilled. With three little ones underfoot and a husband to care for, she could not have been happier. As she lifted her champagne glass, she met the gaze of Dolly Baltmore Creevy and smiled.

Tingles of joy and a mild sensation of ecstasy suffused Dolly's slight frame. From Rose's smile, she looked to her husband, the famous pugilist who had once unwittingly trained her to box. Though their meeting was precipitated by tragedy and mistaken identity, their relationship was firmly founded on trust. In the last year, Dolly had learned that she could be loved for herself, that she didn't have to pretend to be someone else. Her heart she had given irrevocably to her husband, but her eternal gratitude belonged to Devon Avondale.

"As a toast to my new bride, I would like to read something written by a woman I once loved very deeply." His deep voice brought silence to the room as everyone gazed questioningly at Claire. It was well known that Claire had once declared her animosity toward the former Mary O'Roarke. "I hope that my wife will allow me."

Slanting him a flirtatious look, she said, "I think I know what it is, darling. Go ahead."

He picked up the leather-bound journal and opened it to the back page. " 'Tis the last entry she wrote, and till recently, I paid it little mind. After recent events, however, I realize that this is perhaps the most important passage in her memoirs."

Emotion strained his voice as Devon read:

> *Darling, there is one last thing that you must remember. The women I have written about in this diary were once good friends of mine. Not all of them remained so. After boarding school in Switzerland, Dolly and I went our separate ways, never to cross paths again. Rose tried to stay in touch with me, but after what we had been through—what I had put her through—I found her society entirely too painful and too reminiscent of my follies to endure.*

> *As for Millicent, she was such a young thing when I knew her, so full of courage and pluck. She, too, shamed me into realizing the virtues that I lacked—candor, honesty and selflessness.*

> *I tell you these things because as I lay dying, I realize how dearly I have loved these women and how sadly I have neglected to tell them so. You see, I did not become the woman I am today, Devon, by chance or by breeding or because I was enlightened during a spiritual search for goodness. No, dear, it*

was because at last I saw myself reflected against the image of these women . . . I recognized my shortcomings and my failures. I knew they were good . . . and that I could be better.

Oh, I made many mistakes, Devon, darling, too many to recount in this journal. I think of Claire Kilgarren and my heart hurts. I have not said much about what happened between Claire and me during that horrible weekend in the country, and I shall not say more here because to publish my misdeed would only create deeper wounds.

I only hope that if and when you find her, you can somehow make amends for my cruelty, and make her understand what a fine and beautiful woman she must be. For I have no doubt that despite the wrong I committed against her, she flourished and blossomed into a strong, independent soul. I know deep in my heart that she did—I suppose I could not have lived with myself otherwise. Lady Claire Kilgarren was my model for elegance, sophistication and dignity. Perhaps I resented her for what she possessed . . . which was everything I craved.

My time is coming to an end, Devon, but your life will go on. I hope you will take a small measure of comfort in knowing that you, too, contributed toward making me a better person. Because I loved you, darling, I improved myself. Please, please, please, Devon, remember that if you ever cease to love, you will cease to live. I hope you will find someone to share your life with, someone who will cherish you as I have. But most importantly, my beloved husband, I hope you will find someone to love.

Carefully, Devon closed the journal, turning its cracked leather binding over in his hands, as if he were soaking up the spirit of its author. He looked at Claire, and something passed between them, something rare and intimate and intense. A tear sparkled in his eye as he clutched the book with one hand and lifted his champagne flute.

"My darling Claire," he toasted her, "you have given me life and hope and love . . . you have rescued me from loneliness, and for that I am forever grateful. But most of all, you have taught me to be a better person. 'Tis you, Claire, who have taught me to love . . . and for the rest of our days, I believe you will continue to do so."

"Here, here!" cried Dick Creevy.

"Any woman who would kick over a lamp and set her room on fire in order to attract the attention of a stable boy deserves my admiration and respect," added Captain Alec Wolferton. "Much happiness to both of you! Though I don't advise you to revisit the Cork and Clover anytime soon."

"Last I heard, the innkeeper wants to sue you," said Sir Steven. "But don't worry; I believe I can settle your case. 'Twill be my wedding gift to you both!"

In unison, Millicent, Rose and Dolly—*and their husbands*—lifted their glasses, clinked the rims and drank to the newlyweds, Devon and Claire.

Then everyone watched in wonder as Devon

strode to the fireplace, gently kissed the cover of Mary O'Roarke's diary and tossed it onto the flames.

Returning to the table, he stood beside his wife and leaned down to kiss her throat. Eyes closed, she smiled serenely, pressed her palm to his cheek and murmured, "I love you, too, Devon."

wrote to the bedline, gently kissed the corner of
Mary O'Reard's cheeks, and tossed it onto the
flames.

Returning to the table, he stood beside his wife
and leaned down to nibble her throat. Ilsa's closely-
ate stuffed scratch pressed her panties to Stack
and appreciated. A low moan from Devin.

Epilogue

Later that night, their first night as man and wife, Devon and Claire made love for hours. Naked beneath the twisted covers, they slept intermittently, waking whenever desire jolted them from their dreams. Then they made love again until they were exhausted, their breath coming in shallow puffs, their skin slick and their hair damp from their exertions.

With a purr, Claire rolled to her back and opened her eyes. Her gaze locked with Devon's, and instantly she wanted him. Propped up on his elbow, he kissed her, tenderly at first, then with a feverish passion. His tongue was skillful and his flesh warm. He kissed Claire as she had never been kissed, lovingly and patiently.

"Talk to me," he whispered against her lips. "Tell me what you are thinking, what you like."

"I am thinking that I did not know—" She searched for the words to describe her feelings. It wasn't easy to say such things aloud. Claire had never attempted to articulate her sexual feelings or preferences; indeed, it had never occurred to her that married couples talked during their lovemaking.

"You did not know *what,* sweetling?"

"That kissing could be so enjoyable."

"You have a lot to learn, Claire—if you will allow me to teach you." Kneeling between Claire's legs, Devon supported his weight on his hands, stretched over her and teased her flesh with his own, tickling her with his thick chest hair, prodding her damp golden curls with the tip of his penis.

Her pulse galloped so fiercely that for one dizzying instant, she feared she might lose consciousness. Her uncertainty receded, and in its stead flowed an ever-increasing need to wrap her arms around Devon's body and draw him as snugly into hers as she could. The heaviness pulsing between her legs amazed her.

Then, as Devon dipped his head to her breast and gently sucked her nipple, Claire's tenuous grasp on her composure snapped completely. A strangled sound of pleasure emerged from her throat, shocking her. She could not make sense of what was happening to her, and she did not care. For a woman who had spent the last few years swearing that she hated men, she was surely enjoying this one.

And just when she thought she could not withstand the aching heat between her legs a moment longer, Devon rained a trail of kisses from her breasts to her stomach. Expertly, he tongued a delicious swirly pattern on the tender skin below her navel. The sensation was mind-numbing. In response, Claire's hips bucked and lifted. She cried out, begging him to stop, but if he had, she would have wilted with disappointment.

Lifting her head, Claire stared at her body, splayed open, exposed, naked. Her inner thighs sparkled like gossamer. A delightful stickiness coated the folds of her flesh. Between gasps, she whispered Devon's name repeatedly, desperate to be taken by him, eager to feel his body sheathed inside hers.

But her skillful husband was not to be hurried.

Hunkered down between her soft inner thighs, he looked up and met her gaze.

"Devon, what on earth are you doing?" she whispered. The sight of his engorged penis made her throat go dry.

"Loving you," he murmured, pressing his nose against her soft mound.

When his lips found the tiny nub of flesh nestled between her feminine folds, Claire moaned her disbelief. Devon's knowledge of a woman's body had to be more thorough than any doctor's. How did he know these things? Carefully, he kissed and nibbled and sucked the most intimate parts of her womanhood. Crying out, Claire arched her back, deepening Devon's kiss, opening herself up to him as much as she could.

"Does anyone else know about this?" she finally managed to ask. "Do other civilized folk do such things? Is it allowed by law?"

His deep masculine laughter vibrated against her body, filling her with happiness. When he spoke, his voice was thick and muffled, as if he, too, were drunk with pleasure. "When you are in love, darling, anything is allowed."

Relieved and liberated, Claire clasped Devon's head and directed his movements. If she had taught Devon how to love, then he in turn would teach her how to *make love*. And Claire Kilgarren intended to be a very apt pupil.

DO YOU HAVE THE
HOHL COLLECTION?

Celebrate Romance With
Meryl Sawyer

_Thunder Island $6.99US/$8.99CAN
0-8217-6378-4

_Half Moon Bay $6.50US/$8.00CAN
0-8217-6144-7

_The Hideaway $5.99US/$7.50CAN
0-8217-5780-6

_Tempting Fate $6.50US/$8.00CAN
0-8217-5858-6

_Trust No One $6.99US/$8.99CAN
0-8217-6676-7

Call toll free **1-888-345-BOOK** to order by phone, use this coupon to order by mail, or order online at **www.kensingtonbooks.com**.

Name_____

Address_____

City_____ State _____ Zip _____

Please send me the books I have checked above.

I am enclosing	$_____
Plus postage and handling*	$_____
Sales tax (in New York and Tennessee only)	$_____
Total amount enclosed	$_____

*Add $2.50 for the first book and $.50 for each additional book.

Send check or money order (no cash or CODs) to:

Kensington Publishing Corp., Dept. C.O., 850 Third Avenue, New York, NY 10022

Prices and numbers subject to change without notice.

All orders subject to availability.

Visit our website at **www.kensingtonbooks.com**.